LORD OF MISCHIEF

SASHA COTTMAN

To Dean and Laura

Chapter One

LONDON 1817

Eve Saunders wrapped her black woolen cloak about her shoulders and softly closed her bedroom door.

"Are you ready?" she whispered into the darkness.

Her brother Francis stepped out from behind a nearby pillar, a finger held to his lips. "Ssh, Papa is still awake and working in his study. If he hears us there will be the devil to pay." He pointed toward the main staircase, motioning for Eve to follow.

She lifted her skirts and hurried after him.

When she reached the bottom of the wide marble staircase, Francis pulled her into an alcove.

"I have checked the rest of the house and no one else is about the floors. Papa suddenly decided he needed to work on some papers for a shipment of tobacco which is arriving from Brazil on the morning tide," he said.

Eve grinned. Her father could stay up until dawn for all she cared, just as long as he didn't catch her and Francis sneaking out the house.

They had been stealing into the night for as long as she could remember. Occasionally they could entice their sister Caroline to tag along, but she was no night owl, preferring the joy of going to bed early and sleeping late. The nights when it was just Francis and Eve were always the best.

London late at night was a different place. The soul of the city stirred from its daytime order and dared all who ventured out into the dimly lit streets to become someone else. Being out among the crowds at night stirred the heat in Eve's blood.

"Come on, we don't want to be late," urged Francis.

They headed into the garden of their family home and slipped out into the rear laneway through a small gap in the fence, which was hidden behind a bush. Every time the head gardener made noises about repairing the hole, a coin or two found its way into his hand and he managed to find some other more pressing task to take up his time.

Five minutes later Eve and Francis were running down Dover Street, laughing. The hood of Eve's cloak fluttered behind her in the cold night air.

"Papa would skin us alive if he ever caught us!" she laughed.

They crossed over to Hyde Park Corner and found themselves in the middle of a crowd, which was growing by the minute. The crush of bodies all jostling for the best vantage point was thrilling.

"I take it the race is still on," said Eve.

Rumors of a secret bareback horse race along Oxford Street and down to Hyde Park Corner had been circulating throughout their various groups of friends for almost a week. Excitement had now built to fever pitch.

Eve couldn't wait to see who was reckless enough to ride in a horserace through the middle of London in the dead of night. The threat of arrest would deter all but the very wild at the pursuit, and if there was one thing that set Eve's pulse racing, it was wild men.

She smiled to herself. There were not enough wild men in London society; she craved a man who could sate her wickedness.

"This will be the best vantage point to see them as they come through from Park Lane," said Francis.

Eve pulled the collar of her cloak up around her ears. It was only September, but already the nights were chilly. There had barely been a summer to speak of, and now autumn was showing all the signs of a long horrid winter to follow.

She stretched up on her toes, straining to get a better look as the crowd began to cluster tightly around the corner of Hyde Park. She managed to find a gap through which to see Park Lane. Along either side of the street, people held flaming torches to guide the riders.

A ripple of cheers and applause ran through the crowd as the riders finally came into view at the top of Park Lane.

"Here they come!" she cried.

\&

As the horses neared the end of Oxford Street, a sickening feeling of panic began to rise in Freddie Rosemount's mind. He was going to have to do something quickly if he was going to win.

From the moment he'd leapt onto the back of his horse he'd regretted his decision to bareback horse race through the wet, slippery streets of London.

He had been all of ten years old when he last sat on the back of a horse without a saddle. It had been a quiet ride around the mounting yard outside the stables at his family home in Peterborough—a race in the dark against a skillful opponent was something else entirely.

"Blast!" he muttered as his opponent's horse drew ahead. If he didn't do something now, the race would surely slip from his grasp.

He settled down lower over the reins and dug his heels into the side of his mount. He was not done by a long shot. He was not going to lose the first of the Bachelor Board challenges.

"Ha! Come on!" he urged his horse.

His horse lengthened its stride. Freddie gripped on tightly. It would be a disaster if he was to fall.

Slowly but surely, the gap between them and the lead horse closed. Freddie dug his heels in one last time and his horse kicked into another burst of speed.

At the end of Oxford Street, they drew level. Freddie chanced a look at his opponent and his heart leapt.

Lord Godwin Mewburton was wielding his whip like a madman. From his mouth came a never-ending stream of abuse, all directed at his horse.

Unsurprisingly, the abuse did not have the desired effect. Freddie's mount edged forward into the lead.

By the time they reached the turn into the top of Tyburn Lane, Freddie's horse was half a body length in front. Lord Godwin had gone too hard too early and was now paying the price for his uncalculated move.

Tyburn Lane was dark with only houses on one side and Hyde Park on the other. The gaslights on the side of the street added little to light the way. Freddie squinted in the dark and prayed his horse had better eyesight than he did.

He lifted his head and caught sight of a series of lit torches near Hyde Park Corner. The finish line was in sight. Throngs of people crowded the finish line. They cheered and waved, urging the riders on.

Freddie grinned as his horse entered the start of Park Lane. He was in the lead. The cheers were for him. He was going to win.

৯

The second rider crossed the finish line less than a minute after the winner, but Eve barely noticed. Her attention was already captured and held fast by the dark-haired victor who leapt off the back of his stead as soon as they crossed the finish line and was now accepting the congratulations of dozens of well-wishers who were singing his name. Freddie! Freddie!

The grin on his face had her smiling.

Francis took hold of Eve's arm. "I thought I had lost you in the crowd. Did you see the finish?"

Eve nodded, but her gaze remained firmly fixed on the winner. The very sight of him took her breath away. He had dark, wind-ruffled hair, which was the perfect level of sexy wildness. He was tall and perfectly built. Her only disappointment was that in the dark she could not make out the color of his eyes.

"Who is he?" she asked, enthralled.

Francis huffed in disgust. "Freddie Rosemount. Second son of Viscount Rosemount, he was at Eton the same time as me. Just come down from a first-class degree at Oxford and looks like he is planning to tear up the town. And from your lovesick look, break a few hearts in the process," replied Francis.

"Oh, please. I am just excited to see a dashing young man on horse-back. You cannot blame a girl for dreaming of knights and their mighty chargers." She brushed her brother's words away as yet another of his good-natured teases, but at the same time, she knew Freddie Rose-mount had already captured her imagination. She mentally checked her 'must have' list for a potential husband.

Viscount Rosemount was one of the richest men in the country so Freddie had the issue of wealth covered. He had a university degree, so he was no dunce. He was devilishly handsome and had an obvious wild streak.

Tick. Tick. Tick. Tick. He met all the criteria on her list.

Now she had to discover whether a passionate heart beat beneath that broad chest. She was determined to marry before the year was out, but a dull, safe husband was the last thing she desired.

With her heated blood pumping strongly through her veins, she no longer felt the bitter chill of the night air.

Eve placed a hand over her heart and made a silent vow. She would do whatever it took to meet this handsome devil. If he was half as interesting as the way he rode, his name would be added to her list of potential husbands. The list in its current state was both short and disappointing.

Eve tightly fisted her hand. She was not going to see out the year as an old maid. She was determined to find love. She would do every-thing within her power to beat her sister Caroline to the altar. The next family wedding was going to be hers.

Hello, Freddie. You might just be the man I am looking for.

Chapter Two

Freddie Rosemount crawled out of his bed as late as he could the following morning. The post-race celebrations had gone well into the early hours. After his third glass of champagne he had switched to brandy and stopped counting his drinks.

He sat on the edge of his bed and stared down at his bare feet, softly chuckling at the notion of how those feet were walking a different path to the one he thought they would. The dull ache in his head was the victor's price for glory.

He dressed and headed into the breakfast room of his family's London townhouse in Grosvenor Square. The single setting for breakfast was placed at the head of the long, highly polished oak table. As he took his seat, he smiled. With everyone else in his family still in residence at Rosemount Abbey, he had the run of the London house all to himself for the first time in his life.

While waiting for the servants to bring him breakfast, he surveyed his surroundings. He'd always sat further down the table. His father's seat offered a different perspective of the room. Paintings of long-dead family members, which were normally out of sight in his usual place, were now in full view.

He gave the portrait of his great-great-grandfather a respectable nod. The lucrative horse breeding program at Rosemount Abbey had been established by his ancestor in the early part of the eighteenth century, and it now afforded the family a position high in the rarefied air of the *haute ton*.

Being a second son, Freddie would never hold the seat at the head of the table as his own. It was nice to enjoy the pleasant fantasy of being lord of the house even if only for a short time.

He couldn't begrudge Thomas his role as future Viscount Rosemount. Thomas's life was set out for him. He was already in possession of two sons of his own. With an estate to run, tenants to manage, and a huge Elizabethan period house to maintain, Thomas would never have the same opportunities as Freddie in deciding his future. Of one thing Freddie was certain: his brother would never have been found racing at breakneck speed around the streets of London in the middle of the night.

Yet it burnt deep within to know that up to this point in his life he had always been second. The second son to attend Oxford. The second son to finish with a first-class degree. Nothing he had achieved so far had been uniquely his own. He was destined to be a footnote in his family's long and proud history.

A footman brought him a small tray with two boiled eggs on it, which he wasted no time in finishing. When the second cup of coffee did not shift the cobwebs from his brain, he promised himself he would make it early to bed that night.

Grabbing his coat, he walked out the front door, crossed Grosvenor Square, and headed toward St James Street en route to the Houses of Parliament. A cadetship at the House of Commons had unexpectedly come his way via one of his old university professors. The cadetship was only for a few months and it was a rare chance to see the inner workings of the English political system. It was the perfect role for him while he was still finding his feet within London society.

The morning walk gave him time to enjoy the movement and life of London during the early part of the day. With a scarf wrapped around his neck and his hands kept warm inside a pair of dark brown leather gloves, he was well rugged up against the biting wind.

Crossing through St James's Park he looked to his right and gave a respectful nod to Buckingham Palace off in the near distance. The flags were flying. The royal family were in residence.

"Your Majesty," he whispered.

Upon reaching the offices of the parliamentary cadets in Barton Street, he signed the day book and went in search of his fellow cadets. Barton Street to the Palace of Westminster was a five-minute stroll through narrow streets behind Westminster Abbey. He walked in through a side door.

"Caesar has arrived! All of Briton is now mine for the taking," he announced as he stepped into the small meeting room, which had been assigned to the cadets during their short tenure.

"You, sir, are no conqueror. You are a first-class lunatic!" replied Lord Godwin Mewburton. He slapped Freddie hard on the back. "I nearly had you as we reached Strathmore House, but your horse damn well kicked away."

Freddie laughed and gave a wink. Godwin could tell himself all the stories he liked, but they both knew once Freddie's horse had caught the lead, he was never going to yield it.

"I may be a lunatic, but I won the first of the challenges, which means I have one hundred points toward my seat on the Bachelor Board. I tell you, at this rate, I shall be a fully-fledged member before the week is out," replied Freddie.

Seated in a nearby, deeply padded leather chair, the Honorable Trenton Embry snorted. "Yes well, just be grateful my sister and her husband insisted I attend their dinner party last night, otherwise I would have shown the pair of you how we in the west country ride."

Freddie and Godwin exchanged a mutual raising of the eyebrows. In the short time they had known the second son of Viscount Embry they had discovered he was a man prone to little speech, and even less action.

"So, what do you think we will be up to today?" asked Godwin.

Freddie threw himself down onto a nearby couch and placed his boots on a conveniently placed coffee table. If today was anything like any other day at the House of Commons it would be boring meetings, copious amounts of alcohol, and getting up to all manner of dangerous hijinks. And not necessarily in that order.

Freddie promised himself to follow up on a long-standing offer of a role at the British Library once his cadetship was ended. The Harleian Library collection had writings from Ptolemy he was itching to get his hands on.

"Our fearless leader will soon tell us, once he has scraped himself up from whichever gutter he frequented last night," replied Freddie.

They all chuckled.

The man responsible for leading the new cadets at the English parliament, Osmont Firebrace, was a man who led a life strictly by the book. In his case, a small black leather-bound book.

While Osmont was happy to encourage his protégés to make a mess of themselves, he was not one to partake in a single drop of alcohol. Even his weak cups of tea were often left to go cold.

On cue, Osmont Firebrace entered the room.

He was dressed in a black jacket, black trousers, and black hessian boots. His shirt was pure white linen. It was the same outfit he wore every day. Under his arm was tucked the black notebook.

"Gentlemen. I trust you had a successful evening," he said.

His gaze was locked firmly on Freddie as he spoke. When Godwin attempted to mention his own efforts in the race, Osmont put up his hand.

"Second means nothing, Lord Godwin. You either win or you may as well have stayed home and had an early night. The Bachelor Board does not reward also rans."

He untied the string, which held his black book tightly closed, and opened it. He made a great show of running his finger down the open page. "As of this morning we have the Honorable Frederick Rosemount in first place on one hundred points. In second place, Lord Godwin Mewburton, on twenty points. And the Honorable Trenton Embry is yet to open his account." He snapped the book shut and tucked it back under his arm.

"It would appear that Mr. Embry has not understood the rules of the Bachelor Board. So, I shall give you all a refresher," he said.

A servant brought in a fresh pot of coffee. Freddie and Godwin eagerly picked up a cup each and sat back to enjoy an early morning heart-starter. Freddie's head started to clear. The throb in his brain dropped a notch.

Osmont had told them the rules of the Bachelor Board enough times that Freddie felt he could recite them by heart.

"In order to secure your seat on the Bachelor Board you must accumulate enough points from a set of challenges which you are to undertake over the next month. If you are the successful candidate, you will gain unfettered access to some of the most powerful men in the country—men who can guarantee you a life of wealth and exclusive opportunity. You will never have to settle for being anything less than first among equals. Your older siblings will envy you. With all that in mind, I should not have to remind you that only one candidate from the three of you will be offered a seat on the Bachelor Board," said Osmont.

The horse race down Oxford Street and Park Lane had been the first of the challenges. Freddie sat and smiled. He was off to an excellent start.

The crowd at Hyde Park Corner had all been cheering his name as he'd crossed the finish line. He would be the talk of many a breakfast table conversation this morning. By the end of his cadetship, he was determined all the right people in London would know who he was. He wouldn't be known simply as Viscount Rosemount's second son. He would be his own man.

The next member of the Bachelor Board would be the Honorable Frederick Rosemount. Nothing, and no one, was going to stop him.

Chapter Three

E ve stood and stared at her wardrobe. She had tried on two gowns
already and tossed them onto her bed. Nothing seemed to suit
the occasion. Nothing fitted her mood.

Her maid came and stood beside her. "Blue for good luck?" she
suggested.

Eve wrinkled up her nose. Luck was something her cousin Lady
Lucy Radley and her about-to-be husband, Avery Fox, were going to
need in spades.

After having been caught in a compromising position with the
former soldier in the grounds of Strathmore House, Lucy and Avery
were now obliged to marry. Avery, the future Earl Langham, had not
gone quietly into the arms of his impending marriage.

Lucy's two older brothers had both taken brides earlier in the year,
and their respective weddings had been followed by lavish parties and
balls, attended by more than a thousand people a piece. Lucy's
wedding should have also been a glittering occasion.

At Avery's insistence, however, his and Lucy's nuptials were to be a
quiet family affair at Strathmore House.

"Why aren't you dressed?" Caroline Saunders closed the bedroom
door behind her.

Eve spared her fully dressed and ready-to-go sister a sideways glance before going back to staring at the wardrobe. "I just cannot find the right outfit for the occasion. Nothing in there speaks to me. What does one wear to an occasion that is a cautionary tale in not pursuing a hasty marriage?"

Caroline sighed. It was going to be a trying day for all.

"It's not a funeral. Besides, we should wear what we would be wearing if it was a full church service. We owe it to cousin Lucy to give her as much support as possible. Who knows? If we give them all our blessings then they may make a go of it."

Eve nodded. Her sister was right, as usual. Lucy did love Avery. She had set her sights on him a matter of weeks earlier when he was first introduced to London society as the mysterious new heir to the title of Earl of Langham. The fact the groom was not keen on the union was beside the point. He had kissed Lucy and placed his hands on her naked breasts in the garden of Strathmore House. After those facts, marriage was the only possible outcome.

"I shall go with the pale blue dress. It is simple and elegant, and I haven't worn it before today," replied Eve.

"Good. Papa is making noises downstairs about wanting to leave very soon, so you had better get a wriggle on," said Caroline.

Strathmore House, home of the Duke of Strathmore, was located within the fashionable area of Park Lane. The mansion dominated the street, being twice the size of every other house. Its huge Portland stone columns were a physical reminder of the long-held power and wealth of the Radley family. For Eve and her siblings however, it was simply the home of their uncle, aunt, and cousins.

As the Saunders's family carriage drew up outside the front of Strathmore House, Eve's heart sank. It should have been the biggest and most wonderful day of Lucy Radley's life. Crowds should have gathered outside, all craning to catch a glimpse of the elite of London as they arrived for the post-wedding festivities.

The only sign anything was happening at the house was a simple bouquet of white lilies, which had been hung from the front door. They spoke volumes as to the hurried nature of the wedding and the lack of celebration that came with it.

"Now, I want all of you to make a fuss over Lucy and Avery today. No matter the circumstances, it is still their wedding. The wedding breakfast will be a small affair, but since it's the only one they are going to get, it is up to all of us to make the day memorable. Make sure you have your best smiles on at all times," said Adelaide Saunders.

Eve noted the bitterness in her mother's words. Adelaide was heartbroken for her niece, but she was determined to do all she could to make it a special day for Lucy.

Inside Strathmore House, the family were ushered into the Winter Ballroom.

Adelaide shook her head with disgust. "Not even the Summer Ballroom. When Charles and I were married, my father made sure we had the finest of everything at our wedding. A duke's daughter should never have to face such an insult to her station."

The Winter Ballroom was bigger than any other ballroom Eve had seen in London, yet it was still smaller than the famous Summer Ballroom with its towering ceiling fabulously decorated with scenes from Aesop's fables.

The room had been simply decorated with a large vase of white roses next to where the bride and groom were to stand. Little other effort had been made for the wedding decorations. The chill of a forced wedding hung in the air.

Eve and her family took their seats. When the bride arrived ahead of the groom, hot tears sprang to Eve's eyes.

Lady Lucy looked every part the beautiful bride.

Her white lace wedding gown fitted perfectly to her body. In her hands she held a small posy of cream and red roses. Her short veil was held in place by the Strathmore family tiara—a priceless gold and diamond tiara which had been worn by every daughter of the family on her wedding day going back many generations.

Eve wiped tears away, her heart breaking for her cousin.

"I have others if you need them," whispered Caroline, handing her a clean handkerchief.

Lady Lucy Radley stood quietly talking to her mother, the Duchess of Strathmore. There was no grand entrance for the bride. She barely acknowledged the rest of the guests.

When the groom arrived, Eve noticed the stripes of his waistcoat matched the color of Lucy's flowers. It was nice that Avery was making some effort toward keeping up appearances no matter how much he had resisted offering for Lucy's hand in marriage.

Eve and Lucy had always been close. She knew Lucy was in love with Avery, and the heartbreak she faced in marrying a man who did not want her. Eve could only hope the kind-hearted Lucy would eventually win Avery's heart.

"He is rather handsome," said Caroline.

Eve nodded. The dark-haired Avery was lean and muscular. His long, powerfully built legs had her gaze trailing all the way to the top of them. She let out a small sigh, envious that tonight Lucy would be the one who would explore his magnificent, naked body.

Avery was exactly the sort of man Eve was seeking. Someone who had more to him than just a title or money. Those things could make a young woman comfortable in her life, and she wasn't naïve enough to think she could marry a man who could not keep her, yet she yearned for more. A passionate marriage was her heart's goal, and on that she would not compromise.

Avery had been to war and known a hard life before coming into an unexpected inheritance. He had faced real danger and overcome it. His left hand was continually covered with a black leather glove, which hid an unsightly war wound.

Watching as her uncle, the Bishop of London, married Lucy and Avery, Eve wiped away a final tear. She wished the newlyweds nothing but the happiest of marriages, but knowing the circumstances of their union, they had a hard road ahead.

When the groom placed a chaste kiss on the bride's cheek, Eve and Caroline exchanged a sad look.

"He had better treat her well. Or he shall have me to answer to," Eve muttered.

With the wedding service over, Lucy left Avery to talk to the other guests while she sought out Eve.

"Well done. You got through the service," said Eve.

Lucy gave her a tight smile. "Yes, I managed that much. Now I just need to get through the wedding breakfast and it will all be over."

Eve was about to make mention of the wedding night, but the look on Lucy's face gave her pause. The bride clearly had plans contrary to the usual ones for a married couple's first night.

"If I don't get an opportunity to talk to you before the wedding breakfast is over, I shall write to you when I get settled," said Lucy.

Caroline wandered over. "I do love your wedding gown, dearest cousin Lucy. It suits you so well," she said.

Lucy looked down at her wedding gown. Eve had been with her when she chose the fabric and knew how many tears had been shed at the studio of the modiste.

"Thank you. I shall have to keep it well stored. Who knows? I may have a use for it again someday."

Caroline gasped.

"I think Lucy is in jest, Caroline," replied Eve.

Caroline frowned. Eve's sister had turned down eight potential suitors in the past six months. Like her sister, Caroline also had her exacting requirements for a husband, though Eve suspected they were somewhat staider than her own. With looks that far outshone those of Eve, Caroline could have her choice of husband among the most eligible of *ton* bachelors.

Caroline was a true beauty. Her long blonde hair and stunning emerald green eyes ensured whenever she was at a gathering, a cluster of men would soon form around her. Her porcelain skin was flawless. Eve doubted her sister had ever suffered from a blemish on her face.

"Yes, well at least you have managed to get to the altar. This season has been so disappointing that I am beginning to wonder if I shall ever be fitted for a wedding gown. I should save my pennies and elope with Freddie Rosemount instead. He was the winner of that midnight horse race last week. I wonder if he would be up for a midnight flit to Gretna Green," continued Eve.

Her words were met with a huff from Caroline. "You take the whole notion of marriage far too lightly, Eve. I shall go and seek a sensible conversation elsewhere. Excuse me."

Eve pulled a face as her sister wandered away. She and Caroline were always at loggerheads these days, and she took particular delight in stirring up trouble with her sister.

"You are incorrigible, Eve. Why she takes the bait every time you say something outrageous is beyond me. Why do you need to do it?" said a flustered Lucy.

Eve shrugged. Caroline got under her skin. "I don't know why. What I do know is that I need to find a husband and get out of my sister's hair before we both end up hating one another."

Lucy took hold of her hand. "Don't make the same mistake as me and throw yourself at a man. But enough of my misfortune. Who is this Freddie Rosemount? The servants have been talking about a mad race that came past the house and had them all watching from the lower-floor windows. Is he the one responsible for my maid offering to run any errands which happen to pass by Grosvenor Square?"

Eve's mood lifted at the mention of Freddie's name. "Freddie Rosemount is Viscount Rosemount's second son and is making quite a name for himself from all accounts. Oh, and did I mention he is rather dashing? Francis and I were in the crowd that welcomed him across the finish line."

Caroline Radley, the Duchess of Strathmore, walked over from where she had been speaking to other guests. She took Lucy by the hand. Seeing Eve, she smiled. "Hello, Eve, my dear, sorry but I must steal the bride away from you. She and Avery have other guests to speak to before we sit down for the wedding breakfast."

As she watched her cousin and aunt walk away, Eve was struck by the irony of the situation. Both she and Lucy were true believers in love. They had both wanted the fairy-tale courtship and the society wedding, yet fate had not seen fit to bestow its grace upon either of them.

Lucy was now trapped in a loveless marriage, while Eve spent her days being eaten up with frustration over her lack of success in finding a suitable mate.

"I won't make the same mistake as you, Lucy, of that much I am sure."

Chapter Four

"What do you think of Osmont Firebrace?" asked Lord Godwin.
Freddie turned from admiring the fine house in Silver Street, outside which they were standing. The street in which Osmont's house stood was the home of many foreign embassies and diplomatic residences.

"I don't really know him that well. I met him the day we started our cadetship. From the look of it, he must do well from the Bachelor Board. It takes serious blunt to be able to afford a house around Golden Square. Why do you ask?" replied Freddie.

"Nothing. It's just that I find him to be an odd sort of chap. At times I catch him staring at me," replied Godwin.

He headed toward the front steps of the house, followed by a slightly puzzled Freddie. Earlier that morning he'd caught Osmont giving him a long, slow look, which had left Freddie feeling somewhat uncomfortable.

From outside the house, there was nothing to suggest the sort of gathering which was being held inside. A servant opened the front door. His livery matched that of Osmont's day-to-day attire: everything black, with a pure white shirt.

He looked Freddie and Godwin up and down. The look on his face was that which one would normally reserve for debt collectors or beggars.

"Yes?" he snapped.

Taken aback at such a greeting, Freddie hesitated for a moment. Then he remembered the secret entry code for the party.

"My colleague and I are here for a board meeting," he replied.

"Very good, sir," replied the butler, his demeanor instantly more respectful.

No sooner had Freddie and Godwin stepped inside and finished handing their coats and hats to a footman, then a glass of champagne was thrust into their hands. They clinked their glasses together.

"Bottoms up and chase it down with another," said Godwin.

A large, red silk curtain separated the reception hall from the rest of the downstairs area. Upon stepping through the curtain, their senses were immediately assailed with sight, noise, and smell.

Everywhere Freddie looked he saw scantily clad young women and men. They were draped across the various plush couches and daybeds which were dotted around the room. None of them were alone. From the look of it, each of these hosts were busy attending to the needs of Osmont's guests.

Freddie did a quick rough headcount and settled on a figure of fifty people. All were in varying stages of undress and all appeared to be talking at once. The room echoed with the sound of voices.

A heady cloud of smoke hung about the room. Freddie breathed in the mix of burning hashish and tobacco, bringing back memories of his time in the residential halls at university. The air was thick enough to give him an immediate small high.

"Ah. My latest protégés. So glad you could make it."

They turned to see Osmont standing behind them. At his side was a tall, thin youth dressed in exactly the same black garb as Osmont. When the young man ran his gaze seductively up and down Freddie's body, Freddie felt his skin crawl. He knew a sexual predator when he saw one.

"This is my nephew," said Osmont, with barely a nod in the young man's direction.

He didn't bother introducing him by name. Freddie gave Godwin a look. There was likely no blood between uncle and supposed nephew.

"I see you didn't bring Embry with you. I take it he thinks himself above having a spot of fun. Typical west country farmer. He is probably sitting at home right now having a second helping of scones for the night and thinking he is living the high life."

Freddie and Godwin exchanged a grin. With Embry not bothering to take the game seriously it meant one of them would be the eventual winner.

"I don't know why he is even attempting to feign interest in the challenges. Then again, his kind rarely make it onto the board," continued Osmont.

The young man beside him tittered.

"Well, gentlemen, at least the two of you are keen to make your mark on London's more interesting and select quarter of society. Why don't you have a wander around and see what and whom takes your fancy? Everything and everyone is on offer," said Osmont.

Godwin downed his glass of champagne in one long drink before eagerly seeking another. Freddie sipped his drink. He wasn't that keen on champagne, preferring a decent brandy or a good French wine.

The two of them began a slow circuit of the large room, which Freddie surmised had been separate rooms at one time, but now had all the walls knocked out in order to create a large entertainment space.

At the first couch they came across a young woman caressing a much older man. Freddie stifled a laugh when he saw Godwin's eyes grow wide with interest. At the next couch, a young bare-breasted woman beckoned for them to join her. Godwin moved like lightning and took a seat next to her. She pointed to the other side of the couch, motioning for Freddie to take a seat.

"This could be interesting," he muttered.

A footman stopped in front of them, and in his hands, he held a tray of cigars. When Freddie gave the tray a second look it was clear they were not the usual kind of cigars his father purchased from the merchant in London. Tobacco and hashish mixed together gave a long-burning and heady experience.

He took one of the cigars and waited for the footman to light it for him. Sitting back on the couch, he drew on the cigar and inhaled deeply. His brain immediately felt a spark from the hashish. He had smoked enough of the drug at university to know that this cigar was finely made.

Beside him on the couch, Godwin and the young lady were getting well acquainted. When she opened the placket of Godwin's trousers, and went down before him on her knees, Freddie decided three was a crowd. He rose from the couch and made a solo circuit of the room.

Apart from himself and Lord Godwin, there were few other young male guests. The members of the Bachelor Board all appeared to be much older men. Men who were being serviced in various ways by both women and men.

He wasn't naïve enough to think sex involved just women and men in a biblical sense. University had shown him things that had opened his eyes. Several of his friends were known to frequent special clubs in the city of Oxford.

"Bored?" said Osmont's nephew.

"No, just watching. If I find something that takes my fancy I shall partake in it," he replied.

Osmont's nephew sidled up to Freddie and stood close. His breath was warm on the back of Freddie's neck. Any closer and his lips would be on Freddie's skin.

"If you don't see what you like, there are rooms upstairs where you can find some other more intimate gatherings. The more you indulge, the more points you can score. You wouldn't want Lord Godwin to get ahead of you, would you?" he purred.

Freddie was a simple man when it came to sex, but he was determined to beat Godwin in succeeding to the Bachelor Board. Extra points could make all the difference.

He chanced a look toward the couch where Godwin was lying back, his eyes closed, while the young woman ministered to him with her mouth. It was time to venture a little farther afield.

"Lead on," he said.

Upstairs was a series of rooms, all with their doors left wide open. As he walked the length of the upper floor, he caught glimpses of the activities going on in each room.

From the first room came the loud crack of a whip and the thwack of it landing on flesh. A loud groan quickly followed. Craning his head around the door, Freddie saw a woman dressed in a leather corset standing over a portly naked man who was tied to the edge of the bed. From the bright red marks crisscrossing the gentleman's back, it was obvious they had been at the whipping session for some time.

In the corner of the room sat a group of well-dressed gentlemen, sipping drinks and watching the proceedings.

"Lily has a long wait list if you wish to be thrashed by her tonight."

Freddie shook his head. He had no desire to have the skin on his back flayed. It was odd that some men developed a taste for what every ill-behaved child dreaded. Sexual punishment was not to his liking.

The second and third rooms had various orgies taking place on large beds. Men and women were tangled together. The air was rank with the smell of sex and the sound of whimpers and groans.

When he turned and started to head back toward the staircase, Osmont's nephew seized Freddie by the arm.

"You didn't try the last room," he said.

Freddie fixed him with a glare. Osmont's nephew released his grip.

"I take it that is the room where a gentleman can be serviced by a young man. If it is, I am not particularly interested," replied Freddie.

"I was going to offer you my services. You could ride me hard, like you did your horse the other night. I promise I can take every inch. Or if your tastes run more to observing, there is a foreign diplomat in there, teaching a young man about international relations. You are most welcome to watch."

The chuckle which escaped Osmont's nephew's lips made Freddie's stomach churn. He had no ambition to be involved in any of the nocturnal activities taking place. Even the extra points on offer could not entice him. He would chance his luck with future challenges to regain the lead from Godwin after tonight.

"Actually, I am feeling a tad unwell. I gave the wine and brandy a good nudge at luncheon today, so I might call it a night. I hope your uncle won't take offence. Tell him I shall attend more of the parties, and next time I won't stand on the side of the dance floor and watch."

Freddie handed a nearby footman his glass and turned toward the stairs.

Osmont's nephew put a hand on Freddie's shoulder. "Are you sure I cannot tempt you with something, or someone?"

"Not tonight," replied Freddie.

Godwin was heading upstairs with his female hostess when Freddie stopped to inform him he was leaving the party.

Stepping out into the night air, Freddie took a deep breath. The mixture of hashish and alcohol was creating merry hell in his mind. His head was spinning.

He pulled out his pocket watch and squinted as he tried to read the time. It was still this side of midnight.

"You ought to be ashamed of yourself, Rosemount. So much for wanting to mix with the members of the Bachelor Board," he muttered.

He turned and took one last look at Osmont Firebrace's house, silently promising himself he would own a fine residence once he made his fortune with the Bachelor Board.

He was about to hail a hack and go home when he remembered the invitation he had received for a gathering at a home in nearby King Street.

"Come on Rosemount, show some spine and get out into society," he muttered. If he made an appearance at the party, he could still salvage something of his evening.

As he strolled the short distance to King Street, his mind began to clear. He had seen enough of the seedier side of London society for one evening; it would be good to spend the rest of the evening with people his parents would consider respectable.

Climbing the front steps of the house, he promised himself he would go back to one of Osmont's parties and sample some of the attractions for himself. If Godwin scored valuable points over him by virtue of having indulged this evening, then Freddie Rosemount would rise to the challenge next time.

Chapter Five

With a glass of brandy in his hand, Freddie began to make a circuit of the party. He stopped and greeted several people who were friends of his parents. He promised to write to his mother and let her know he had made their acquaintance.

He was beginning to wonder if it was physically possible to die of boredom and whether he had been too hasty in leaving Osmont's sordid soirée when he received a tap on the shoulder.

"Devil of a ride you showed the other night. There was never any doubt you were going to win."

Freddie turned to a hand held out in greeting.

"Francis Saunders. A pleasure to meet you. As I was saying, Lord Godwin didn't stand a chance once you were halfway down Tyburn Lane leading onto Park. The fool was thrashing the hide of his horse right to the very end."

Freddie took Francis's hand. He blinked when he beheld the shock of white hair on the other man's head. It couldn't have been any whiter if he had stolen one of the Queen's swans and used it as a wig.

Francis laughed. "The hair? My father swears there is a strong Viking vein in the family's blood and that's where my coloring comes from. Something about Ragnar Lodbrok and the siege of Paris."

"Or more likely that you took one look at your first horse and went white with fear, but don't let the truth get in the way of a good story."

Freddie looked to one side of Francis and caught sight of the dark-haired beauty who had spoken. Her smile warmed his heart.

Beside her was another young woman with fair hair. As with Francis, her appearance made Freddie gasp. It was as if a porcelain doll had come to life and was standing before him. But, beyond her beauty, she also had the coldness of something made of delicate china. Her gaze held a disapproving look.

"My sisters, Evelyn and Caroline," said Francis.

Freddie bowed. "Freddie Rosemount. A pleasure to make your acquaintance."

The dark-haired girl stepped forward and eagerly offered him her hand. She gave an air of self-confidence which delighted him. He guessed she only curtseyed when the situation demanded it of her.

"My friends call me Eve. Such a pleasure to meet you, Freddie. I must confess I was screaming at the top of my lungs by the time you reached the finish line at the end of the race. It was so exciting. You rode like a god," she said.

Freddie's mood and evening immediately lifted. He had met a few well-wishers on the night of the ride but hadn't thought his fame had spread as far as the elegant ballrooms of cultured society. It was odd that a young lady such as Eve Saunders would be out late at night, watching illegal and dangerous night rides. She stirred his interest.

"I am surprised you were at the race. It was very late. I take it your parents were not aware," he replied.

Caroline rolled her eyes, while Francis and Eve shared a conspiratorial grin.

"There are ways and means of getting about after dark in London without stuffy parents finding out. Your ride has been the talk of the young set for most of this week," said Eve.

Something within him sprang to life at her words. She wasn't as beautiful as her sister, but she had a charm about her that could have a man begging to be at her beck and call. Her brown- and green-flecked eyes held a thousand unspoken promises.

"You wicked thing," he replied, with a grin.

She raised an eyebrow as he spoke, and he immediately recognized a kindred spirit. He had wondered if there were mischievous girls among the unwed misses, and the one standing before him immediately raised his hopes.

"So, are you all residents here in London? I'm still finding my feet and only know people I have met over the years through my parents. I don't know many of the younger set, so I am at a disadvantage," Freddie said.

"We live permanently in London. Papa and I are in the import trade, mostly from South America. I was at Eton for a year the same time as you, but I don't' recall us ever having met," replied Francis.

Freddie heard Francis's words of explanation, but his gaze and mind were firmly fixed on the hazel eyes of Eve Saunders. Her long black lashes tempted him with their every blink.

Eve smiled, and Freddie could have sworn she batted her eyelids ever-so-slightly. His manhood gave a twitch. He had been offered all manner of sexual delights this evening, yet none of them had stirred his soul like the girl who now stood before him. He let out a soft breath and tried to cool his blood. *Interesting.*

"And apart from mad horse racing, what else do you do, Frederick?" asked Caroline.

Freddie caught the death stare Eve shot her sister, and chuckled. The Saunders siblings were fast becoming the highlight of his evening's entertainment. "I'm engaged in a short-term cadetship at the House of Commons at the moment. Learning about the inner workings of parliament and all that. I am expecting to take up a post with the British Library just after the New Year," he replied.

Caroline looked down at her pale green evening fan and proceeded to make a subtle show of flicking it open and fanning herself. She made no attempt to hide her displeasure and obvious boredom with their encounter.

Freddie and Eve caught each other's gaze.

"Francis, dear brother, I think Caroline would like to take a turn about the dance floor. She is in dire need of entertainment," said Eve.

"And what about you, Eve dearest? I thought you promised Lord Towell the next dance. He is on your list, is he not?" replied Caroline.

"Not anymore he isn't. He is paying particular attention to another young lady this evening and has not even bothered to acknowledge me," replied Eve.

Francis looked from one sister to the other, and Freddie caught the look of pained resignation on his face. This was obviously not the first, nor probably the last time he would have to deal with headstrong siblings.

"Come," snapped Francis.

Caroline took his roughly offered hand and allowed her brother to lead her away. As he watched them go, Freddie caught wind of Caroline rebuking her brother for his lack of manners toward her. His sympathies went with Francis. Caroline was a shrew.

Eve turned to Freddie.

"I am so sorry about that. She gets jealous if any gentlemen show an interest in me. She thinks because of her beauty she should be the first of us girls to be married. God forbid I ever beat her to the altar, she would never forgive me. Mama says I am stubborn, but Caroline could give lessons in the art."

Freddie wasn't too concerned with Caroline Saunders and her disappointment—his attention was fully captured by her sister. There was a feistiness about Eve that had him quietly imagining what it would be like to have her naked and in his bed.

Chapter Six

E ve was relieved beyond words when Francis took Caroline away and left her alone with Freddie Rosemount. She had been searching for him at various parties and balls since the horse race, hoping he would eventually surface at one of them. His unexpected appearance at the gathering this evening afforded her the opportunity to ask some of the long list of questions she had compiled for him.

Standing this close to him was a pleasure she was silently relishing. The spice of his cologne had her taking in long appreciative breaths.

When she had first seen him at the end of the horse race, it had been dark and there had been a sizeable crowd gathered around him. She had barely managed to get a glimpse or two of him amongst the mass of people.

Here at the ball, she had him all to herself.

After Lucy and Avery's wedding, she had gone home and looked at her private list of all the men she knew in London who might be candidates for matrimony. She had scratched several men from the list, only stopping when she realized nearly everyone on it had good reason to be removed.

But, tonight, she was intent on discovering if Freddie Rosemount was true to the wickedness of his horse riding.

He was taller than she had expected, only realizing it when he had stood next to Francis. At six feet four inches, her brother towered over most other men. Freddie, she guessed, was perhaps only an inch shorter than her brother.

Freddie was well built. Francis was a long, tall string bean, whereas Freddie had wide shoulders. The sleeves of his evening coat showed his well-developed muscles to their best advantage. His tailor knew exactly how to cut the cloth to the man. Well-dressed men always caught her approving eye.

"So how are you finding London on your own?" she asked.

He gave her a sideways glance before replying. "How do you know I am in London on my own? Have you been spying on me?"

Eve gave him her best coy look. She straightened her back, allowing her ample bust to be displayed to its best advantage. It wasn't every day that a young lady was afforded the opportunity to talk to a young man barely of her acquaintance, and she knew it wouldn't be long before Francis tired of Caroline and returned to her side.

Freddie and Eve's gazes met. They were only a matter of a foot or so apart. Too close by accepted social standards, but Eve was not about to take a step backward.

His deep, brown eyes were pools of dark, rich coffee. His long black eyebrows added the perfect frame to his chiseled features. Even the small crow's feet, which appeared at the corner of his eyes when he smiled, had been crafted by artisans. Eve could stand there all night and make a slow, luxurious assessment of his handsome face. She was in no particular hurry to be anywhere else. "Well actually, yes. Yes and no. I have lots of friends and relatives in London, and one of them happened to mention you have the run of your father's house to yourself. I did consider breaking into your house if I couldn't run you to ground before the end of the week," she replied with a smile.

Freddie laughed at her reply, and Eve felt emboldened. In the time available to her she decided she would push the barriers a little further.

"So, tell me about the horse race. Why were you racing against Lord Godwin Mewburton in the middle of the night? It was so exciting."

Freddie looked around the room. There were plenty of guests close by, some close enough to be within earshot. "I could tell you, but we may need to go somewhere a little more private. Are you game?"

It took all of Eve's self-control not to clap her hands with glee. Freddie Rosemount was beginning to sound like the perfect candidate for a husband. She was always game.

She offered him her arm and they walked a short distance away to a nearby private alcove. They were still in sight of the dance floor and other guests, so propriety was theoretically being observed. He stood with his back to the dance floor ensuring no one could see his face. He leant in close.

"Now if I tell you, I need you to promise it will stay our secret. If you dare to tell your sister or your brother, I shall know," said Freddie.

Her heart pitter-pattered with excitement. She had never before felt these sorts of sensations when near a young man. Freddie and his delicious secrets would be all hers.

She eagerly nodded her agreement.

"It was part of a game. Winner gets to join a secret society. Tomorrow we are to be given our next challenge," he explained.

Eve's heart felt fit to burst with excitement and disappointment. A secret game. But why did the men get to have all the fun? Young, unmarried ladies such as herself were never afforded that level of amusement. A piano recital or the opera was dictated to be suitable entertainment for her, none of which were exhilarating.

"Any idea what the next challenge is going to be?" she asked.

He shook his head.

Out of the corner of her eye she saw Francis and Caroline approaching. From the angry look on her brother's face, the dance had not gone well. It wouldn't be long before Caroline was demanding he take her home, which would also mean that Eve would shortly be leaving the party.

It was time to take a chance.

She leant in close and placed her hand on his arm. If Francis saw, he could take her to task over her familiarity with Freddie later on.

"Promise me, if you need a friend to help you win the game, you will consider me. I know lots of people and places in London. I could be of immense assistance to you," she said.

Her cousin Lucy had done the exact same thing for Avery Fox when he had newly arrived in London, and she had managed to snag him as a husband. While Lucy had made a mess of things in the end, Eve was determined to take all the lessons from Lucy's heartbreaking experience and use it to her own advantage.

She held her breath. *Please say yes. Please say yes.*

He looked down at her hand, which was still placed on his arm, and then, to her delight, placed his hand on hers.

"If there is an opportunity for you to help me win the game, then yes I shall ask. But we would need to be mindful of your reputation. You are an unwed young woman. What was it your sister was saying about Lord Towell?"

Eve schooled her features into blandness. Trust Caroline to mention Lord Towell who, until this evening, had sat at the top of Eve's list of potential husbands. Her interest in the earl had not been reciprocated, but Freddie's appearance at the ball had taken the sting out of her sense of rejection.

"Oh, nothing. Lord Towell was on my dance list for later this evening, but I have discovered he has two left feet and an eye for another young lady. By not dancing with him

I am saving my feet and making sure the path of true love runs smooth," she replied, ignoring the slight raise of Freddie's eyebrow.

Francis and Caroline drew closer and, true to form, as soon as they got within earshot, Eve could hear her sister complaining about wanting to leave. Eve stepped back from Freddie and schooled her features into a calm, placid look, which would make her mother proud.

Caroline could protest all she liked. Eve's evening had been a success. She had caught Freddie's attention. He now knew she existed and had taken her into his confidence.

It was time to go home, tear up her potential list of husbands, and prepare her battle plans to win Freddie's heart.

There was only one man on her list, and she was going to have him.

Chapter Seven

"Gentlemen, I must voice my disappointment in your efforts to secure a seat on the Bachelor Board. There are only so many challenges left, and the clock is ticking."

Freddie had been waiting for the moment when Osmont would make mention of the previous evening's party.

Osmont marched over to Godwin who was seated in his usual chair by the fireplace at the Barton Street office and came to a hard stop behind him. He reached out and gave Godwin a hearty pat on the shoulder.

"This young man had the balls, and I mean *balls*, to sample the delights of my hostesses. I know you came to the party Rosemount, but Godwin was the only one who actually *came*."

Freddie ignored the tavern-grade, vulgar remark, while Godwin sat with a huge self-satisfied grin on his face. Embry, who had his nose stuck in the newspaper didn't respond.

"Ah, but your nephew did offer me points if I came upstairs with him," replied Freddie.

Osmont harrumphed. "He meant you were to go upstairs and participate in the entertainment. So, you get nothing from last night.

Lord Godwin here got his cock well and truly sucked, and therefore collects himself a solid fifty points," replied Osmont.

Freddie gritted his teeth. While Godwin had scored points and numerous sexual favors the previous evening, Freddie was still in the lead for membership of the board. He began to wonder if he truly had the measure of Lord Godwin.

"So, what now for the next challenge?" asked an eager Godwin.

"Well the board and I have had a think, and we have decided that the challenge needs to be spiced up a little. As from today, the Rude Rules apply," said Osmont.

"And pray tell us, Firebrace, how do the Rude Rules work?" asked Freddie.

"Quite simple, actually. If you play the Rude Rules, you must take every opportunity to be a complete arse. If, for example, you can be rude to a lady and get away with it, you score points. The higher the social standing of the person you cause personal offence to, the higher the point score. Though I must caution you on attempting to be cheeky with the Prince Regent. Considering his temper and the current situation with his father's mental incapacity, you might just find yourself in the Tower of London if you try to play the Rude Rules at the Royal Court," replied Osmont.

Freddie sat back in his chair and considered this latest development. While the Rude Rules were simple in their plan, he could see how they could cause serious trouble while being executed. He was suddenly very grateful for the fact his parents were back at Rosemount Abbey. If his mother found out her youngest son was going about making a complete fool of himself in London society, she wouldn't hesitate to box his ears. His being of age meant nothing to his mother when it came to dishing out punishment for real and imagined transgressions.

Godwin sat back in his chair and softly chortled. His father was a duke, and Godwin had easy access to the highest levels of society. He was also known as being a bit dim among his family, so he had the advantage of having said many inappropriate things already. He could get away with the Rude Rules, and no one would think anything unusual about it. He could become a serious threat to Freddie's plans.

"Oh, and one other part of the rules. You need to have a willing partner. Someone who will play the game alongside you. While you are making a complete arse of yourself, they are to keep a straight face and not give any indication anything is amiss. They will be the person who writes a report each day of your Rude Rules efforts, which you shall hand directly to me. Of course, if I discover your partner has been untruthful in their account of your efforts, you will be immediately disqualified from the challenge."

Freddie chuckled as the smile on Godwin's face disappeared. No one wanted to be tarred with the same brush as socially awkward Godwin Mewburton.

"Just how much are we allowed to tell this other person about the Bachelor Board?" asked Freddie.

He had made mention of the game to Eve Saunders the previous night, and she had been keen to aid him in his quest. He didn't know anyone else in London he could ask, or at least no one as enticing as her.

"Only that you are playing a secret game and they have been selected to play along. I shall leave it up to your judgement, but I would suggest the bare minimum of details should be imparted. Just enough to secure their ongoing assistance in the challenges," replied Osmont.

This suited Freddie's plans. Eve had already sworn to keep the game secret. She looked like the sort of girl who would be up for some hijinks. As soon as he finished at the House of Commons, he would head home and search through the pile of invitations which no doubt had arrived at the house during the day. The Saunders siblings did not strike Freddie as the kind to sit at home all evening and do needle-work; they would be out and circulating within the social set. He was comfortable with his assumption that he could catch up with Eve at one of those parties and get her on board as a member of his Rude Rules team.

Chapter Eight

The moment Eve walked into the ballroom she knew she was being watched. The chill that ran down her spine had her searching for hidden eyes.

She caught a glimpse of a tall figure, in part shadow, near the entrance to the supper room. She sucked in a startled breath, then quickly turned her head, pretending not to have seen Freddie.

With a glass of champagne in her hand, she moved to the other side of the room. Much as she was tempted to cast a backward glance she kept her gaze forward. *Patience, Eve. Patience.*

She had learnt enough from Lucy's ill-fated plans to make Avery fall in love with her to know she should not appear to be overeager to gift Freddie with her attention. He would have to come to her.

"Good evening, Miss Saunders."

She turned, and feigned surprise.

He had followed her across the floor and sought her out. She liked that he appeared to be eager to see her again. "Mr. Rosemount, when did you arrive? I have been here for some time and did not notice you before," she replied, coolly.

Freddie bowed. As he did, she caught him looking up at her, a sly smile painted on his lips. A bubble of excitement began to dance in her stomach. He was just what she had been looking for all these years. "I must have arrived after you," he replied.

Eve laughed, and gently tapped him with her closed fan. "Oh, you liar! I saw you as soon as I arrived. Don't pretend you weren't trying to be the dark and mysterious stranger hiding in the shadows."

Freddie gave her a look of mock horror, then settled into a playful chuckle. "Ah, you have me. How are you this evening, Miss Saunders?"

"I am well, but I would be better if you called me Eve. My sister likes to be called Miss Saunders; it helps to keep a distance between her and her crush of admirers. For myself, I prefer to bestow a little familiarity on my friends. It makes cultivating relationships that much easier." She met his soulful gaze, swallowing deeply as she felt herself drawn to him. Freddie wasn't like the other young men she knew. There was depth to him … a certain mystery that enticed her.

Her imagination fleetingly took hold and she wondered what it would be like to wake up beside a man such as him every morning. Those eyes and that hardened body would keep her abed until late after the dawn.

She licked her lips. When she blinked back to the now, she saw that he was staring at her. She wasn't alone in the moment.

He cleared his throat and looked away briefly. "Do you recall our discussion of the other night, when I mentioned the secret game I am currently playing?"

Eve licked her lips a second time. She had thought of little else but Freddie over the past few days. In bed at night, she had lain awake thinking of all the wicked things they could do to one another. Her imagination had run to the edge of her knowledge of sexual matters.

What the man standing opposite her would say if he had any inkling of the effect he had had on her, she dared not think. Her nipples grew hard at the memory of how she had stroked herself when she had let her mind run wild with thoughts of Freddie's naked body.

"Yes," she replied through a sensual haze.

A strange look appeared on Freddie's face. A worried look. "Are you alright? You appear a little faint."

Eve snapped immediately out of her erotic daydream, then died a little of embarrassment. "Oh. Ah. It must be the champagne. I sometimes drink it a little too fast and it goes to my head."

She looked around and, finding a nearby footman, offloaded her glass of champagne onto his tray. She returned to Freddie, desperate to salvage the encounter. "You were saying about the secret game. Do go on."

Relief flooded her mind when his countenance returned to its previous state. "Yes, well, as I was saying. The game I am playing has entered a new phase. One in which I am going to need a partner. I was wondering if perhaps you might be interested in helping ..."

"Yes!"

They both chortled at her overly enthusiastic response.

"I am so sorry. I don't seem to be able to put two sensible words together tonight. You must think me a complete ninny," she said.

He reached out and placed a hand gently on her arm. "No. I find it rather charming. I am going to assume it's because you find me devilishly attractive, and even now you are falling hopelessly in love with me."

Eve prayed her cheeks were not bright red. Her heart was racing as she felt herself slowly die inside. How could he possibly be able to read her mind? She could not think of a moment in her entire life when she had been more embarrassed and awkward.

He released her arm. For a moment, she could have sworn he wore a worried look, then it all changed. A wicked grin appeared on his lips. "I'm only in jest, Eve. I was testing to see how good a player of the game you will make. I need someone who can keep a straight face while the farce is played out in front of them. You passed the test."

A player? He was asking her to join him in the game.

"Really? You want me to help you in the secret game? I didn't know if they would let girls play," she replied.

"Yes, of course you can play. The next phase of the game is called the Rude Rules. I have to act the fool in front of other people, preferably causing offence but not enough for them to be able to take public umbrage with me. You have to assist me as well as maintain the pretense there is absolutely nothing wrong with my behavior. At the end of each day you need to write a short note saying how I went.

Points are awarded based on how well we managed to play the Rude Rules. We cannot lie, of course, otherwise I shall be disqualified."

Eve had never heard of anything so preposterous. The plan was mad. It was also brilliant in its simplicity and attraction.

All her life, social behavior had been drummed into her. Public decorum ran in the blood of every young woman in London society. To use the wrong knife at a private dinner party was unthinkable.

She needed no press gang to get her to jump on-board this particular ship before it sailed.

"Tell me. Are there limits to this game? Anyone we should agree we cannot play the game with?" she asked.

"The Prince Regent is absolutely out of bounds unless you wish to find yourself on the scaffold at Newgate. The only other people who I would consider too dangerous to cross would be my parents. My mother is in town in a week or so for a few days, during which we shall have to suspend the Rude Rules. In the meantime, we shall have to work hard to score as many points as we can before she arrives."

Freddie stopped speaking and took a step back. Eve frowned at his sudden change in behavior, only understanding the reason why when she heard Caroline's voice.

"Rosemount," Caroline said.

"Caro," Freddie replied.

An indignant hiss escaped Caroline's lips. She and Freddie barely knew one another. It was inexcusable for a gentleman to call a young lady by anything but her formal name.

Eve gritted her teeth. The game was on.

Freddie turned to Eve and gave a snort. "Fancy a brandy, Evie? Champers is only for the weak and the French."

She kept her gaze firmly on him, not daring to look at her sister. Every muscle in her body was tensed in excitement. She knew full well that Caroline would be staring daggers at Freddie, while expecting Eve to rebuke him for his behavior. The French heritage of their family must be defended.

When she didn't support Caroline, her sister huffed angrily. Eve desperately wanted to clap her hands with delight, but she kept her poise.

"Of course. I always find champagne to be sickly and sweet," she replied.

Champagne was actually her favorite tipple and she hated brandy with a passion, but the game now held her in its grip. She would poke sticks in her eyes before she backed down and gave in. Especially in front of Caroline.

Arm in arm, Eve and Freddie walked away. She chanced a look back at her sister who was standing open-mouthed and visibly outraged behind them.

"She is going to kill me when we get home," muttered Eve.

"I am sure we can do better than your sister in the Rude Rules, Eve. She is an easy target. We need to find some bigger prey with which to score those vital points."

They found a footman and were soon making their way around the party with brandy glasses in hand. As they passed by other guests, they began to accumulate odd looks and whispers. It was not proper for a young lady to drink brandy in mixed company, nor to wander around a party on the arm of a gentleman with whom she was barely acquainted. They were skirting dangerously close to the edge of acceptable behavior, but Eve didn't care.

"I must say, you are a natural at this rebellious behavior. Were you a naughty girl as a child?" asked Freddie.

Eve took a sip of her brandy, trying her best not to screw up her face at the horrid taste. To say she had been naughty as a young girl would be a gross understatement. Her mother had been forever making Eve sit and mend clothes as punishment for her misdeeds.

"I have been accused of being a little too willful," she replied.

He leant in close and whispered seductively. "And I expect you were spanked enough times that you developed a taste for being bent over someone's knee."

Eve's mouth opened in a shocked 'o'. A young man had never said such an overtly sexually suggestive remark to her face before. Heat raced through her body and pooled in her loins. Freddie was a refreshing and mischievous delight.

They stopped at the edge of the dance floor, where a small group of guests were enjoying a waltz. The sight of the dancers twirling around the floor gave Eve a wicked idea.

"Do you dance, Freddie?"

"A little. Why?"

She pointed in the direction of the dancers, smiling when she saw Freddie's eyes open a little wider at the sight before them. He reached out and took her brandy glass from her hand, downing its contents in quick time.

Francis appeared at Freddie's side and tapped him on the shoulder.

"I say, Rosemount, my sister Caroline is most put out by your behavior. She claims you have been rude to her," said Francis.

Freddie nodded and thrust the brandy glasses into the hands of the bemused Francis. Freddie quickly took hold of Eve's hand and led her away.

"I think we are doing well in the point-scoring stakes tonight. Time to up the ante. If I am not mistaken, that is Lord Cullins dancing with his wife. He is a senior member of the prime minister's cabinet," said Freddie.

Once on the dance floor, they began to track toward their prey. A member of the parliamentary cabinet would help garner a handsome tally of points in the game.

Eve relaxed into the dance, enjoying the pleasurable sensation of being held close by Freddie. He was a skilled dancer, and her body fitted well against his as they moved through the dance steps. The warmth of his arms holding her radiated throughout her body.

They slowly worked their way around the dance floor, their target in their sights. As they reached the minister, Freddie cleared his throat. "That is a particularly lovely gown you have on this evening, my dear. If I dance close enough I can see right down the front of it. If you lean over a little more, I am certain I shall be rewarded with a glimpse of your nipples," he said.

Eve bit down on her bottom lip in an attempt to stifle a snigger. Out of the corner of her eye she caught the look of horrified disgust on Lady Cullins's face.

"Really? Can you? I don't believe it," she replied.

Freddie chuckled. "Well, lean forward and I shall tell you exactly the color of your nipples. Do you have any hair on them, by chance?"

The minister's wife cleared her throat as Eve leant forward. Freddie closed the distance and very obviously looked down.

"Young man. That is entirely unsuitable behavior for the dance floor. And as for you, young lady, I shall discover who you are and have a word with your mama. You should not have been allowed to come out if you were not properly finished," scolded Lady Cullins.

Eve watched as Freddie fixed an idiotic look to his countenance and turned to the minister's wife. "Scientific research must be conducted in all manner of places. I am more than happy to do the same research with you if you feel the statistics will be skewed by such a small sample."

The ugliest of scenes was only avoided by the fortuitous ending of the music, which signaled the end of the dance. The minister and his equally outraged wife marched from the dance floor. They approached a footman who quickly escorted them out into the foyer.

"I say. Are they leaving? Was it something we said?" asked Eve.

Freddie turned to her. His lips were held tightly together. His eyes shone brightly with suppressed mirth. "A British cabinet minister—this calls for another drink. Then we need to decide who to target next."

"I could do with a spot of night air before we get another brandy," replied Eve.

They found a door and headed out onto the garden terrace. The cold night air immediately had Eve's brandy-affected brain spinning. She reached out and took hold of Freddie's arm to steady herself.

"Are you alright?" he asked.

She sucked in a deep breath. Then began to laugh. "I cannot believe we just did that! My mother will skin me alive if Lady Cullins ever discovers my identity."

Freddie gave her a worried look, which she laughed off. The thrill of danger coursed through her veins. If this was devilish behavior, it was a heady drug she wanted to experience over and over again.

Eve's evening of mirth and dangerous delight eventually ended on a sober note. Caroline sat silent in the carriage on the journey home. Eve didn't bother to look at her sister. She could feel the imaginary daggers being plunged into her heart, but after an evening spent with Freddie Rosemount, she refused to let it get to her. Once inside their family home, they both headed upstairs.

Eve entered her room and was about to close the door when an angry Caroline barged into the room behind her.

"How dare you treat me like that?"

Eve gave her a weary look. She was tired from too much dancing and far too much brandy to conduct a full-scale row with Caroline. Her evening with Freddie had been a triumph. Her long game of baiting Caroline was beginning to lose its luster in comparison to the sharp, shiny newness of the Rude Rules.

"I don't know what you are talking about," she replied, with a tired wave of her fingers.

Enraged, Caroline reached out and grabbed a hold of her hand.

Eve winced in pain. "Let go of me, you self-important bore."

The look on Caroline's face immediately changed. Eve took deep satisfaction in knowing the spiteful remark had stung liked a slap to the face.

"Oh, don't go looking all offended and upset, Caroline, just because someone doesn't fall on their knees in front of you. We can't all be fawning members of your royal court."

Caroline pointed a finger at Eve. "You take that back. You take it all back now."

Eve shook her head and walked away. She undid the ties of her cloak and let it fall with satisfying dramatic effect onto her bed. She walked over to her dresser and picked up her hairbrush.

Her maid entered the bedroom and stopped when she saw Caroline. Eve beckoned her over, and her maid busied herself with pulling the pins from Eve's hair. Caroline remained standing to one side of the doorway, her fists tightly clenched.

Eve looked at her through the dressing table mirror, giving her a *why are you still here* glare.

"You cannot hold me to account just because I am finally getting a little attention and you don't like it."

"What I don't like is being treated so poorly by my sister and her newly minted friend. I shall expect your apology in the morning," replied Caroline angrily.

Eve's maid jumped as Caroline slammed the door behind her as she left.

Eve sat quietly while the rest of the pins and ribbons, which had held her hair in place, were removed. Her heart was thumping a loud tattoo in her chest. Tonight, she had crossed several lines of socially acceptable behavior.

The thrill she had experienced with Freddie on the dance floor had emboldened her so much that Caroline had never stood a chance when she'd sought to correct Eve. Hell would freeze over before she apologized to Caroline. Hell, or the wrath that her mother would bring down on her if Caroline decided to cross another line tonight and tell their mother about Eve's encounter with Freddie Rosemount.

Chapter Nine

E ve rose late. Keeping up with Freddie and the game was beginning to take its toll. Instead of going out socializing once or twice a week, she was now seeing him every night. Adelaide had made mention of the late hours Eve and Francis were keeping when they arrived home the previous evening.

Francis was gifted with the ability to stay out late but still be up and fresh with the dawn. Eve was not so fortunate. Adding to her problem was the fact she was a young lady. It would only be a matter of time before her mother decided a quiet word about reputations was in order.

Fate, fortunately, had other plans for Adelaide Saunders that morning. As Eve sat in front of the mirror of her dressing table, her bedroom door crashed open.

"He's coming home. He's leaving Gibraltar within the week!" announced an excited Adelaide. In her hand she brandished a letter.

Eve didn't need to ask to whom her mother was referring. Her older brother, William, had been away in France for five years and had recently written to the family announcing his intention to return permanently to England. Every day since then, Adelaide had checked with the family butler to see if further letters from Will had been received.

"That is wonderful news," replied Eve. She looked at her teary-eyed mother and smiled. It was more than wonderful. It was a huge relief.

Will had been a secret agent for the British government in the war to overthrow Napoleon. His ability to speak his father's native tongue, and fit in with the local population in Paris, had made him an effective spy.

The war had been over for two years, and Will had made his first trip home to England during the summer. His family had been expecting him to stay and were dismayed when he'd returned to France. Her mother had felt the pain of disappointment harder than the rest of the family. Eve and Caroline had temporarily put aside their differences and rallied around her, but Adelaide had continued to weep for many weeks after Will's departure.

"He has spent some time in Spain and is now in Gibraltar. Oh, Eve, he says by the time we get this letter he will already be on the boat. My boy is coming home. My boy!" exclaimed her mother.

"What did Papa say?" asked Eve.

"He doesn't know. That's why I am here. You need to get dressed and come with me to your father's offices at once. Both he and Francis need to know the marvelous news without delay. Caroline has gone shopping with Harry Menzies's mother and sister, so we shall have to wait until she returns to tell her."

Eve frowned. What was Caroline doing going shopping with the female relatives of Francis's best friend? A best friend who, as everyone apart from Caroline seemed to know, was head over heels in love with her?

Caroline had made no mention of having developed any romantic attachment for Harry. He came from a good family and had a sizeable fortune from importing goods from the Americas, but her sister had never treated him with anything other than cool politeness. All the nights Eve had watched Harry worship Caroline from close quarters proved her sister's interest in him bordered on indifference.

But Caroline was no fool. She would have seen Eve and Freddie together enough times to know Eve had likely set her sights on him. If Caroline made a sudden and decisive move to be the first one married, Eve was likely to be caught wrong-footed.

A more pressing problem also now presented itself. The chances of her being able to get out the house each night to see Freddie would be severely curtailed in the first weeks of her brother's return. There would be family reunions and special dinners held in his honor. Much as she wanted him safely home, Will's return could not be coming at a worse time. If Will was already on the boat back to England, she had only a matter of a week or so to force Freddie's hand.

"Now get dressed. I want to go and see your father within the hour," said Adelaide.

She turned on her heel and rushed out the door.

Eve stared at her reflection in the mirror.

A small smile formed on her lips as she remembered Freddie having made mention that his mother was coming to London in the next few days. He had not formally requested permission from her father to court Eve, but Adelaide and Lady Rosemount knew one another.

If she could manage to get the two mothers together, and drop some subtle hints, the wheels of future matrimony would begin to turn. If Caroline had indeed decided to settle on Harry Menzies as her future husband, it was going to be a race between the two sisters as to who could get to the altar first.

"I'll be damned if I am going to be the second bride of the family. I am going to get married before she does, even if it means having to elope," muttered Eve.

Her fingers gripped the side of the dressing table. Eloping would be scandalous. An elopement would put Lucy and Avery's hasty marriage to shame. She and Freddie would be the talk of London society. Her mother would be mortified, and Caroline would be furious.

She was falling in love with Freddie, every moment spent with him was magic to her heart. But until now he had shown no indication of having formed any sort of emotional attachment to her. Unrequited love would be a bitter pill to swallow if all her plans amounted to nothing.

Chapter Ten

F reddie took a walk to clear his head. Osmont Firebrace had given the Bachelor Board candidates their next challenge the previous morning. They were to purchase an animal and name it something outrageous. They were then to take the animal with them everywhere for an entire week and address the animal at every opportunity.

Trenton Embry had shown his usual level of interest in the game by promptly buying a mouse. He'd named it Tiger, which he found highly amusing. For the first time since he had met the dour Trenton, Freddie actually heard a chuckle escape his lips. His efforts at the game had become nothing more than tokenism, which suited Freddie just fine. Only Godwin was any real threat to his success.

Godwin had done little better. He'd bought a baby turtle and named it Flash. It had relieved itself in his coat pocket several times already that morning, and by the time Freddie left Barton Street, the stench had seeped into the wool of his friend's clothes. Godwin was regretting his hasty decision.

That left Freddie open to come up with something a little more imaginative. But what?

As soon as he arrived home the previous day, he had sent word to

Eve of the new challenge. She was an intelligent girl, and one he knew would have plenty to say on the matter of beast he was to purchase.

He made it as far as the Thames before turning back to head for home. On the way he strolled from Piccadilly into Old Bond Street, his mind still fixed on the problem of the animal he should purchase. He needed those valuable challenge points if he was to hold Lord Godwin at bay.

What sort of animal could he take everywhere with him? He was still pondering the question when Eve and her brother Francis came into view.

He immediately questioned his decision to send her details of the next challenge.

Leading both Eve and Francis—though dragging could have been a closer word to the truth—was a huge, lumbering, Irish grey wolfhound. His brother had once owned one while at university and had constantly complained about how much it had cost him to feed the dog.

As they drew closer, he began to pray the dog was a member of the Saunders's family. From the look of displeasure on Francis's face, he knew he was in for no such luck.

Eve, on the other hand, was grinning from ear to ear. A laugh threatened with every step she took. Her hands were wrapped tightly around the end of the lead and she appeared to be holding on with all her might.

When they finally reached where Freddie was standing, Francis took the lead out of his sister's hand and passed it to Freddie. Freddie's heart sank as he took possession of his unexpected gift.

Eve gave up on her attempt not to laugh and broke out into a cackle. "Oh, you should have seen us, Freddie, it was hilarious. We got up at the crack of dawn and went all the way out to Spitalfields market to buy him. Francis here thought a small cat would do the trick, but as soon as I saw this monstrous beast I knew he was perfect for you."

Francis gave his sister a deathly glare, obviously not enjoying the jest as well as she. Freddie caught sight of the drool stains on the front of Francis's trousers and coat, and guffawed.

"Laugh all you want, Rosemount. Just remember how funny you

thought this all was when he has made a complete mess of your clothing. I expect by day's end the joke will have worn thin. I don't know what the two of you are playing at, but this beast is beyond ridiculous," replied Francis.

Eve rolled her eyes. "Saintspreserveus."

"No! You are not calling the dog that. You are the niece of the Bishop of London. Please try to have at least a half ounce of decorum," snapped Francis.

Eve and Freddie's gazes met. They knew the rules of the game. The pet had to have a ridiculous name. She smiled back at him. Those dark hazel eyes held him in their sway. He couldn't go against her in front of her brother; she would never forgive him.

His gaze drifted to her lips. He wanted to kiss them. He also wanted to kiss several other places on her body.

"Saintspreserveus. I like it. It rolls smoothly off the tongue," said Freddie.

Francis let out a sigh. "I see I am in the company of two fools. So be it. Eve can accompany you and the dog for the walk back to Grosvenor Square. I shall send the carriage around to collect her as soon as I get home. But for heaven's sake, Eve, try to avoid being seen by anyone who knows you."

"Saints preserve us," Eve muttered as Francis walked away.

Freddie looked at her and chuckled. "Are we really going to give this beast that name? Poor creature."

The dog held its head high and seemed to be doing its utmost to ignore both of them. If Francis thought the name was foolish, so, it would appear, did the dog.

"Yes. You told me you needed an animal for the challenge. I thought we could kill two birds with one stone. Plenty of people will take offence at the name, so we can get Rude Rules points as well. I would have thought you would understand, but clearly a demonstration is in order," Eve replied with a huff. She snatched the lead from out of Freddie's hand and let the end fall to the ground. The dog took one look at the lead and bolted.

Freddie didn't have time to question the recklessness of what Eve had done. He was too busy running after his new pet as its long legs loped along the street. A giggling Eve trailed behind them.

"Call his name!" she shouted.

"Saintspreserveus!" cried Freddie.

The jest finally landed. Two fools were running after a dog, crying "saints preserve us" at the top of their lungs. Eve, in her cunning, had found a way for them to score extra points. The Rude Rules would allow points for idiocy and public offence, while the new challenge was covered with the name of the dog. A dog who was fast putting distance between its new owner and itself.

As they rounded the corner into Bruton Street, they both skidded to a halt. Saintspreserveus had made it all the way to Berkley Square and was busy relieving himself on the leaves of a low green hedge.

"Walk slowly to the right side of the square, and I shall take the left," whispered Freddie.

The scene was farcical. Here was a huge, furry beast nuzzling the well-kept greenery of the garden, while two humans attempted to sneak up on it.

They got closer. At one point the dog lifted its head and looked back down the street. Eve hurried and hid in the doorway of a nearby shop. Freddie, caught out in the open, froze.

"Here, boy. Saintspreserveus, come, boy," he called.

Several people passing by gave him strange looks, Freddie simply smiled at them.

Eve stepped out from the shopfront. "Saintspreserveus!"

Side by side, the two of them walked the length of the street, repeatedly calling the dog's name. Both managed to keep their faces straight.

Finally, they reached where Saintspreserveus was standing. His head was over the side of an ornamental fountain and he was happily lapping up the water with his long pink tongue. Freddie swiftly took a hold of the lead and wrapped it firmly around his arm.

Eve came to his side but uncharacteristically said nothing.

"Eve, what's wrong?" he asked, reaching out and touching her arm.

She turned to him, her face a sudden study in seriousness. "What will your family say when they see the dog? Will they think I am a foolish young miss who should be at home under the watchful eye of her mother?"

Freddie paused for a moment. He hadn't actually thought what his family would say about the dog. When it came to the subject of Eve, they were completely in the dark.

His heart went out to her. When their relationship came to the attention of their respective parents it would put Eve's behavior in particular under scrutiny.

The thought pulled him up short. A relationship did exist between them. He couldn't deny he felt a strong attraction to the free-spirited Eve. Looking at her now, standing beside him, he was possessed of the need to kiss her until every single one of her worries was gone.

"It's alright. I won't mention that it came from you. My family are very keen on dogs, so they will likely take to this big furry beast with gusto," he replied with a smile.

It was a good thing his family did like dogs. While Saintspreserveus had been purchased as part of the challenge, it was now his dog to feed and look after.

He bent down and gave Saintspreserveus a scratch behind the ear. "I promise, when this is all over, you will go and live at my family estate in the country. There are lots of places where you can run free and be happy."

Freddie stood and offered Eve his arm. Overbearing brothers could go hang. He wanted to walk with Eve by his side, and he would damn well do it.

❧

Eve sighed with relief as she took Freddie's arm. It had been a risky move to go and buy the dog, but as soon as she had seen him she knew he was exactly what the game required. A small animal, who could fit in a coat pocket, would never be enough to cause the sort of mayhem the Bachelor Board challenge required. Chasing Saintspreserveus through the streets of London while crying out his name would earn Freddie more points.

She reached into her reticule and pulled out a piece of paper. She wrote a few notes on it and then handed it to Freddie.

"Today's score sheet for the challenge, I have added in the dog," she said, handing it to him.

He smiled as he took the paper and put it in his jacket pocket.

"Thanks, you are the best partner a chap could ever ask for."

His words were exactly what her heart longed to hear. With every win, he would see how important she was in his life. If she kept to this path, in time, Freddie would come to the realization their futures were inevitably linked together as one, and that she deserved a place by his side at Rosemount Abbey.

With Saintspreserveus safely on his lead, they made good time in getting to Grosvenor Square. Eve had attempted to slow their pace, but Freddie and the dog had other ideas.

Crossing Grosvenor Square, she was relieved to see the Saunders family town carriage was not waiting out the front of Rosemount House. As they reached the front steps of his home, Freddie gave a quick glance around them and pulled a surprised Eve inside the front door.

"We don't want the neighbors seeing you arrive. It will get back to your parents," he said.

He waved away the footman who came to enquire as to whether he and the young lady required refreshments. Instead, he handed him the dog's lead and instructed him to find some food and water.

"We can wait in here until your carriage arrives. We should be able to see it out the front window," he said. He showed her into a ground-floor sitting room and closed the door behind him.

Eve had taken two steps toward a nearby couch in order to sit down before Freddie grabbed her by the arm and pulled her back to him. Before she could utter a word of protest, he wrapped his arm around her waist and pulled her hard against him. "I've been wanting to do this since the first day we met," he said.

His lips descended and she felt the soft heat of his mouth as he took her in a searing kiss. She tilted her head back and relaxed into the embrace.

He ran his tongue along the bottom of her lip, and when she

opened her mouth, his tongue swept inside. The kiss deepened as their tongues met and slowly began to move against one another in a passionate dance. This was everything she had ever hoped for in a first kiss. Heat and passion.

His hand drifted down lower and he took a firm grip of her bottom, pulling her even harder against him. The layers of her cloak and gown could not disguise the hardness of his manhood as he held her in this tight embrace. The knowledge she was arousing him both frightened and thrilled her.

She softened her lips. He kissed exactly like she had hoped he would. There was no youthful fumbling in his actions.

"Oh, Eve," he murmured, pulling away from her lips.

She looked into his eyes and saw the glaze of passion in them. She reached up and put a hand to his cheek, drawing him back to her. Their mouths met once more in a soft kiss, which rapidly grew in its intensity. A kiss that spoke of an understanding of the change in their relationship. His hands pushed open the folds of her cloak and she felt fingers brush against her nipples. When he took her nipple between his fingers and gently squeezed, she let out a low groan of satisfaction.

Desire stirred within her body, and she sensed she was about to lose the little power she had over the situation. If Freddie decided to lower her to the sitting room rug and take her innocence here and now, she would let him do it.

He pulled out of the kiss and let out a stuttering breath. "Sorry, I got a tad carried away there for a minute."

Eve stepped back and tidied up the front of her gown and cloak. Through the lace curtains of the sitting room window she saw her family town carriage draw up out the front. Disappointment descended on her happy mood. The moment between them was at an end.

"I have to go," she said.

"Yes, of course. Thank you for the dog. He is exactly what we need."

An awkwardness descended on what had been an intimate moment only seconds before. Freddie ushered Eve toward the door, but he no longer met her gaze.

As she climbed into the carriage, she gave him a hopeful smile. He returned it with a friendly wave and closed the door. When the carriage drew away from the edge of the road, Eve looked back.

A second carriage now drew up outside Rosemount House, and Freddie turned away from her. She silently wished he would look back, but whomever was in the other carriage had captured his attention.

She sat back and faced forward. They had shared a kiss—one which spoke of desire and a hungry need. She could only hope he felt more than mere lust for her. With her heart now in dangerous territory, her greatest fear was that he would be guided by society expectations and be forced to offer for her. She might beat Caroline to the altar, but a loveless marriage would be the most hollow victory of all.

It would be the greatest gamble of her life to risk both her heart and reputation, and it was a decision she was going to have to make alone. With Lucy on her honeymoon in Paris, and Caroline barely on speaking terms with her, there was no one to turn to for advice. Freddie was a risk she was going to have to take on her own terms.

Chapter Eleven

F reddie stood and watched as Eve's carriage pulled away. He had half turned away when another carriage drew up outside the house.

It was the Rosemount travel coach. Seated at the nearest window was his mother. A footman stepped down from the coach and opened the door.

"Frederick, what perfect timing. One guest leaves as the other arrives," she said, taking his hand.

Freddie schooled his features into that of the dutiful son, while inwardly thanking the gods his mother had not arrived five minutes earlier.

His mother was spending a few days in town to check up on him, and once she was satisfied he had not burnt the house to the ground, she would head back to Rosemount Abbey. Hopefully.

Freddie Rosemount was not the first son of any family to wish his parents would stay out of his life.

"Who was that you were saying farewell to? The footman on the back of the carriage looked to be wearing the livery of the Saunders family," his mother said.

Freddie's heart sank. His mother had seen the carriage with Eve leaving and he had no time to find a lie. Within the hour his mother would have penned a note to Adelaide Saunders mentioning having just missed the family member who had been visiting at Rosemount House.

He could not stand by and let Eve's reputation be called into question. It was time to step up and defend his girl.

"Come inside, Mama. You must be tired from the journey. Then we can talk."

&a.

Eve kept a low profile for the next day or so. Freddie had sent word that his mother was in town and they would have to wait a few days before attempting to resume the game. She took his note as a blessing in disguise; a rest from the game gave her the opportunity to catch up on some well needed sleep. Going out night after night with Freddie was taking its toll.

It also gave her time to think on how she could get Freddie to reveal his feelings for her. The kiss had been all that she had hoped for, but whether it led to him declaring himself to her was uncertain.

"Ah, just the person I wish to speak to," said her mother, catching Eve in the upstairs hall.

Eve held her breath. Those words were never ones she enjoyed hearing. It usually meant she was either in trouble or, worse still, about to spend an evening listening to the latest gossip from among London society. She wasn't sure which she hated more. Gossip never transpired to be half as good as it was initially reported.

With reluctance, she followed her mother into her formal drawing room and took a chair near the window. She straightened her back and sat with hands clasped ladylike in her lap. She waited for her mother to speak.

Instead, her mother came and sat next to her, taking Eve's hand softly within hers. "I received a note from Lady Rosemount this morning. Apparently, you have become acquainted with her son, Frederick, and she would like to meet you. Isn't that lovely news?" asked Adelaide.

Eve stilled. She had thought of several things her mother could take her to task over, including her treatment of Caroline. The news that Freddie's mother wanted to meet her was a lightning bolt she had not seen coming.

"Yes," she replied.

She felt Adelaide's gaze boring into the side of her head. Nothing got past her mother. If Freddie had decided to make mention of their friendship, then it made sense she do the same.

"We met a few weeks ago at a party. He knows Francis," she replied.

Throwing her brother's name into the mix could only help to steer her mother away from thoughts of impropriety on her daughter's part. She privately prayed the sibling code of silence would still hold.

"I'm surprised you didn't make mention of him until now. Or was it your intention not to tell me about this young man?" asked Adelaide.

Eve swallowed deep and turned to her mother. "We are friends. Though matters may eventually head in the direction of something more, I cannot at this point say."

Adelaide met her gaze. Eve suddenly felt naked. Why did mothers know when their daughters were not telling the whole truth? "Well, Lady Rosemount has invited you and I for tea later this week. I have accepted the invitation on our behalf, assuming you would want me to do so."

Eve nodded. There wasn't much else she could do. It felt odd that while she had been making secret plans to win Freddie's heart, he had made several unexpected moves of his own. The kiss had taken her completely by surprise, and she had thought of little else since.

Meeting his mother took things several miles past where she thought they were in their budding romance. With Adelaide now aware of the relationship, it wouldn't be long before the discussion turned to the matter of a betrothal.

"Yes. That would be lovely. I am looking forward to meeting Lady Rosemount. Though of course, if you think Will's impending home-coming will disrupt our visit I would be happy to postpone it."

Adelaide smiled. "Absolutely not. Your happiness is as important to me as is your brother coming home. Once he is back here in Dover

Street, I shall be able to see him every day. The opportunity for you to meet with your potential future mother-in-law is something to be treated with the dignity and reverence it deserves."

Mother-in-law.

The very words sent shivers of fear down Eve's spine. What if Lady Rosemount was a stickler for protocol and behavior? She would see right through Eve's charade of a well-bred young woman and know she was entirely unsuitable for her son.

Then where would she be?

Chapter Twelve

"Where can he be?"
Eve and Caroline shared a knowing look and went back to writing notes.

Will's ship from Gibraltar had docked in London early that morning. Word had been sent from Charles's shipping agent as soon as the *Canis Major* had berthed at the docks. Adelaide had taken up a post in the downstairs sitting room nearest the front door to wait for Will's arrival.

By mid-morning she was pacing the front hallway. By noon she stood just inside the front door, arms crossed. Waiting.

Will's luggage arrived early in the afternoon, but there was no sign of Will himself. At three o'clock, Adelaide marshalled her troops. Eve and Caroline were each given a small pile of cards with instructions to write to everyone in London who could possibly tell Adelaide the whereabouts of her first-born son.

"That boy owes me three years of my life. I lost count of the nights I sat up and worried about him while he was on his secret mission in Paris. He is a wicked and cruel son if he thinks I should have to wait a day longer for his return."

"He may have some pressing business matters he needs to finalize before he comes home," offered Caroline.

Eve's heart went out to her mother. For as long as she could remember, the arrival of the morning post had been an occasion of silence and dread within the family. Dread that among the letters and invitations would be a communication from British army command that the French authorities had uncovered Will's true identity and he had met his fate at the hands of Madame Guillotine.

"Mama, he will come. If not today, then tomorrow. His luggage has arrived, so he clearly intends to come home," said Caroline.

A knock at the door heralded Charles Saunders. Adelaide rose from her chair, a handful of notes held tightly in her hand. Charles came to his wife and gave her a gentle kiss on the cheek.

"Will sent word. He has urgent army business to attend to which he cannot discuss. Suffice to say, he is in London and will be with us as soon as he can. In the meantime, I suggest we go on as we have done for the past one thousand, eight hundred and however many days since he has been away," said Charles.

Adelaide took her husband's advice and as a result, Eve found herself sitting in Lady Rosemount's drawing room late the following morning. If her mother was still anxious about not being home when Will eventually did arrive, she hid it well.

The talk meandered through various safe topics, while Eve sat quietly waiting for it to land on the real reason for her and Adelaide's visit to Rosemount House. She was nervous, all her self-confidence having fled the moment she set foot inside the front door.

"So, Eve, Frederick tells me you and he have recently become friends. I cannot begin to tell you how pleased I am he has found new friends since his arrival in London. He is not the most outgoing of young men and finds it difficult to socialize," said Lady Rosemount finally.

Eve continued to chew on her cake long past when it was well and truly ready to be swallowed. It allowed her time to gather her thoughts and frame a suitable response.

The Freddie his mother described was nothing like the man she knew.

"Oh, so he is a shy young man. I hadn't realized," replied Adelaide.

Eve crossed her toes in her slippers and prayed. One of the lessons she had learned from playing the Rude Rules challenges was that keeping a straight face at all times was imperative. If people thought you found humor in a situation, they were likely to do one of two things: they either wanted to be in on the jest, or they got angry. *Very* angry, in the case of several people she and Freddie had managed to offend during the game.

"He is a quiet young man, almost bookish I would say, which is why it is encouraging to see he has caught the eye of a lovely young lady. Especially, may I say, one from such a respectable and well-connected family," replied his mother.

She caught her mother's eye. Adelaide was beaming proudly at her daughter.

Eve picked up her cup of tea and took a hesitant sip. She was content to let her mother and Lady Rosemount do the talking. It allowed her to add to the long list of questions she was going to ask Freddie when next they were alone.

"Do you enjoy the countryside, Evelyn?" asked Lady Rosemount.

Eve felt the heat of two pairs of eyes looking straight at her.

"Yes. I've always enjoyed going to Scotland at Christmas. Mama's family castle, Strathmore Castle, is in the wilds of Scotland, and I do love long walks among the hills and the valleys," she replied.

Both her mother and Lady Rosemount sat back in their chairs, smiles evident on their faces. It was a morning for smiles. Eve had given the correct answer. They would see little point in a marriage between a headstrong city girl and a bookish lad from the country, but Eve had set their minds to rest.

"Well, then. May I suggest you and your mother come and visit us at Rosemount Abbey. I am certain the rest of the family would like to meet you both. My eldest daughter-in-law, Cecily, most especially would be interested in meeting Evelyn."

A small bubble of excitement and fear formed in Eve's stomach. Lady Rosemount had invited her to visit Freddie's family home, which could only mean he had told his mother he was intending to make an offer for her hand in marriage.

"Mama?" she replied, suddenly in need of her mother's reassurance. Things were beginning to move at a pace Eve could no longer fully control.

"That would be lovely. My eldest son is returning to England this week after a number of years abroad, so a visit would have to be after he has settled in at home. Would the end of the month suit your convenience?" asked Adelaide.

Lady Rosemount placed her hands together and nodded. "The end of the month it is. I shall let Frederick know. He will be most pleased. And in the meantime, I shall head home and make preparations for your visit."

Chapter Thirteen

With the matter of their visit to Rosemount Abbey agreed upon and settled, the two older women now spent several hours working through their respective social connections.

At one stage, Eve wished she had a pen and ink to map out the interconnected families of England's nobility. Every family had married into the other family at some point or other. Blood lines crossed over many times down the centuries. By the time she and Adelaide left Rosemount House, Eve had calculated she and Freddie were forty-third cousins, twice removed. Distant enough for her to know they shared little blood.

Eve's musings over her future with Freddie were set to one side as soon as she and Adelaide set foot inside their home. They were greeted by a familiar and very welcome face.

"William!" Adelaide promptly burst into floods of tears and threw herself into her son's arms. Will stood, eyes closed, holding his mother, while Eve watched through a veil of her own tears. Will was finally home for good. He was safe. Her brave big brother had been returned to her.

"Francis says he is not moving out of your old room," Eve said.

Will chuckled. "Yes, we have already had that conversation. Now he is taller than me, he thinks he can push me around. But to be honest, I am happy just to have a room to sleep in. He is welcome to my old space."

"Where have you been, you wicked boy? Your father said you had some army business to attend to, but haven't you done enough already for your country?" asked Adelaide.

"Sorry, it was unplanned business that could not wait. It was late by the time I had finished so I stayed at Bat and Rosemary's last night."

Adelaide nodded. The Earl and Countess of Shale had been under-cover operatives with Will during the war; a special bond existed between Will and his cousin.

Will and Eve embraced. "And I hear you have news of your own," he said.

Eve looked away, sheepish at the thought her secret love was now becoming public knowledge. "Freddie Rosemount and I have become friends. It is nothing more than that at this moment, but we shall see."

Adelaide said nothing, for which Eve was grateful. She wanted to keep news of the impending visit to Rosemount Abbey a secret until she had had a chance to talk to Freddie. It was all well and good to start making wedding plans, but when she and he had not even discussed the matter of possible affections held, the idea of marriage was a little premature.

"Speaking of married people, I hear we have much to thank you for in the turnaround in Lucy and Avery's wedded fortunes," said Adelaide. Eve gave her brother a second hug. For Lucy.

"I played a small part—nothing more. We menfolk can be blind sometimes to what is in front of us. It was obvious when I met Lucy and Avery in Paris that Avery was in sore need of someone to clear the scales from his eyes. Once he accepted he was already in love with Cousin Lucy, there was nothing left for me to do," replied Will.

His remarks were typical of Will. From Lucy's letters it was clear he had been instrumental in putting her and Avery's faltering marriage onto solid footing, yet he would never seek to claim the accolades he so richly deserved.

"So, when do I get to meet this young man?" Will asked Eve.

"Soon. Your father and I are planning on a small gathering of friends to celebrate your return. Nothing big, as per your instructions. We shall invite Frederick to the gathering," replied Adelaide.

A prick of worry entered Eve's mind. Hearing her family openly discuss Freddie was becoming a little too real for her comfort. While their relationship had remained a secret from her parents, she had a sense of control. With their respective parents stepping into the picture, she was going to have to renegotiate the terms of the Bachelor Board challenges with him.

Before he met with her family, they would need to agree on what was to be done with the Rude Rules. It was fun to be rude to strangers —and even Caroline at times—but she dreaded to think what would happen if something untoward was said to one of the senior members of her family.

Chapter Fourteen

"**B**loody hell!"

Freddie marched in the front door of Rosemount House and swore. He had held his tongue the whole of the walk from Whites club, but as soon as he got home his pent-up rage got the better of him.

As his voice echoed around the walls, he gave thanks his mother had left London the previous day and gone home to Rosemount Abbey. He had several other words he intended to use, none of which would be fit for his mother's ears.

Godwin had got the better of him in the Rude Rules this morning and he was livid. In front of a dozen witnesses, the Duke of Mewburton's youngest son had managed to act the goat and offend the Archbishop of Canterbury, three foreign ambassadors, and a representative from the Papal delegation.

To top it all off, he had done so while Osmont Firebrace had been enjoying a meal in the dining room of Whites club.

Freddie's mind was awhirl with the sheer number of points Godwin would have scored for his outrageous efforts.

A footman tentatively offered him a tray upon which sat a note. Freddie gave it a quick glance, then seeing the handwriting, picked up the letter.

It was from Eve.

The thought of her brought his rage down a notch. She would understand the predicament he was in. He hurriedly opened it.

My family want to meet you at a small gathering to welcome Will home. We need to discuss the Rude Rules. I don't think offending my family will go down well.

This was precisely not what he needed. With their families now aware of their relationship, Eve would no doubt be asking for him to exempt her family from the game. With Godwin's stroke of genius now hanging over his head, Freddie was going to have to convince Eve of the opposite.

Everyone they knew, family included, was going to be fair game from now on.

⁂

The moment Freddie's gaze landed on Will and her father, Eve knew her evening was going to be torture.

He looked down at her and placed her hand on his arm. Leaning in close, he whispered, "It has to be done. There are only a handful of challenges left. If Godwin beats me, everything will be for naught. The life you want with me will be nothing compared to what we can have if I win my seat on the Bachelor Board. I need you to support me, Eve."

She gritted her teeth. There was nothing she could do.

As they approached her father and older brother, she began to silently rehearse the apology she knew she would have to make after this evening. "Papa, Will, may I introduce my friend, Frederick Rosemount?"

Freddie reached out and shook her father's hand. "A pleasure to meet you Mr. Saunders."

Eve let out a small breath. So far, so good. Her father would be the one to decide if she was going to marry Freddie. Offending him might be counterproductive to her plans.

"And Will. You must be pleased to be able to speak the King's English once more. French is a God-awful language to learn at school. I would hate to have to speak it every day," said Freddie.

A look of bemusement appeared on her father's face. Charles Saunders was French-born, having only changed the family name from Alexandre after losing his father during the bloody French Revolution. He was a proud patriot to his boots.

"Yes, I do so love English as a language," added Eve.

"But French is the mother of the romance languages," replied Will.

Freddie let out a derisive snort and pulled Eve closer. "Yes, well, we English have the edge over all those foreigners when it comes to romance. Just ask Eve here. She would never marry a Frenchman when she can find fine English stock like myself within her reach."

And so, it went on. Thirty minutes of excruciating embarrassment in front of the two senior male members of her family. Eve was relieved beyond words when Freddie finally announced he was leaving.

She followed him out to the foyer. "Did you really have to insult my family heritage? And I will have you know that not all Frenchmen are short," she said.

Freddie finished putting on his coat. "I'm sorry. I know that was hard for you, and believe me, I didn't enjoy it much either. Though I have to say your brother held his temper well. I was watching his jaw while I told him that French food is terrible, and he was clearly grinding his teeth. I am certain he would love to have punched me in the face if he had got the chance." He brushed a hand on Eve's cheek, then bent down and placed a soft, tender kiss on her lips. As he pulled away, their gazes met. "I'm proud of you. You stood by me tonight. I won't forget it, *mon doux amour*," he whispered.

As he walked out the front door, Eve closed her eyes. He had told her he loved her, but at what cost had those words come?

She turned and went back into the gathering, the beginning of an apology already on her lips.

Chapter Fifteen

"Yes, Mama."

Those words had become Eve's mantra over the past few days. Anything to placate her mother's mood.

Freddie had played the insufferable fool in front of Eve's parents and siblings. Eve had been forced to stand by his side and act as if nothing was amiss. His behavior had cast a shadow over the evening, and her mother and gone to great lengths to continually remind Eve of that fact.

Adelaide was busy ordering about the servants and anyone else within earshot. A quiet family dinner with her brother Hugh and his wife Mary would not normally be the cause of such anxious behavior, but her mother had been in an odd mood all week.

"So, Frederick knows what time supper will be served, and he shall endeavor to be here on time?"

"Yes, Mama."

"And he will be on his best behavior. I do not need to remind you any foolish remarks in front of the Bishop of London will get back to Lady Rosemount. I know you think it is because he is shy and struggles in social gatherings, but you are going to have to teach him he cannot just say whatever is on his mind. People tend to take offence."

Remembering that part of the Rude Rules was that she was not to show any indication that there was anything wrong with Freddie's behavior, Eve said nothing. Offending her uncle was exactly what Freddie had told her he had in mind for this evening. It was an unfortunate but necessary part of the game. They had managed to close the point gap on Godwin over the past few days, but they both knew he was far from finished.

Under any other circumstance, Eve would have been eager to introduce Freddie to her relatives. Especially her uncle, the Bishop of London. The Radley family were a close-knit group. It wasn't even the likely repercussions from her mother that was bothering her. These were people she loved. Hurting them was something that went against everything for which her family stood.

She headed up to her room. It was late in the afternoon, and her maid would be waiting to set Eve's hair in preparation for the evening. As she took a seat at her dressing table she forced herself to stop wringing her hands with worry over the impending evening.

The Bachelor Board challenges will be over soon.

The winner was to be announced early in the new month. Once the game was over and Freddie had won, she could take the time to make whatever amends were needed to all those whom they had offended.

When the time came for their guests to arrive, Eve headed downstairs. She was dressed in a simple pale pink gown, with a cream ribbon threaded through the bun on her head. It was the most demure look she could muster, a balm for the harsh looks she had been receiving from her mother all week.

Will was waiting downstairs. "Mama is in the kitchens talking to cook. I don't recall her ever doing that before."

He didn't need to mention the likely cause of their mother's concerns. *Freddie.*

I shall be so glad when this foolish game is at an end.

"Oh, and this came for you." He handed her a letter. It bore the crest of the Rosemount family on the outside. She opened it.

A mix of disappointment and relief coursed through her body as she read the short note. Freddie wasn't coming. Osmont Firebrace had arranged an impromptu four-in-hand race for the evening, and valuable challenge points were on offer.

She folded the letter up. "Freddie is unable to attend. He has other pressing matters. He sends his heartfelt apologies," she said.

Will reached out and put an arm around her, pulling her into a brotherly hug. It took all of Eve's willpower not to cry.

By rights she should be relieved that he wasn't coming. The Bishop of London was a kind-hearted man, but not one who would stand the antics of a foolish young man. The evening, and family relations, had escaped the antics of the Rude Rules.

It still hurt to think he had put the game ahead of her, ahead of them. In her heart, they now existed as a couple. She was certain of her love for him, no longer in doubt that she wanted his whole heart for herself.

"He will come to his senses, and if he doesn't, I can assure you Francis and I shall step into the fray," said Will.

She looked up at him. The big, strong brother she had missed all those years was back in her life. Will would not stand idly by and let Freddie hurt her. "Have I told you how wonderful it is to have you home once more? To know that I can get out of bed every day and see you? To know that you are safe?"

"Good to see some members of this family are able to be punctual. Now where are the others?" asked Adelaide.

Eve turned to see her mother and father arriving in the foyer. Adelaide was clearly flustered. "Freddie sends his apologies. He is unable to attend," she said.

She watched as her words registered with her mother, and a look of relief appeared on her countenance.

As soon as the game was over and Freddie had won his place on the Bachelor Board, Eve would tell her mother the truth. While the game was important to Freddie and his future plans, she still owed a great deal of loyalty to her mother. It pained her to see her mother in such distress.

On the other side of Richmond, Freddie was doing his best to get his horses under control. He had never driven a team of horses before and had to rely on his memory of sitting up alongside the driver on the top of his father's travel coach.

Lord Godwin, on the other hand, was showing far more skill than he had done during their earlier race in central London. Freddie risked a look at him, only to see a self- satisfied grin plastered across Godwin's face. *He thinks he has a real shot at this now. Bastard.*

The carriage was smaller than his family travel coach and thus able to turn in tighter circles. Upon receiving Osmont's note earlier that morning Freddie had raced out of the house and headed for the nearest coaching inn. He had eventually managed to find a willing carriage owner who would let him rent his horses and outfit for the day. Heading out to Richmond as soon as he was able, he spent the afternoon trying to best come to terms with handling a team of horses.

The last thing he did just before leaving Rosemount House was send word to Eve. It wasn't the ideal situation, crying off so late in the day, but he trusted she would understand. Their kiss in the foyer of her family home had been poor payment for the pain he had caused her while he stood and insulted her family and heritage. He longed for the moment when the game was over and he could be himself with her. To hold her close and indulge in showing her how much she had come to mean to him.

It had been a shock to hear himself says the words—to call her his true love. But he was becoming more comfortable with that unfamiliar emotion.

"She knows how much this means to me, which is why I have to win this bloody race," he muttered.

He pushed the thought of Eve from his mind; he needed all his concentration focused on the job at hand. He pulled back on the reins, and his team drew to a halt. He looked across as Godwin pulled up alongside him.

"Embry sends his apologies. Something about cakes in the oven!" shouted Godwin with a laugh. Freddie nodded. Trenton Embry had long ago given up on the challenges—it was Godwin he had to beat.

A starting line had been roughly fashioned with a stick in the dirt.

They were both to take their teams to the top of a nearby hill, then bring them down along a long winding path back to the start. The first to cross the line with his team and coach still intact, would be declared the winner.

Freddie hadn't seen this move coming, and he was fuming about it. Osmont knew Godwin was handy with a coach and four, and to Freddie's mind had thrown this challenge in to make things difficult for him. If he didn't win tonight, the points would be level.

He pushed the worry of the outcome from his mind as best he could. He needed to concentrate on the task at hand. He needed to win.

He missed hearing the starter's gun go off, and only reacted when he saw the first of Godwin's team leap into action. With a flick of his whip, Freddie's horses started forward.

The ride to the top of the hill was a flat-out race. Neck and neck, they battled. By the time they reached the top Godwin had managed to snatch the lead.

"Blast!" Freddie did his best to harness his rage. Losing his temper at this moment would serve him no good. He settled over the reins and pulled his horses ready for the first turn.

Godwin stood up from his seat and raised his whip. His team kicked away, increasing the lead over Freddie. They swept through the first turn while Freddie had to haul back on the reins to keep his horses under control.

He was going to lose. Godwin was too strong. Freddie settled in the seat, accepting that the second-place points would have to suffice. He would have to find another way to get ahead of Godwin after today.

The upcoming third turn was a simple one from where Freddie could see it. Even he knew he could go through it at a fast clip.

He watched with fading hope as Godwin, who was still standing, cracked the whip over his team when they reached the top of the turn. His horses kicked again.

To Freddie's shock, Godwin suddenly teetered on his feet and appeared to lose his footing. Time slowed as he leant further and further over to the left, before finally disappearing over the side of the coach. His horses continued on, taking their now driverless coach toward the finish line.

As Freddie reached the turn, he looked down and caught sight of Godwin getting to his feet on the side of the hill. He turned back and concentrated on the task at hand. Godwin did not appear to be injured; there was no need to stop and render assistance.

Closing in on the finish, Freddie passed Godwin's coach and horses. He crossed the finish line and pulled up his team.

Relief, mixed with jubilation, coursed through his veins. Only a miracle could see Godwin reclaim the lead in the final week of the Bachelor Board challenge.

The look of anger on Osmont's face was a fleeting one. By the time Freddie had climbed down from the coach, Osmont was once more displaying his usual emotionless countenance.

"Well done, Rosemount. Though you have to admit that Lord Godwin assisted in his own demise," he said.

Freddie bit down on his bottom lip. As far as he was concerned he had won because Godwin had become cocky, nothing more. The points were his; he needed no ovation.

Osmont stepped back and another older gentleman stepped forward, his hand outstretched. A nod from Osmont quickly told him this was a hand he should take.

"Well, when the gods decide they are on your side you have to take all they give you. James Link is my name. Hopefully you and I shall be seeing a lot of each other shortly. If you do succeed in winning your seat on the Bachelor Board, I will be one of your first mentors. We will put up the cash for your first venture, and of course share in your rewards. You are about to have a whole new set of wealthy and powerful friends," said Link.

"Thank you, I am looking forward to working with you. I promise I shall endeavor to be worthy of my place on the board," replied Freddie.

With the race won and his standing in the competition almost unassailable it was encouraging he was now being introduced to the men who would be the secret to his future success.

"Bloody unlucky. That's what I would call it," said Godwin,

jumping down from the back of the horse which had been sent to collect him.

"More like bloody foolish. You had the race won, Lord Godwin, and you threw it away," replied Link.

He refused Godwin's offered hand and turned back to Freddie. He placed a hand on Freddie's back and smiled. "Soon, young Rosemount, the world will be your oyster. Soon. Good evening."

Godwin shrugged. "Oh, well. At least I can say I gave you a good run for your money. Though the game is not yet over. I may still find a way to win."

Freddie slapped him on the back. If he was to beat Godwin, then at least he knew there wouldn't be any hard feelings. Now he would just have to hope Eve's take on his non-appearance at her home this evening was as charitable.

He watched as James Link walked away and got into a gleaming black coach. Freddie noticed the horses, and from the look of them guessed at least half came from the Rosemount stables breeding program. Link had a team of six staff on his coach, all in full livery. If Freddie needed any further reminder of the wealth that would soon be within his reach, he saw it James Link's ostentatious trappings of success.

Chapter Sixteen

With her and Freddie's relationship now on a more formal footing, Eve was disappointed to discover her mother had decided to place rules on their meetings. They were only to meet in public with other members of her family present at all times. As Freddie had not yet asked for permission to court Eve, they were not to dance together at social functions. They couldn't even meet for walks in Hyde Park unless both Francis and Caroline were present. At all times.

Eve would have protested, but the sudden appearance of a new young lady in Will's life added some unexpected complications. Within a week of his arrival in London, Will had secured his own home on nearby Newport Street, and much to Adelaide's consternation, had moved out of the family home.

Her mother's constant tears told Eve it wouldn't be wise to make mention of Freddie for a short time.

Miss Harriet Wright had appeared in public on Will's arm a little more than a fortnight after his return. He had received her family's full approval to court the young woman, and he was playing everything strictly by the rules of society. Her widower brother's gallant behavior left little room for Eve to make her own demands when it came to

Freddie.

With the Rude Rules still in place, Eve did not want to make her connection with Freddie a public matter. She was counting the days until she and Adelaide left London to stay at Rosemount Abbey. Once out of sight of the *ton,* she would be free to press her case with him.

Will may have been moving on with his own life but that did not mean he'd forgotten his brother and sisters. An invitation to a night of entertainment at Vauxhall Gardens was extended to them. With all of them keen to meet Will's mystery woman, Francis, Caroline, and Eve readily accepted.

In the early evening, the Saunders's family town carriage stopped outside a house in Newport Street, a short distance from Will's new home. Will got out.

"Hattie lives two doors from me, but we must still respect social conventions. I won't be a moment," he said.

Caroline was seated on the bench opposite to Eve. "So, you know this Hattie Wright? Mama said you and she came out the same year," asked Caroline.

"Yes, poor girl. Her father got a dose of puritan religion and pulled her out of polite society to go and work with the poor in the London slums. From what I understand, she is now living under the care of her married brother," replied Eve.

The door of the carriage opened and Will assisted Hattie inside. She took a seat in the carriage, and Will made introductions.

"I am very pleased to have finally met you all. Will has told me so much about your family, I feel like I already know you," she said.

"I remember you from the year we both came out," replied Eve.

"Yes, you had the most wonderful dress at the official Royal ball. I must confess, I was so jealous," replied Hattie.

Eve nodded and leant over, taking Hattie's hand. "My mother had the fabric smuggled in from France; my father was livid. Caroline and I both got new gowns from that cloth."

Eve and Caroline smiled at one another. They had been the best-dressed girls at several parties that year in their illicit gowns.

"Will tells us you run a soup kitchen that feeds the poor of St Giles. How ever do you manage such a thing?" asked Caroline.

"Yes, I've been in charge of the soup kitchen for a number of years now. You find that after a while you develop the skills to ensure that over a hundred people get fed every day. I'm very good at making a penny stretch a long way when it comes to haggling with the shop keepers at Covent Garden Market," replied Hattie.

It didn't take long for Eve to understand why Will was moving forward with such haste in courting Hattie. She was the right mix of intelligence and caring soul he sorely needed in his life. She was pretty and possessed a warmth that immediately made Eve want to welcome her into the family.

"It's been a long time since I visited Vauxhall. I am really looking forward to this evening," said Hattie, settling into her seat.

Eve ran a fashion-conscious gaze over Hattie's attire. Her gown, while simply cut, was still of the latest season colors. Her matching slippers met with Eve's silent approval.

Will had adopted his social face at this point, but he couldn't hide the glint of happiness in his eyes. There would be wedding bells ringing very soon if her brother had his way.

Vauxhall Pleasure Gardens was situated near the River Thames, not far from the newly built Waterloo Bridge. A long line of carriages slowly snaked its way along the road, gradually depositing the elegant members of London society at the entrance to the gardens.

Vauxhall at night was the destination for the cream of London society. The famous pleasure gardens were full of various entertainments. Food and drink stands were dotted throughout the gardens with all manner of delights for patrons to purchase. A full orchestra played in the center of the gardens where a raised dance floor was situated.

Anyone who could afford the entrance fee could attend. That anyone also included the second son of Viscount Rosemount who, by no matter of chance, happened to be standing outside the main entrance to the gardens as the Saunders family and Hattie Wright finally alighted from their carriage.

Eve hadn't seen Freddie since Will's welcome home function. The long days apart were quickly forgotten as Eve tossed aside all efforts at decorum and leapt with joy into his arms. Her exuberance was rewarded with a deep passionate kiss. She ignored the rest of her family.

When Freddie finally ended the kiss, Eve searched his face, looking for an echo of the joy she felt in her heart. The briefest of smiles came and went.

"Rude Rules I am afraid tonight, my love. As you and I have not been out together for some time we have some catching up to do. Lord Godwin insulted Christopher Smith, the lord mayor of London this morning, and Osmont gave him extra points for bravery. We are still ahead, but the gap is closing. This battle is going to go to the very end, I am afraid," he whispered.

Eve tried to dampen down her initial disappointment. She had hoped the Rude Rules were a thing of the past. Instead, she focused on his other words. Once more he had called her my love.

"Of course. Though Will has a guest who I am not sure will take kindly to being mocked. She is from a family of missionaries, so we may need to tread carefully," replied Eve.

The raising of Freddie's left eyebrow told her exactly what Freddie thought of that piece of news. Hattie Wright was going to be fair game tonight, and Eve was going to have to back him all the way.

His gaze moved from her face to over her shoulder. "I see you dragged the rest of your family out tonight," he said, loudly.

The Rude Rules were in play. She hurriedly turned to the rest of the group. "Sorry, I forgot to mention Freddie was going to join us. I am sure he is welcome as one of our party," she announced.

She tried her best to ignore the tension within the group. Caroline looked away.

"Oh, and who is this?" said Freddie, rudely pointing at Hattie.

Will stepped forward. The look on his face was a hard-set social mask. Eve feared the moment when he let his mask drop and Freddie got a taste of Will's wrath.

"Miss Harriet Wright, may I introduce the Honorable Frederick Rosemount. Frederick is the second son of Viscount Rosemount."

Freddie looked down with undisguised disgust at Hattie's outstretched hand. "You work with the dirty poor, don't you? How very noble of you," he sneered. He turned away.

"I think we should go inside now," said a clearly unimpressed Will.

Eve and Freddie trailed behind the rest of the group. Freddie took a hold of her arm and placed it within his, but quickly removed it when Will turned and gave him a steely glare. Eve returned his look. It was unfair he was allowed to walk with Hattie on his arm, yet she was not allowed to be accompanied by Freddie.

They made their way through the crowd, eventually reaching a large, grassy clearing, which was ringed with elegantly set out supper boxes. Will had reserved one for their party. Within minutes, a servant appeared with champagne and glasses. Eve eagerly downed her first glass; grateful brandy was not on offer. She called for a second and made short work of it.

Francis leant over and said loud enough for everyone to hear, "Take it slowly, Eve. You are supposed to sip champagne, not drink it like beer."

Eve ignored him and called for a third glass. Will stepped in at that point and took the glass out of her hand. "The night is still young," he said.

Eve pouted. No one questioned Francis when he drank to excess. "You are not the only one who changed while you were away, William. I am no longer a child. I shall decide if I want another glass of champagne, not you."

On cue, Freddie stepped in to intervene. He put a hand on Will's arm, ignoring the heated glare that Will was sending him. "Now, Will, my good chap, how about I take Eve for a turn around the gardens? The fresh air might return her to good humor. Rest assured we shall remain in full public sight on the main paths."

Eve could have clapped her hands at his words. He was offering to diffuse the situation, but it came with a price. Will was going to have to allow Freddie and Eve time alone at Vauxhall. Everyone who attended the gardens knew all manner of wicked behavior went on in the bushes and secret paths around the gardens. Will, the master strategist, was being beaten at his own game. He wouldn't dare risk an ugly scene in front of the woman he was intending to marry. Freddie had Will exactly where Eve wanted him.

Eve rose quickly from her seat and seized the moment. Taking a firm grip of Freddie's hand, she quickly led him out of the supper box and away from the group, before Will had a chance to fully protest.

As they cleared a nearby corner and disappeared into the crowds, Eve slipped her arm into Freddie's. "That was rather well done. Will didn't want to look like an overbearing brother in front of Hattie, so he had to agree. Now we have some time alone," she said.

Freddie turned to her, and she saw the questioning look on his face. She huffed. Why did men have to be so dull at times? Here she was, free and available to him. "Alright, but not too long. I have to get to a card game in Duke Street later tonight. There are several members of the Bachelor Board whom Osmont wishes me to meet," he replied.

Eve said nothing, but his words stung. Apart from the unexpected kiss and a few words of endearment, Freddie had not made much of an effort to woo her. She yearned for stronger signs of affection from him.

"Through here. There are some nice private spaces at the end of this path," she said. If Freddie wasn't going to take the lead in the area of romance, then she would.

At the end of the path was a hedge with several gaps through which a body would easily fit. They tried the first gap, but another amorous couple had beaten them to it. The second spot was similarly taken. They finally had luck with the third.

As soon as they passed through the gap in the hedge, they entered a different world. The light from the path disappeared, leaving them in near darkness. She turned to him, intent on making her position clear. He pulled her roughly to him.

"Come here, you naughty little minx. You need to be kissed thoroughly," Freddie said, gruffly.

His lips and hers met in a hungry exchange. He wasted no time in opening the folds of her cloak and fumbling with the laces of her gown. She felt the kiss of the cold night air on her breasts and exalted in the knowledge he did indeed want her. He was everything she yearned for in a man. Her love for him shone brightly in her heart.

He bent down and took one of her breasts into his mouth. When he suckled on her hardened nipple, heat pooled between her legs. This was the passion and desire she so desperately craved.

"Tell me if you want me to stop," he murmured.

With her back hard against the hedge, Eve let her head fall back as she closed her eyes. She felt her skirts being lifted and told herself to remain calm. If he was going to ruin her this night, she would let it happen.

His hand glided up the inside of her leg. His knee gently pushed her legs apart. She swallowed and held her breath.

"Are you ready for me to begin your education in the art of sexual pleasure?" he whispered in her ear.

"Yes," she murmured.

His fingers reached the thatch of hair between her legs. Her whole body silently screamed for him to go further. She felt the tip of his thumb enter her womanhood. She groaned.

"Through here, lads! I'm sure that bloody dog came this way," bellowed a voice.

Two burly men crashed through the gap in the hedge and broke the private moment. Freddie immediately dropped Eve's skirts and stood over her, shielding her naked breasts from sight.

The interlopers held a lantern high enough that the dark, private space was now well lit. The man with the lantern caught sight of them. "Oh. Sorry. We didn't see you there. Have you seen a hound come through here?"

Freddie shook his head but kept his back to them. Putting a hand to her gown, he pulled the folds back into place. A frustrated Eve took her cue and began to lace the gown back up. By the time the dog hunters had searched the immediate area, her gown and cloak were set back to right.

"We had better get back to the others. I don't want to test too much of Will's patience, and I must leave soon," said Freddie.

She reluctantly took his offered hand and allowed him to take her back out to the main garden path. The mix of champagne and disappointment made her feel sick.

By the time they reached the supper box, she was ready to go home. Every step forward with Freddie felt like she was wading through thick mud. She was constantly struggling to gain traction.

Chapter Seventeen

Eve was up early. She sat in front of her dresser and watched as her hair was set high in an elaborate and elegant chignon. Today, Will and Hattie would become man and wife.

Having watched the betrothed couple over the past few weeks, it was clear Will had met his match in Hattie. She was as stubborn as he, but they both brought out the caring and tender sides of each other. Will loved Hattie, and Hattie made no secret of the affection she felt for her future husband.

Eve smiled, remembering when she'd caught the two of them kissing in the garden the night they arrived to announce their betrothal. The kiss had not been a gentle social kiss between two innocents. Rather, it had been one of passion between two people who couldn't wait to share the marriage bed.

Eve privately doubted Hattie would be going to her wedding night a virgin. She was already living in Will's house, which was scandalous enough, and Will had been widowed for nearly four years. Lust and desire would not keep them sleeping in separate beds.

Her and Adelaide's visit to Rosemount Abbey was only a matter of days away. Given half a chance, while she was in residence, Eve would let Freddie have his way with her. She didn't regret any of what had happened at Vauxhall Gardens. In fact, the sooner he had his hands on her naked body, the better. She yearned for long nights in his arms.

A long, slow breath did little to settle her aching hunger. With the Bachelor Board close to being Freddie's, she would need to move forward with her plans to forge a permanent future with him. His declarations of love had her believing that a betrothal would be announced not long after she and her mother arrived at Rosemount Abbey.

The wedding at St Paul's cathedral was a delight. Eve's uncle Hugh, the Bishop of London, conducted a beautiful wedding service. All the Saunders and Radley women cried.

It was only as they were leaving St Paul's that Eve caught sight of her cousin Lucy. She hurried over to speak with her.

"I didn't know you were coming today. Mama said you were still in Scotland," said Eve.

Lucy kissed her cheek. When she pulled away, Eve noticed the sparkle in her eye.

"We did head to Scotland after we returned from France, but Avery is keen to start working with Lord Langham on understanding how to run an estate," said Lucy.

She was about to ask Lucy how things with Avery were going when her cousin's new husband appear from out of the crowd of well-wishers. He slipped a hand around his wife's waist and whispered something to her. Lucy's eyes opened wide and she smiled.

Eve took a step back as Lucy looked her husband up and down with barely concealed lust. If she were to put words to what she was watching, she would say Lucy was stripping Avery naked with her eyes.

"Good morning, Cousin Eve. I hope you are well. Lovely day for a wedding," said Avery.

Eve was momentarily lost for words. It felt like only yesterday that Avery and Lucy had stood in front of the Bishop and struggled to say the words to commit to their marriage, yet here they were acting like all the other love-struck newly-weds.

"Lucy, my love, I must go and speak with your father. I promise to come back as soon as I can," said Avery. He nodded his farewell to Eve, and they watched as he headed off in the direction of the Duke of Strathmore.

Lucy laughed as a stunned Eve turned back to her. "Miracles do happen. Mind you, it took Will's efforts with Avery in Paris, and some soul searching on both our parts to finally face the truth of our marriage. Oh, Eve, I could only wish that you marry a man half as magnificent as Avery. From the depths of despair, I found happiness beyond anything I could ever have imagined. You must get out and find yourself a husband."

Eve took her cousin by the arm and pulled her over to one side of the front steps of the church. She pointed to where Freddie was standing alongside his mother. They were enjoying a friendly chat with Adelaide. "Mama and I are off to Rosemount Abbey the day after tomorrow. Lady Rosemount has invited us to visit," she said.

Lucy leant toward her cousin and whispered, "And I take it your visit has absolutely nothing to do with that rather dashing young man who is standing in the midst of those ladies. Oh, Eve, do tell. Do you think he might be the one?"

Eve shrugged, adopting her best nonchalant attitude. She gave Lucy a sideways glance. "Who is to say? I love him, and he has told me the same. I am determined to know what is beyond those words. I know he feels passion and desire, he just needs to be brave enough to let me see the real him. Once that is accomplished then I will know that he is truly the one," replied Eve.

Stolen kisses and the liberties she had allowed him at Vauxhall were enough for her to be confident when she returned to London after her visit to Rosemount Abbey she would be wearing a betrothal ring.

The smile disappeared from Lucy's lips. A worried frown took its place. "Be absolutely sure of him before you allow yourself to be put in a position where marriage is the only possible outcome. Promise me, Eve, you won't do anything rash like I did. Matters between Avery and I could so easily have gone the other way," she replied.

Eve waved her cousin's concerns away. She was sure in the knowledge Freddie wanted her. Men like Freddie wanted fresh and frisky wives. If his heart wasn't hers already, it would be by the time they were wed. She had plans in place to make the most of her stay at the abbey. Plans that included long walks with Freddie far from the main house and, if she was lucky, a convenient wood or two to get lost in.

She took Lucy's hand and placed it on her arm.

"Come on, Lucy. Today is not the day to discuss my forthcoming wedding. We must go and find Will and Hattie. You should see the lacework on her dress. It is absolutely divine."

Chapter Eighteen

Freddie sat through Will and Hattie's wedding feeling like the Sword of Damocles was hanging over his head. How soon would it be before Adelaide Saunders and his mother had him measured up for a wedding suit?

Lady Rosemount had arrived in London for the wedding and then returned home as soon as the service was over. Her appearance at Will and Hattie's wedding was not just to wish the bride and groom well. He had watched with interest as his mother had worked her way through the assembled guests, dropping small hints here and there about the next wedding that would be held at St Paul's.

It had been his mother's idea to invite Eve and Adelaide to Rose-mount Abbey. The theory was, it would give Eve and himself time to decide if they were suited. The reality was, as far as his mother and likely future mother-in-law were concerned, the only thing left to decide was the color of flowers for the church.

Finally, he consoled himself with the idea if he did end up marrying Eve it wouldn't be such a bad thing. His mother approved of her. She had been a great sport when it came to the Bachelor Board challenges, and likely deserved her place by his side as he reaped the rewards of his new position.

She was a hot-blooded girl who would satisfy him in bed. She was well-read and well-bred. Eve Saunders would do him just fine for a wife. When his thoughts turned momentarily to the question of whether he was actually in love with her, he frowned. Love wasn't something he had really considered. He was prepared to accept he had developed warm feelings for her. He had even told her he loved her. Where the truth lay was something he had not fully explored.

What was love anyway? Real men didn't feel all the soppy emotions that women and small children did. Men were providers. With his membership of the Bachelor Board all but secure, he was well on his way to being the sort of man a wife would want. Fine food on the table in exchange for a lusty sex life was a solid bargain for marriage.

He had it all figured out.

He shook the thoughts from his mind. This morning he had other matters to attend to in town. The foremost being to receive the last of the Bachelor Board challenges. He had established a commanding lead, so much so it had long ago stopped being a real race. Nonetheless, he had to finish the game and be declared the victor.

After bidding Eve, a hasty farewell at the wedding breakfast, Freddie headed over to Barton Street. He bounded up the steps of the office and strode confidently into the room set aside for the House of Commons cadets.

As expected, Godwin was not present at this hour of the morning. Osmont had introduced him to the delights of the opium dens in the East End and Godwin was more than likely still lying in a drug-induced haze in some lodging house. A naked prostitute no doubt slept beside him.

As for Trenton Embry, most days he didn't bother even coming to the office. His interest in the Bachelor Board challenges had never got past tepid. His absence was barely noted.

The only person who was present was Osmont Firebrace.

"Ah, Rosemount, at least one of you can live the life of a libertine and make it into the office the next morning," he said.

Freddie walked over to the sideboard, which was laden as usual with pastries and a pot of hot coffee. He picked up a cup and poured himself a brew, then settled comfortably in one of the office armchairs, quietly imagining himself as a king on a throne.

"Yes, well, enjoy my company while you can. I won't be here tomorrow or the next week. I am off home to Rosemount Abbey," he said.

Osmont snorted in obvious disgust. Only mama's boys went home to the family estate. True men stayed in London where the action was centered.

"What about the challenge?" replied Osmont.

Freddie sipped at his coffee. "Well, I was thinking since I am so far ahead of the others and you were going to call the result in a matter of days, perhaps we should announce now. Godwin appears to have finally given up and conceded defeat," he replied.

Osmont looked at him from over the rim of his reading glasses. Freddie sensed he was being scrutinized, something he found unsettling when it came to his boss. There was always an undercurrent of sex when Osmont looked him up and down.

"Tell me. Why are you going home? Your father is not ill, and even if he was you have an older brother to inherit the title."

Freddie tried to ignore the callous remark about his father. Much as his father was a stickler for protocol and behavior, he still loved his sire. Lord Rosemount was a good man. He was true to his wife and he had been even-handed in the raising of his two sons. Freddie knew he had been gifted a good family upbringing.

"I have been courting a young lady, and she is coming to Rosemount Abbey with her mother to meet my family. My mother has arranged it," he replied.

Osmont took his black notebook from out of his coat pocket and unfastened the string. He flipped through a few pages, then paused at one and quietly read it.

Freddie had finished his coffee by the time Osmont finally closed the book and retied the string.

"There is one final challenge for you. Successfully complete it and you will be admitted to full membership of the Bachelor Board. I cannot begin to tell you the powerful friends and wealth you will find at your disposal. The real power brokers of London will be revealed to you. A new uncharted world where you will be among firsts. No one will ever again see you as merely a second son," said Osmont. He headed back into his office and closed the door. Several minutes later he returned, a letter folded up and sealed in his hand.

"Here is the last of the challenges. Now, there are strict instructions which you are to follow to the letter. Break them, and your membership will be forfeit." Osmont handed Freddie the letter.

Freddie would have broken the seal if Osmont had not stopped him. He took a slow, deep breath to calm the nervous excitement which coursed through his veins. He was so close to success, he could taste it.

"You must wait until the third day after you have arrived home at Rosemount Abbey before you open the letter. In the meantime, you can spend your time sampling the delights of your lady friend. Though, if my reading of you is correct, I am certain you have already had your hand up her skirts. From what I have seen of her, she would be the type to suck your cock dry if it meant getting you before a priest." The sneer he loaded into the final of his remarks was enough that Freddie should have taken Osmont to task for the sake of Eve's honor.

He couldn't exactly call him a liar though. If they hadn't been disturbed at Vauxhall Gardens, Eve would have let him bring her to climax. He longed to hear her soft sighs at her moment of crisis. He enjoyed lustful dreams of her most nights. His body ached for the touch of her naked body beneath him.

"How will you know I have completed the last of the challenges?" he asked.

Osmont straightened the lapel of his coat and nodded sagely. He bowed low, which caused a chill of premonition in Freddie's mind. What exactly was written in the letter? What if, after all he had achieved, he still fell at the final hurdle?

"When next you and I see one another, young Rosemount, we both shall know."

Chapter Nineteen

"I wish you every success on your journey and I hope to be sharing your good news upon your return," said Caroline.

Eve looked up from her travel trunk. She rose and approached her sister, taking her by the hand. "Thank you. I know I have been horrid to you lately, but I promise when I come back everything will change," said Eve.

She felt a prick of guilt over her sister's good wishes. It would hurt Caroline to know Eve had initially pursued Freddie out of spite over her own popularity.

One day, when they were both long settled in their own marriages, she would confess her guilty secret to her sister. Today, however, was the day to seize her future.

A tearful Caroline hugged her.

"You had better get your cloak. Mama has already said goodbye to Papa three times."

Freddie left London the day before Eve and Adelaide. His mother was insistent on him being home and settled before his prospective new bride arrived.

With Lady Rosemount having returned home in the Strathmore travel coach straight after Will and Hattie's wedding, Freddie was left to take the main public coach to Peterborough. There he was met by one of his father's grooms who brought a spare horse.

The ride back home through the countryside was invigorating. The feeling of wind in his hair and the thud of the horse's hooves on the country lanes had the blood in his body pumping. Reaching the top of a rise a half mile from his home, he reined the horse in and sat for a moment looking down on his family estate.

It was good to be home.

Below him, at the top of another small rise sat Rosemount Abbey. The main house dated from the mid-sixteenth-century. The first Viscount Rosemount had been one of Queen Elizabeth's favourite courtiers.

Over the ensuing centuries the house had been extended and elaborate gardens created around three sides. While the Rosemount family had only risen to the rank of viscount over the years, they had been astute enough in their business dealings to be near the top of the list of wealthiest families in England.

London was full of life and distraction but here, in the Northamptonshire countryside, he could breath. The fields before him were full of sheep, covered in their coats of wool for the oncoming winter. Beyond them were the red coats of his father's prized herd of Sussex cattle.

The main fields closest to the long, stone stables were reserved for the highly prized horses of the Rosemount breeding program. Every nobleman in England owned at least one horse from the Rosemount stables.

He sat back in the saddle and thought of the unopened letter sitting in the pocket of his coat. Membership of the Bachelor Board would afford him the opportunity to carve out his own piece of England for himself and his heirs.

His son would not be merely the cousin of the future Viscount

Rosemount. He would hold his own place in society, his father's new wealth behind him.

He spurred his horse on. Two more days and he could open the letter and find out the very last challenge. With Eve by his side, he would successfully complete it and head back to London ready to claim his future. Frederick Rosemount was ready to take his place as a first among equals in the rarefied air of English high society.

※

Eve climbed down from the travel coach, laughing with joy as she saw Freddie approaching from the stables. He hurried to meet her.

"I am so sorry I am not properly dressed to greet you. I only got word your coach was arriving as it reached the top of the drive," he said.

The drive was long, some two thirds of a mile from the main Peterborough road. Eve had struggled to stay in her seat when they had finally turned off the main road and she'd caught sight of the house.

Her gaze now was fixed firmly on Freddie's open-necked shirt, and she was too busy thinking wicked thoughts of what he could to do to her to be concerned about his lack of suitable attire. He had awoken a near constant, sexual hunger within her, and keeping to society's social expectations was becoming increasingly difficult whenever he was near. She hoped he had already chosen some perfect private places for them to finish the business they started at Vauxhall.

"Lady Adelaide Saunders. Miss Saunders. How wonderful for you to visit with us."

Eve turned at the sound of her mother's formal title and saw Lord and Lady Rosemount coming toward them. Eve dipped into a respectful curtsey. Adelaide would be expecting the utmost of impeccable behavior this week. Eve intended to be the perfect, innocent daughter around her mother and the viscount and viscountess. It was Freddie she intended to practice being disgraceful with during their stay. Practice that she intended would make her perfect material for his wife.

A second couple emerged from the house. The man, who Eve

assumed was Freddie's older brother, Thomas, was carrying a young boy. The woman beside him held a baby in her arms.

"Welcome, I'm Thomas Rosemount, and this is my wife, Cecily. This curly haired rascal is James, my heir, and the baby is Jonathan," said Thomas.

"Yes, I had to convince them not to call the baby Frederick. One Freddie in the family is quite enough," added Freddie, with a smile. A polite laugh rippled through the gathering.

They climbed the steps into the main house, while the household servants unloaded Adelaide and Eve's trunks from the coach.

Eve glanced around as they entered the main foyer. A magnificent marble staircase hugged the wall to the left of the entrance. It rose several floors into the air. When she looked up, she quickly understood the need for the staircase to have been built to one side.

A huge white dome dominated the roof of the entrance. Her mouth dropped open as she stood under the center of it.

"It is rather magnificent, isn't it? Mind you, it costs a fortune to have it cleaned and repainted every few years," said Freddie.

Eve caught the look of disapproval from Lady Rosemount. Freddie had mentioned money which was considered crass to discuss in mixed public. The Rude Rules may have finally come to an end, but it was clear some aspects of the game had now become habit.

He turned to Adelaide and bowed. "Would it be acceptable for Eve and myself to take a short stroll in the grounds? I have told her much about the abbey and I am most keen to show her the gardens."

Eve's heart began to race. He wanted to be alone with her. She turned to her mother. "A walk would be just the thing after such a long journey, Mama. A short stroll around the gardens before coming back to freshen up."

Adelaide nodded. "Of course," she replied.

Freddie offered Eve his arm and they made for the front door.

"Don't look back. They will be watching and talking about us," he said, as they stepped outside.

Eve kept her head still. Her every move would be under close scrutiny at this point.

As they reached the end of the house, Freddie made a great show of pointing out the ornate gardens. But once they were out of sight of the main house, Freddie steered her toward a nearby stone building.

"The flowers can wait. I can't," he said.

As soon as they reached the building, he checked no one was in sight. Quickly opening the door, he ushered Eve inside and locked it behind them. Her heart raced as her blood heated with anticipation. She ached for his hands to be on her naked body.

He wasted little time with pleasantries. A hasty kiss and then Eve's skirts were lifted. His thumb parted her swollen, wet folds and he began to stroke.

"No men and their dogs to disturb us this time," he said.

With her back against the cold, stone wall, Eve relaxed and let Freddie minister to her sexual needs. Her hands began to work at the opening of her gown, but he stopped her.

"Not enough time for that. I can guarantee you my parents and your mother will be following us out into the garden within a few minutes. I think I have just enough time to make you come before we have to leave," he said.

Eve looked at him through a haze of arousal. His thumb was creating tension throughout her body.

"Close your eyes. Lie back and feel," he ordered.

She did as he said. With her eyes closed, she experienced the full pleasure of his thumb as it rubbed over her sensitive nib. When he pushed two fingers into her heat, his thumb tortured her clitoris, and she whimpered. On and on the torture continued as a slow heated tension built higher and higher within her. A sob escaped her lips.

He threw back the folds of her cloak and took hold of one of her nipples through her gown. As the bud hardened, he twisted it hard.

She cried out as her orgasm hit with blinding intensity. His lips closed over her mouth to soften her cry. His fingers continued to stroke, gradually slowing as she came down from her climax.

"There. That is what you needed after that long journey. I knew you had it in you to come at my command. Good girl," he whispered.

Her clothes were quickly fixed back in place, and they had just made it out into the formal garden when the sound of approaching footsteps on the loose stones of the garden path heralded the arrival of Adelaide Saunders and Freddie's parents.

"The house was designed by Robert Smythson. The roses were planted by my grandmother. The walls and folly were designed by Capability Brown. We employ twenty gardeners," Freddie hastily murmured.

Eve turned and smiled as her mother and Lord and Lady Rosemount approached. With a nod toward Freddie, she spoke. "Mama, Frederick was just telling me about the gardens, and that Capability Brown designed much of them. How very interesting."

Lady Rosemount's eyes lit up, and a delighted smiled appeared on her lips. "Frederick is such a well-studied young man. Though I must warn you not to let him ramble too much about architecture and ancient philosophers. I am sure there are other things young ladies are far more interested in," she said.

Eve swallowed. She could still feel the sensation of Freddie's fingers on her body, and she was certain anyone who looked closely enough would be able to see the afterglow of climax on her face.

I can assure you that Freddie knows exactly what this young lady is interested in.

Chapter Twenty

The following morning Freddie and Thomas went out for an early morning ride. Settling into the saddle, Freddie grinned at his brother. It felt like forever since they had shared time together away from friends and family.

They rode their mounts hard into the nearby village of Thorney. Freddie dug his heels in as they reached a bend in the narrow road. It was just like rounding the corner from Oxford Street into Tyburn Lane. He showed Thomas a clean set of heels, the same as he had done with Lord Godwin.

Coming out of the bend he came upon a shepherd and his flock. Sheep scattered in all directions, and Freddie hooted with laughter as he heard the bellow of the angry shepherd. He kept on the road until the shepherd and his sheep were out of sight.

When Thomas did not appear out of the bend, Freddie slowed his horse, and waited. After a few minutes, he tired of waiting and turned back.

When Freddie finally came upon his brother, Thomas had dismounted and was helping the shepherd to gather his flock. Upon seeing Freddie, Thomas gave him a look that didn't need explanation.

They were the local nobility, and it did not behoove them to go tearing about the countryside causing mayhem.

Freddie dismounted and spent the next half an hour helping to set right his misdemeanor. He slipped a coin into the palm of the shepherd to ensure his father did not get wind of his early morning antics.

He was about to mount his horse and make ready to head back to Rosemount Abbey when he had a second thought. He dipped his head toward the nearby village tavern.

"Fancy an early ale and some cheese bread?" he asked his brother.

Thomas accepted the peace offering. "You, genius, read my mind."

The tavern owner was just beginning to set up for the day and was happy to assist with pouring the sons of the local nobleman a fresh pint of ale. The brothers took a seat outside the tavern and watched the early morning to and fro of the villagers.

"So, are we expecting an announcement sometime this week, brother dear?" asked Thomas.

Freddie sipped at his beer. He had been waiting for the moment when Thomas would raise the question of his and Eve's relationship. "I expect so. She seems eager to get things on a more formal footing. Mama is also keen to get me thrust into the arms of wedded bliss."

Thomas set his tankard down and sat up straight. Sensing a serious conversation was about to take place, Freddie gave his older brother his full attention.

"And what about you? What do you want, Freddie? Don't be sitting on the sidelines while the battle for your future is being fought. If you are not completely sure of how you feel about Eve Saunders, you need to do something about it before it is too late."

Freddie raised an eyebrow. He hadn't expected Thomas to say anything against him marrying a girl from such a fine family. Indeed, he had expected Thomas to press for him to hurry up and propose to Eve. "I think we will do fine together. She is a bright girl and has spirit. I don't see why we wouldn't be happy," he replied.

"You don't sound convinced."

Freddie shook his head. Of course, he was convinced. Eve and he had had a brilliant partnership during the Bachelor Board challenges.

In fact, she was one of the main reasons he was about to claim the prize. He couldn't imagine life without her.

There was also the small matter that she and he had indulged in several sexual activities that demanded he make her his wife. Eve wasn't technically ruined, but she was no longer an innocent by any social standards.

"Expect to hear an announcement by the end of the week. Our wedding will be a little grander than yours and Cecily's, but that's what comes of the bride having uncles who are bishops and dukes. Her brother was recently married at St Paul's Cathedral, so I expect that is where we too will be wed. Anywhere else would not be right," he replied.

Thomas said nothing and went back to drinking his beer and eating his cheese bread.

Eve was up early that morning as well. She was walking the grounds of Rosemount Abbey, her mind full, imagining what it would be like to live there. The lush green of the English countryside was a soul-enriching contrast to the grey and filth of London.

Life at the abbey and its relative close proximity to London meant she could easily move between both worlds. With Freddie about to secure his position on the Bachelor Board they would need to spend a great deal of their time in London, but they would be able to spend time at the abbey.

Long summer nights spent lounging on the stone terrace with her siblings, their respective spouses, and children, beckoned.

She passed by the stables and was heading toward the ornamental lake when Cecily Rosemount hailed her.

"Good morning, Eve. Lovely day," she said.

Eve smiled. She had immediately taken to the future Viscountess Rosemount. She was a fresh-faced young woman who clearly had the eye of her husband's love.

"It's beautiful out here at this hour of the day. I was watching the sun burn through the early morning mist over the lake," replied Eve.

Cecily came to stand beside her. She was dressed in a simple olive-green gown with a large woolen shawl wrapped around her shoulders. Her manner of dress was that of someone who did not care for the fancy gowns of London.

Eve turned to her. "Have you lived around the district all your life?"

She assumed Cecily was the daughter of some local landed gentry or minor noble, and Thomas had chosen someone who would fit in well with the rural life at Rosemount Abbey.

Cecily shook her head. "Lord, no. Before I met Thomas, you would have had to hold a pistol to my head to get me into the countryside. I was very much a daughter of the *ton*. I grew up at the home of the Duke and Duchess of Devonshire, amongst a veritable menagerie of children from various noble families. I ran absolutely wild until I came out, after which my parents began to pressure me to marry."

"And so, you made them proud by marrying Thomas Rosemount, a future viscount," replied Eve.

Cecily burst into a long and hearty laugh. "Oh, you have no idea. The first time I set eyes on him, I thought he was the most handsome devil I had ever seen. My mother and father were horrified when I told them I was considering marrying him. They thought he was this dull, country mouse who would bore me into an early grave."

Thomas Rosemount wasn't the most sparkling man Eve had ever met, but he appeared to be genuine. Nice would be the word to describe him if she was pressed for an answer. He most certainly was not Freddie with his penchant for hijinks.

"But you married him anyway. Why?"

Cecily turned to face the green lawn that ran down to the edge of the lake. "Because of this place. Well, at first anyway. Rosemount Abbey offered me the chance of the first real home I could call my own. A place where I could be settled in life. Thomas brought me here before he offered for my hand; he wanted me to understand what being his wife would entail. The life I was living in London would be a thing of the past."

Eve followed Cecily's gaze. At the bottom of the long stretch of lawn a flock of ducks were waddling their way toward the lake. The mother duck was in the lead, followed by five little ducklings.

"So, do you return to London very often?" asked Eve. She understood the appeal of living part of the year in the countryside but couldn't imagine giving up the English capital.

"I can't remember the last time I went to London—it holds little appeal for me now. The first time I saw this place, my heart told me my children would be born and raised here. I would gladly turn my back on all that London had to offer for the chance of being with the man I loved."

The abbey was truly a beautiful place. Eve had seen enough stately homes during her life to know it would hold its own against all of them. But to completely sacrifice life among the *ton,* and live in the country, was something she could never do.

Cecily turned to her and smiled. "Thomas gave me my own self. With him, I have been able to become the person I wanted to be, not the person London high society dictated. I see so many others of my acquaintance in miserable marriages and thank God every day that Thomas chose me."

The look of happiness on Cecily's face made Eve's heart light. Her countenance was not full of the flush of new love, as Lucy's had been; rather, it reflected a deep contentment. Eve wondered if she would ever feel that with Freddie. Theirs was a relationship based on something else. The heat which fueled the passion between them was more primal than simply love.

If she married Freddie, she knew it would not be a marriage based on contentment. She lusted for excitement, as did he. With the Bachelor Board games coming to an end, she would have to find other ways to keep the passion and interest alive in their union.

Walking back to the house, she pondered her situation. She had been invited here, the same as Cecily had been when Thomas had decided she was the one for him. If Freddie had also come to that same decision she had her part to play. They had been afforded few moments of privacy in the day or so since her arrival. It was up to her to find a way to be alone with him and help move things forward.

Reaching the house, she saw Freddie and Thomas coming down the long driveway of the estate. They were riding slowly, deep in conversation. When Thomas pointed her out to Freddie, she gave him a friendly wave.

Freddie bowed to her while still seated in the saddle. A flush of heat raced to her cheeks. He was perfect.

Tonight, she would ensure they were alone.

Their hunger for one another would finally be sated.

Chapter Twenty-One

F reddie brushed the dust from his boots and quickly headed into the house. He intended on catching up with Eve, to steal a moment of her time—and hopefully a kiss or two. Every time he had been close to Eve since her arrival, he had wanted to pull her hard against him, and take her mouth in a searing kiss.

Disappointment greeted him instead. Once inside, he discovered his mother and Adelaide had beaten him to Eve. They were making plans to take her into the village and show her the Norman era church.

As he made his polite greetings and farewells to them, he prayed they wouldn't be encountering the local shepherd and his flock as they made their way. His mother would tear strips off him if she knew he had been racing about the countryside disturbing the local inhabitants.

In his bedroom, he sat at his writing desk and penned a note to Lord Godwin. He would soon be a member of the Bachelor Board but felt an obligation to share his financial good fortune with his friend. Being the fifth son of the Duke of Mewburton, little money would trickle down to Godwin during his lifetime.

As Godwin was not the sort of young man cut out for the army, nor did he show the slightest interest in taking up a position in the church, he would be among the first people Freddie would assist once he had his own fortune established.

He finished the letter to Godwin and then looked at the date he had written at the top. It was the third day since he had arrived home, time to see what Osmont had set for the final challenge.

He was going through the motions now. With no one else left in the game, the challenge could only be a formality.

He retrieved the letter from his travel trunk and stared at it.

"It had better not be a naked ride through the village," he muttered.

He opened it. Read the instructions quickly. Frowned. Then read them a second time. Slowly. Word for word.

He sat back in the chair and stared at the page.

> To the Honorable Frederick Rosemount,
> The final challenge to secure your place on the Bachelor Board
>   is to win the heart of a woman and then crush it without
>   mercy. Only a man capable of such an act is truly deserving
>   of the keys to the kingdom. Cowards choose love over power
>   and wealth.
> You have one week to complete this final challenge and report to
>   me in London.
> Your future awaits.
> Osmond Firebrace

Freddie sank his head into his hands. His world had been rocked to its foundations by this cruel blindside. "Fuck."

The price of winning the challenge would be to break Eve's heart.

His head felt light, and for a moment he was sure he was going to faint. His fingers fidgeted with the ties of his cravat that were suddenly too tight. He rose from the chair and began to pace the room. Scuff marks on the carpet soon appeared, showing the trace of his boots as he walked back and forth.

If the letter had been from anyone else, he would have challenged it. Offered them any other challenge for him to undertake. But he knew Osmont Firebrace was not the kind of man you negotiated with over such a prize. This was not Royal Ascot, and this was not an argument over the weight of a jockey. Horse racing and gambling were games for children; the Bachelor Board was for men who knew what they wanted in life.

Membership of the Bachelor Board would guarantee him and his heirs a life of wealth and power. Men were waiting to hand him the means to making his fortune. Doors would open that he did not know even existed. To throw away the chance of securing such a life would be madness.

He closed his eyes. Images of Eve filled his mind. Her smile. Those luscious lips were soft, yet when he kissed her they held a power over him stronger than anything he had ever known. He had told her he loved her. While she hadn't said it in so many words, he thought she loved him.

He would be a fool, not a coward to give her up. To treat her so cruelly. Either way he chose, he would lose.

He picked up the letter and looked at it. Osmont had given him a week. He still had time.

He folded the letter back up and left it on his desk. He couldn't stay in his room all day and ponder the choices set out before him—he would go mad. He pulled at the remainder of the knot of his cravat and released it from his neck. After throwing it on the back of the chair, he took off his jacket.

The one place he could be sure of having his mind occupied was the stables. Mucking out the stalls had been a childhood punishment, but today it was exactly what he needed. The smell of horses, hay, and manure would buy him at least a few hours of sanity.

Time in which to make a decision.

Chapter Twenty-Two

The morning trip into Thorney village was a pleasant one. Eve sat quietly in the carriage while her mother and Lady Rosemount discussed suitable menus for a wedding breakfast. Lady Rosemount was all for a large spread of various roast meats, while Adelaide gently pushed for dainty hors d'oeuvre such as Will and Hattie had served guests at their wedding.

Eve frowned as the conversation continued. Freddie had not yet asked her to marry him. It was encouraging, however, that everyone else considered the deal all but sealed. From Freddie's look of hunger when he caught sight of her at Rosemount Abbey a little while earlier, Eve sensed it wouldn't take much to push him into proposing.

When they finally returned to the abbey, it was late afternoon. Eve was itching to get inside and hunt down Freddie. Another semi-formal dinner had been agreed upon by the two mothers for the evening and if she played her cards right, it might be a night for champagne and toasts to the newly engaged couple.

"Have you seen Master Frederick?" she enquired of one of the household footmen.

"Yes, Miss Saunders. I believe he is working in the stables. He has been there most of the day cleaning out the stalls," he replied.

Freddie had never struck her as someone who would be working in the stables, but if that was where he was, then she would seek him out.

The stables were in a long stone building situated some way from the main house. Lord Rosemount had an extensive stud of horses both within the stables and in the nearby fields. His breeding program was well known throughout the *ton* and his horses came with both an expensive price tag and a long waiting list for prospective buyers.

Her father owned several horses which had been bred at Rosemount Abbey, and he was at pains to make sure his investments were properly looked after by his stable staff. Francis had been working hard to put together enough funds to buy his own Rosemount horse.

Eve walked inside the stables and immediately felt the stillness in the air. The horses were all in their stalls. The only sound to be heard was the soft crunch of hay being chewed. There were no stable hands to be seen.

She walked the length of the stables looking for Freddie. She was about to give up and go back to the house in search of him when she came across an empty stall.

Seated on the floor was her quarry.

"There you are. I was beginning to think you had returned to the main house and I had missed you," she said.

Freddie looked up and smiled. He patted the straw next to him.

"Come sit with me. The staff have finished for the day. It's all clean and dry straw; I was just having a rest before I went back to the house. I shall need a bath after this afternoon's exertions," he said.

Eve happily plopped down beside him. "I have missed you. I thought when Mama and I came away to the country you and I would get time together, but it's actually harder here than when we are in London."

He nodded. "I know what you mean. I was going to grab you this morning and drag you into a room for a thorough kissing, but my mother and Adelaide had already got a hold of you. This visit has been frustrating to say the least."

She leant over to him and placed a soft kiss on his cheek. When she went to pull away, he grabbed a hold of her head and drew her back to him. "All the stable hands have finished up for the day and gone back to their cottages. You and I are the only ones here," he said.

When their lips met a second time, Freddie gave her no quarter. He took her mouth with a kiss that had her praying it would never end. Their tongues tangled in a sensual dance. She groaned, knowing it would make him hard.

"Eve," he murmured.

She had been waiting for this opportunity. To show him she was serious about moving matters to their logical conclusion.

"I'm not leaving here until you and I have lain together. The announcement of our betrothal would only then be a mere formality. My mother could send word to my family with the morning mail carriage. I have already penned a note to Caroline, I just need to date and seal it," said Eve.

With her intent made clear, Eve put her thoughts into action. Her hand slid down and rested on his crotch. She exalted in feeling how hard his manhood had become. She gave a gentle squeeze and was rewarded as Freddie deepened the kiss.

The buttons on the front of his trousers were an easy task for her nimble fingers. With the placket of his trousers open, she slid a hand inside and took a hold of him. She began to stroke him slowly.

"Oh god, Eve, you know how to tease a man," he said through gritted teeth.

Eve rose onto her knees and bent down before him. She had heard enough talk amongst her married friends to know the basics of pleasuring a man with her mouth. Hopefully she had a good enough understanding.

"Tell me if I am doing it wrong," she said.

"Just bow down and take the tip of it in your mouth. Then take as much of it as you can and slide it in and out. Mind you don't use your teeth," he instructed.

With his cock in her mouth, she ministered slow, long strokes of him. The salty taste of his essence sat on her tongue.

Freddie lay back and his fingers speared into her hair as she continued to pleasure him. The tension in his breathing gave her all the encouragement she needed. From his soft gasps and groans she knew the moment when the rhythm was just right.

She would have continued to the inevitable conclusion, but Freddie whispered, "Stop."

Lifting her head, she saw the glaze of passion in his eyes. His face was flushed. He pulled her to him and took her lips once more.

Now it was his turn to play with laces and buttons. Eve's breasts were soon released from the confines of her gown and chemise. The cool early evening air made her nipples hard.

She whimpered as Freddie took them between his fingertips and gave them a gentle twist. He lowered his head and took the nipple of her right breast into his mouth. He suckled. Gently at first, then harder. His hand slid up her skirt, and she opened her legs wider as he slipped his thumb inside her heat.

"Oh, Freddie. That feels so good," she whispered.

As he stroked her wet passage, she reached out and took a hold of his hard member a second time. The air in the stall grew heated. The only sounds in the stables were the soft groans from the two lovers and the occasional swish of a horse's tail.

Eve rolled over onto her back and lifted her skirts. Her womanhood was completely naked to his gaze. She was his for the taking.

"Eve," he murmured.

He sat back on his haunches, and for the first time she sensed he was hesitant to come to her. She nodded. This was a major moment. Once he had taken her, there would be no going back. They would be forever bound together.

"It's alright. I am ready," she said.

A look passed over his face, which gave her pause. Was he unsure? She held her breath, only releasing it when he finally nodded. They were going to finally become one.

He pulled his trousers down, freeing his erection. Eve licked her lips. Her whole body ached for him.

He straddled her and kissed her once more. She put her heart and soul into the kiss. This was the moment. Her maidenhead was about to become his prize, but this would be her victory.

She tried to take hold of his manhood once more, but Freddie inexplicably pushed her hand away. He pulled back from her and his head dropped.

Their faces were close. She searched his gaze, desperate for answers.

"I am ready. Make me yours," she urged.

He closed his eyes and stilled over her. His breathing began to slow. "I can't do this."

A cold dagger of disappointment pierced her heart. She did her best to push the pain away. For all his reckless behavior in London, at the very moment they should be making love, Freddie had decided to be a gentleman.

"It's alright. I want to give myself to you now. I don't want to wait until the wedding," she said.

He rolled off her. She watched in stunned silence as he got to his feet and began to button up the front of his trousers. He offered her his hand, but Eve refused it. "Are you really going to tell me you are that much of a prude you will wait until our wedding day to take my virginity?" The anger of rejection was edged on her words.

He puffed out his cheeks. "There is not going to be a wedding. I don't want you. The game was fun while it lasted, but I never signed up for marrying you. You only set your sights on me to annoy your sister. You don't really love me."

He wouldn't meet her gaze and turned his head away as Eve began to cry.

"You should get dressed as soon as possible and return to the house," he said.

And with that he was gone, leaving Eve still in a state of undress on the pile of straw. She closed her eyes as her world crumbled around her.

Chapter Twenty-Three

F reddie woke with a stiff crook in his neck. He was lying under a tree in the woods that abutted the Rosemount estate. Just how long he had been there he could not be certain. From the way his head protested furiously at his first attempt to sit up, it had to have been for a number of hours.

After leaving Eve alone and rejected in the stables he had gone back to the house and helped himself to a full bottle of his father's best whisky. With coat and whisky bottle in hand, he had headed out into the night with the sole intention of drinking himself into oblivion.

In the early morning light, the full force of his elephant sized hangover weighed heavily on him. He dragged himself to his feet, brushing leaves from his coat. The rest of his clothes were damp from the early morning dew.

"Time to face the music," he muttered.

He would have to spend the rest of the time Eve and her mother were in residence at the abbey trying to avoid them. As he trudged back across the fields, empty whisky bottle in hand, he prayed their visit would be cut short. The thought of having to see Eve's crestfallen face once more filled him with dread.

"I am not a coward, I did what I had to," he muttered. The words of Osmont Firebrace's letter were his only source of comfort.

As he rounded the corner of the house, he came upon his parents, Thomas, and Cecily standing out the front. They all turned to him.

Cecily and Thomas exchanged a few words, and she walked back inside. Lady Rosemount followed closely behind. The look his mother gave him as she passed him by would have frozen the sea.

"Morning," he said. The nonchalant air with which he attempted to deliver his words fell flat on delivery.

Thomas marched over to him and fixed him with an angry stare. "So, the fox has finally decided to come skulking out of his hole. You are a bloody disgrace," he said.

Freddie didn't answer, unsure as to what Eve had told his family about the events of the previous evening. He was certain she would not have mentioned their sexual activities in the stables, but he also knew it would take far less than that for his father to demand he marry Eve.

"What has she said?" he asked. His nauseous stomach was not helping the situation. If he had not encountered his family, he would be throwing up the remains of the whisky still in his stomach into a nearby bush.

"Eve didn't say anything. She went to her room last night, and a short while later Adelaide Saunders spoke to Mama and said that they were leaving at first light. The only thing we can be certain of is you have jilted her," replied Thomas.

"How could you do that? You obviously gave the girl all the signs you intended to offer for her and then turned coward at the end. It seems to me you have no sense of honor or decency in your body. What sort of a son have I raised, I ask you?" asked Lord Rosemount.

Freddie's muddled mind listened to their outpour of anger, and he held the requisite contrite face. Inside, however, his mind was filled with thoughts of burning ambition.

Eve and Adelaide Saunders were gone. He wouldn't have to face them. This was an unexpected turn for the good. A day or so of his family being angry with him would see things set to right. He would apologize to his parents, explain it away as him being not ready for the commitment of marriage, and then head back to London with all due haste to secure his seat on the Bachelor Board.

Once he had established himself among the wealthy and powerful members of the board, his family would understand. They would accept he had had to make sacrifices in order to be a success. It was just unfortunate Eve's heart had been one of them.

In his mind he had done the honorable thing by not ruining her, and in time she would thank him.

Thomas loudly cleared his throat, rousing Freddie from his dreams of grandeur.

"Eve Saunders was a delightful breath of fresh air. She is intelligent, well-read, and would have made the perfect wife for you. But no, you had to go and make a mess of things. I tell you, if our father was not standing right here, I would knock you to the ground," said Thomas.

Lord Rosemount sniffed in obvious agreed disgust. "Don't let that stop you. It's taking all my self-control not to throw the first punch. Frederick, you have caused heartbreak to that poor girl and brought shame on your family. Your mother is utterly disgusted with you."

Thomas and Lord Rosemount both headed into the house, leaving Freddie standing alone, words of rebuke ringing in his ears.

By mid-afternoon, the situation had become intolerable. Every female member of his family he encountered constantly had tears on her face, while every male greeted him with stony silence.

The niggling thought he had treated Eve terribly sparked in his brain. As much as he tried to push the thought away, it refused to budge, and by the end of the afternoon it had taken root. He consoled his growing guilt with the unmistakable fact the damage was done. There was nothing he could do to assuage Eve's broken heart. She was on the road back to London, his heartless words likely still ringing in her ears.

He pulled the letter from Osmont Firebrace out once more and read it. He had played the final challenge and succeeded. Victory, however, was cold and hollow. He could only pray that in the years to come power and riches would dull the pain of destroying a young woman's heart.

"It had to be done."

He toyed with the notion of downing another of his father's bottles of whisky or even moving on to brandy. His parched throat and dry lips convinced him otherwise. His body would not thank him for another night of sleeping rough in the cold, damp woods.

Finally deciding he was wasting his time remaining at home, he asked the head stableman to take him into Peterborough. He packed a small travel bag and left a cursory farewell note on the dining room table for his parents to discover. He then took his leave of Rosemount Abbey and once he was in Peterborough, he caught the evening coach back to London.

The coach was only half full, which enabled him to settle down in one corner and get comfortable. Fatigue and the remains of his hangover soon caught up with him and he fell asleep.

Sleep did not bring rest or comfort to his mind, and his dreams were filled with tears and black clouds. The constant memory of Eve's look of heartbroken despair as he pushed away from her sat constantly in the middle of his nightmare.

Winning his seat on the Bachelor Board had come at a terrible price.

Chapter Twenty-Four

E ve managed to hold herself together for the first few hours. After Freddie had thrown her over, she had slowly dressed and fixed her hair somewhat. Then she wandered the grounds of Rosemount Abbey in stunned silence for an hour or so before finally making her way back to the main house.

She cried off the invitation to dine with the Rosemount family that evening, claiming a severe headache.

It was only as she lay in her bed that the tears finally came. Nothing in her life had ever come close to the deep body-shaking sobs that held her in their grip for hours.

Her mother came and sat beside her. She didn't need to ask what was wrong. Adelaide spoke with Lady Rosemount in the late hours and it was agreed that it was best she and Eve leave for London the next morning.

It was with a heavy heart that Eve climbed aboard the coach. The Rosemount family, except the still-missing Freddie, had gathered stony-faced in the courtyard. A soft thank you and goodbye was the best Eve could manage in her current state.

After travelling through Peterborough, they joined the Great North Road, turning south toward London. Adelaide offered for them to overnight at one of the coaching inns en route, but Eve asked they simply change horses and continue on.

She slept a little in the travel coach but refused all offers of food. Her mind was a constant whirl of questions and what-ifs. All her plans had been shattered to a thousand pieces. The Freddie she thought she knew was most certainly not the man who had told her he didn't want her.

The inside of the carriage began to feel increasingly hot and cramped. The palms of her hands became sweaty and her breathing labored. Inside she was screaming.

"Mama, please stop the carriage. I must get out," she pleaded.

Adelaide immediately got to her feet and rapped on the roof just below where the coachman was sitting. The coach slowed and pulled over to the side of the road.

Eve flung open the door and, gathering her skirts, leapt down onto the roadside. She made for a nearby empty field.

She made a few steps into a run but found she had not the energy for it. Instead, with head bowed and shoulders slumped, she slowly walked the field, heading farther and farther away from the coach.

When she finally stopped and turned around, she was a long way from the road. Sinking to her knees, she sucked in a great lungful of air before letting out a loud howl of heartbroken despair.

No one had ever told her that a broken heart came with physical pain. She wrapped her arms around herself and tried to hug the ache from her heart. Wave after wave of hopelessness crashed over her.

A gentle hand stroked her hair. "I know it hurts like the devil at the moment, and believe me, the only thing you can do is to cry it out. Let all the anger and pain come out of you," said Adelaide. She knelt in front of Eve, and in that moment, Eve was so grateful to have such a strong and supportive mother.

"I don't know how to deal with it, Mama. I think my heart is going to give out."

"You have to deal with heartache—you cannot avoid it. I know all you can see right now is the blackness of it, but you will come out the other side. Time is the one thing you can count on to help heal yourself.

Not today, and probably not for some time, but your heart will heal," replied Adelaide.

Eve pulled her knees up to her chest and lay over them. Staring over the field of long green grass, she let her mind speak its truth. A truth she had refused to accept since the day she had set her mind on marrying Freddie.

It wasn't just the pain of a broken heart that troubled her. She had been stubborn and reckless in her pursuit of him. His words, though they had cut through her like a knife, were filled with truth. Spite against Caroline had been the reason she had first pursued him. But that had long ago fallen away. She loved him with her whole heart, and he had smashed it to pieces.

"You will rise from this a stronger woman, Eve. The woman you become shall have been forged in the fire of heartbreak. Your future love is out there. Give yourself time, but never abandon the hope of love."

"It's my fault," replied Eve, unable to look at her mother.

"You cannot blame yourself. Lady Rosemount told me Freddie thought you would make a suitable wife. If he had not thought so, she would not have extended the invitation for us to visit. He is a young man simply not ready for marriage. It is a good thing you both discovered the truth now," replied Adelaide.

Her mother's words would have brought comfort if it had been a simple matter of two people not ready to marry. Eve knew the situation was more complicated.

"I pushed him into a tight corner and when he realized he was going to have to offer for me, he did the only thing he could and ran away. The pain of rejection hurts, but what hurts more is the sense of utter humiliation. I left London telling everyone I expected to be engaged by the time I returned. Freddie told me I only went after him to spite Caroline, and I am ashamed to say there is a deal of truth in his words."

She heard her mother's soft intake of breath. A hand took hold of her chin and raised it. Eve met Adelaide's loving gaze.

"You are not the first girl who wished desperately to be married. And if Lady Rosemount and I hadn't thought the two of you could have made a go of it, we would never have arranged this visit. I think you will find in time that Freddie comes to realize he could have handled things better with you.

"As for you and Caroline, I have never been able to understand how the two of you went from being best friends all your lives to becoming outright rivals. You used to be so close."

Eve didn't reply. Her mind was still trying to come to terms with the truth. Jealousy was an ugly word, and it had hardened her heart toward her sister.

Eve and her mother sat in the field for a while longer, only returning to the coach when the driver came and mentioned they would not make the next major inn before nightfall if they didn't leave soon.

As Eve settled back into the soft leather seats of the coach, she sensed her mood beginning to change. Going home and sleeping in her own bed would no doubt help. She opened a book and began to read. By the time they reached the outskirts of London, it was night and she was falling asleep.

As she drifted off, she felt the comfort of a warm blanket being wrapped around her. Her mother softly whispered, "Sleep, my girl. Find your inner peace, and in time, when you are ready, you will find your prince."

Chapter Twenty-Five

Wwhen Eve and her mother arrived home, Eve headed up to her room without greeting any members of the Saunders family. She couldn't bring herself to face them. Especially Caroline.

A maid brought up a plate of supper. She was accompanied by Adelaide. After the maid set the tray down and left the room, Adelaide came and sat beside Eve.

"I've told your father the bare bones of what happened. To say he is furious would be a gross understatement. Your father was prepared to overlook some of his foolishness because you clearly loved the boy, but after today I will say Freddie is lucky he is not within a hundred miles of here tonight," she said.

Eve picked up a small cheese sandwich and took a bite. For all the fine dining at Rosemount Abbey, it was good to be home, back eating simpler fare. As she sat and chewed, her mother gently held her hand.

"What have you told Caroline and Francis?" asked Eve.

"Nothing."

Having intelligent, caring parents was a priceless gift. While both Adelaide and Charles Saunders would be livid at the outrageous injury inflicted upon their daughter's heart, neither of them would be making a fuss in public.

The events at Rosemount Abbey had taken place far from London. It was unlikely anyone outside of the Rosemount family would know what had transpired to compel the Saunders women to suddenly up and leave the abbey. Lord and Lady Rosemount were respectable, decent people, who Eve knew to be shocked and disgusted by Freddie's actions—or what they knew of them.

"You might want to talk to Caroline in the morning, after which your father and I will decide what we shall tell Francis. Your father will no doubt speak to Will."

The conversations with her brothers were, to Eve's mind, the easier of the tasks. What she herself would tell Caroline was far more difficult. In confiding in Caroline, she would finally have to give voice to some of her inner demons.

Eve slept late the next morning. The trip home in the coach had been long and uncomfortable. She woke to soft rapping on her bedroom door. As she opened an eye, she caught sight of Caroline's face in the doorway.

"Are you awake?" asked Caroline.

Eve sat up in bed and settled the blankets neatly around herself. She beckoned for her sister to enter the room.

Caroline closed the door gently behind her and walked slowly across the floor toward the bed. She took a seat at the end of the four-poster, her back against one of the upright posts.

"So how was your trip?" she asked. She was slowly wringing her hands and wouldn't meet Eve's gaze. Her discomfort was evident.

Eve sucked a deep breath in, then slowly let it out. "It was an utter disaster. He rejected me," she replied. Facing the cold, hard truth was the only way she would ever get over the heartbreak. Part of that cold, hard truth was also accepting she had been a willing participant in her own downfall.

Caroline wiped away a tear. "Oh, Eve, I suspected something terrible had happened when you and Mama arrived home last night. I heard you downstairs and I waited for you to come racing up and be full of happiness, ready to show me your betrothal ring. When I heard you go straight to your room and close the door, I knew. I knew that beastly boy had broken your heart." She climbed off the bed and moved closer to Eve. She leant down and kissed her sister softly on the cheek. "He doesn't deserve you. He never did."

"He was not the only one to blame for what happened," replied Eve. While Freddie was now in her past, there were still things she needed to resolve before she had a clear path forward.

"What do you mean? If Freddie behaved in an ungentlemanly fashion toward you, I cannot see how that is your fault."

Freddie may well have been the one who'd torn all her hopes and dreams to pieces, but she had been very much the architect of her own destruction. She had ignored everyone and their not-so-subtle hints about him. She had been a willing participant in the foolish Bachelor Board games and stood by while he insulted her family and friends. She was now paying the price for her reckless behavior and for having given up her heart.

"I was in such an almighty rush to get married. I thought Freddie was the perfect mix of rake, brains, and money, all wrapped up in a heavenly masculine body. I fell in love with him. What I failed to see was he was playing me all along. That I wasn't a part of the hunt—I was the prey."

Caroline dropped down onto the bed beside Eve and studied her sister for a moment. Eve knew Caroline well enough. Her beauty hid a clever mind. Little got past Caroline.

"Why were you in such a rush to get married? As I recall, you were the one who was saying Lucy and Avery were a cautionary tale for all young women. That none of us should act with haste when it came to marriage."

Eve sighed. The time had come to have the most difficult conversation of her life. A conversation where she would have to bare many of her deepest secrets.

"I originally set my sights on Freddie because I wanted to beat you to the altar. I was desperate to be a bride before you. To have my one moment in the sun."

Caroline sat for a moment and stared at Eve. "But why?"

Eve closed her eyes as fresh tears began to fall. "Because you are so beautiful, and you are always the one the young gentlemen want to talk to and dance with at parties. There have been so many times we have been in a group of people, and while you were the bright and shining center of attention, I stood on the side invisible to all. Freddie was the first one who paid me attention. I was filled with bitter happiness when instead of falling at your feet, he treated you with such horrible disdain." She put her face in her hands and began to sob. The shame of finally acknowledging she had spent much of her life being bitterly jealous of her younger sister threatened to overwhelm her.

Caroline had been nothing other than a loving and supportive sister. She had been Eve's rock so many times, yet all the while, she had been the cause of much pain in her sister's life.

"And that is why you threw yourself at Freddie Rosemount, just to spite me? Oh, Eve, how could you do such a thing to yourself? I cannot believe you hate me so much you would throw your life away in the hope it would make me miserable."

There were no words for the depth of Eve's pain. She had taken a sisterly love and twisted it into an unnatural shape. "I am ashamed beyond words. I am jealous of you. My own sister."

Caroline climbed off the bed. She rummaged around at the end of the fire and picked up a poker. She came back to Eve and jabbed at her gently with it. "I've a good mind to strike you with this and throw your foolish, jealous body on the fire. Mama may be none too pleased, but she will get over it. As you say, I am the golden child so clearly, I am the only one who matters," said Caroline, her voice breaking.

Eve looked up. Caroline was still beside the bed, the poker pointed at her. Her words had dripped of sarcasm but her cheeks were shining with tears.

"You think you are the only one in this family who is jealous of their siblings? I would give a pound a day to be allowed to work in Papa's business, like Francis does. To have travelled the world like Will. As for being the center of attention, men don't see me. They see my looks and figure. Truth be told, I was jealous of you and Freddie. Much as I thought Freddie a fool, I was prepared to accept I had lost you forever because he clearly made you happy. You were always laughing and having secret conversations together."

The poker slipped out of her fingers and onto the floor where it landed with a thud. Caroline looked at it but made no effort to pick it up.

Eve wiped her eyes. She struggled for words. She did not have the monopoly on jealousy. Caroline, too, had felt the ugly emotion. "I'm sorry, Caroline. I had no idea of the pain you have suffered."

Caroline walked over to Eve's wardrobe and pulled out a deep blue and white striped day gown. She marched over and threw it on the bed. She drew in a shaky breath.

"Get dressed. You and I need to go out and have a day together. At the end of it we shall apologize to one another for all the horrid things we have said. Then we shall say no more of our stupid petty insecurities. From this day on, we work together as loving sisters to find the Eve and Caroline Saunders we deserve to be, and men such as Freddie Rosemount can all go hang." She headed for the door but stopped as she took hold of the handle. "And I promise if Freddie does cross our paths again, I shall heat up the end of that bloody poker and stab him with it in a most unpleasant place."

Eve stared at the door after Caroline had gone. Both her sister and Cecily Rosemount were right, she did have a choice in the type of person she would become. Freddie had shown her the folly of her actions. It was time to pick herself up and become the Eve Saunders of which she could be proud.

Chapter Twenty-Six

A fter arriving back in London, Freddie decided it would be prudent of him to lie low for a few days. He still had time up his sleeve before he had to go and see the Bachelor Board. He sent word to Osmont Firebrace that he had completed the final challenge, after which he spent the best part of two days trying to make a sizeable hole in his father's wine cellar.

Being blind drunk meant his brain only had to worry about breathing, sleeping, and throwing up. It had no time to consider Eve or the pain she must be in at that moment. Staying out of sight also meant that if any of the Saunders family decided to pay him a visit, he could hide behind the doors of Rosemount House.

By the fourth morning, he had reconciled himself to his new life. The hangover of the past few days was fading into the background and he woke sober and ready to claim his prize.

His membership of the Bachelor Board would ensure he was the first self-made member of the Rosemount family since the very first Viscount Rosemount. He felt like Alexander the Great on the cusp of conquering the known world. He would soon have an army at his back.

ᐡ

After a quick breakfast, he took Saintspreserveus for a long walk before readying himself for the trip to Barton Street. Leaving home, he cheekily picked up one of his father's walking canes.

Standing on the front steps of Rosemount House, he stood twirling the stick in his hand. Then, with a firm tap of it on the stone front step, he set off for Barton Street, a swagger in his step.

The morning was crisp, with a chill in the air that spoke of snow. He was too wrapped up in the warmth of his triumph to feel the cold. He made quick time across St James's Park, bowing at, and greeting, every passer-by he encountered. The occasional odd look from strangers was met with a laugh. If people didn't know who he was now, give him a year and they would be begging to make his acquaintance.

Arriving at Barton Street, he verily danced up the steps of the office and into the entrance hall. He rapped on the door of Osmont Firebrace's office with his father's cane and stood back, waiting for his grand entrance.

The door opened. Osmont Firebrace bowed low as Freddie stepped inside. "Rosemount. You didn't waste your time. I thought you might struggle with the final challenge, but I clearly underestimated your cold-blooded nature. My spies tell me the Saunders chit arrived back in London before you did. I trust you have not been challenged to a stupid duel by any members of her family?"

Freddie accepted the veiled congratulations with good grace. With his future all but secured, he could afford to ignore Osmont's derisive nature. One day he would wield enough power and influence he would not need to rely upon men such as him. "I did as you asked in every challenge. My ambition can no longer be in any doubt," he replied.

"Please do sit," said Osmont. He picked up a small bell and rang it, then took a seat behind his desk. When a servant opened the door a few minutes later he was carrying a bottle of brandy and a glass. He set them down on the table in front of Freddie before bowing low and leaving.

Freddie sat forward and picked up the bottle. "Croizet Cognac. Very nice. Will you break your abstinence from alcohol and join me?"

He was at pains to maintain a disinterested air about himself, but his heart was racing. Croizet had been the sommelier to Napoleon. His cognac was considered to be the best in the world. The bottle he held in his hand was worth a small fortune.

"Go on, open it. I shall take my enjoyment from having watched you drink it," said Osmont.

Freddie opened the bottle and poured himself a glass. Behind the desk Osmont sat with a look of absolute self-satisfaction written on his face. Freddie was his shiny new protégé.

Freddie sipped at the cognac. It was smooth with the perfect blend of dried fruit and citrus themes overlaying one another. He intended to develop a taste for such fine brandy and the means to be able to afford it.

Osmont rose from behind the desk and held out his hand. "Well done. You are almost there. There is the final matter of payment of your annual subscription. After you pay one hundred guineas into the Bachelor Board bank account at the Bank of England, I shall hand you your letter of introduction."

Freddie finished his drink. He had known there would be one final twist. The matter of one hundred guineas was a problem he could overcome. His annual allowance would not cover it, but he had been canny with his money while at university, and his savings would see him make the mark. He would simply have to ask his father for access to his money. Once Lord Rosemount understood his son's need, he would no doubt send instructions to his bank within a day or two and Freddie would be set.

"Of course. I shall have to write to my father to access funds, but I would expect to have the money by the end of the week. I trust that won't present a problem," he replied.

Osmont waved his words away. "I am sure your father will understand the imperative nature of your need. It's not every day a young man such as yourself sets out on his own path. He will be glad of your news. And just in case you still have some small remnant of guilt over the Saunders girl, don't worry. The Bachelor Board will find you a well-trained, docile wife who meets with your parents' approval. One who will do as she is told in the bedroom and not question where your money comes from. Pretty gowns and sparkling trinkets keep women in line."

Freddie poured himself a second drink. By the time he left Barton Street an hour later, he felt he could take on the world. He returned home the same way he had come. On foot. With two glasses of expensive French cognac under his belt, he had an extra spring in his step.

He had passed all the challenges and was about to be admitted to the Bachelor Board. He had finally arrived in London society. Soon he would be mixing it with the powerful and mighty.

When a girl with a similar-colored deep blue cloak to the one Eve had worn at Rosemount Abbey passed him by, a twinge of guilt stirred in his heart. He pushed it aside. Eve Saunders had thrown herself at him to spite her sister. She should be grateful he had had the good sense not to ruin her. They had their fun playing the game together, and it was at the behest of his mother that she and Adelaide Saunders had come to Rosemount Abbey. He most certainly was not to blame for the mess that had eventuated.

He put the sudden dry and bitter taste in his mouth down to the burnt coffee he had drunk at Barton Street before leaving.

Arriving home at Grosvenor Square, he was well into a long list of the people he would invite to his first party at home. He was going to have a long and wicked celebration to herald his success. New friends beckoned. His life was good, and it was about to become magnificent.

Stepping in the front door, he was surprised to see one of the footmen from Rosemount Abbey had opened it for him. He frowned. That could only mean someone from the family was in town.

He sighed. His party would have to wait a few days. As he took off his hat and coat, the footman pointed him toward his father's study.

"Lord Rosemount has instructed you attend him as soon as you arrive," he said.

Freddie walked across the foyer and stood outside his father's study door. His father had made no mention of coming to town. Freddie silently chided himself for having left the abbey without speaking further to his parents. An apology was clearly in order.

He took a deep breath before knocking. It was time to grovel. His mind began to race; he had to get back into his father's good graces in order to access his money. He was going to have to tread very carefully.

As he stepped into his father's study, he saw Lord Rosemount was hunched over a pile of papers on his desk. The first spark of concern lit in Freddie's brain when his father failed to acknowledge his presence.

Freddie stood in the middle of the room, hands held loosely by his side, and waited.

Finally, Lord Rosemount folded up the last of the papers and placed it on the top of a nearby pile. He picked up a small bell and rang it.

Within a minute, a footman entered the room. Lord Rosemount handed the papers to the footman who stole several glances at Freddie as the viscount spoke quietly to him. At the end of the short conversation with Lord Rosemount, the footman left the room, taking the papers with him. As he passed Freddie, he averted his gaze.

Lord Rosemount remained at his desk. "Those papers are instructions to all my creditors and merchants with whom I have accounts. The last one was to my banker. That is, of course, if you are the slightest bit interested in matters of the Rosemount estate. Though after what I have to say, you might be very interested." He rose from his desk and tidied up the remaining pens and items on its surface. He then closed his drawer and locked it. Freddie scowled when, instead of putting the key to the desk in its usual secret place, he put it in his pocket.

Freddie was about to mention to his father he would need the key in order to access letterhead which he used to place orders on the family's various accounts, but the hard glare on his father's face stopped him. He made a mental note to remind his father—after he had finished admonishing Freddie for his behavior.

"Before you ask, it was no mistake I kept the key. It's time you were given a hard lesson in life, my boy," said Lord Rosemount.

"I'm sorry if I embarrassed you and Mama over the Saunders girl. I did not behave well and I should have spoken to you before I came back to London. I offer you my most humble apologies," replied Freddie.

His father closed his eyes, and a sad huff escaped his lips. "Oh, Frederick. So little, so late."

Freddie ground his teeth as his jaw set hard with fear. There was ice in his father's voice. His father was not a man for great displays of anger. He had never known him to speak much louder than a raised voice. The quiet rage of his father was more powerful than any man who bellowed at the top of his lungs. "I—"

His father shook his head. "The letters which have left the house are instructions to cease extending any form of credit to you. Merchants will not honor any orders for goods or services that you place from today. I am cutting you off for the foreseeable future."

Freddie swayed on his feet as raw shock took hold.

Cut off.

His brain struggled to register the words. "How … how am I to live?" he stammered.

His father pulled a small money pouch out of his jacket pocket and threw it on the desk. "There is enough money in there to last you and the dog for a good six weeks if you stretch it tight. And when I mean stretch, I mean you are going to have to watch every farthing."

Freddie shook his head. "You cannot be serious. How are the servants to maintain the house if I do not have funds?"

When his father flinched at the mention of the servants, Freddie saw an opening. He could survive well enough if he cut back on his spending, but the servants couldn't very well walk around London paying cash for items for the household of Viscount Rosemount. It wasn't the done thing.

"They won't be maintaining the house. Those who are normally based at Rosemount Abbey will be travelling back tonight. The rest I have given paid leave for the rest of your six-week banishment. And when I say banishment, I mean it. If things get a little tough for you here, don't think of getting in a coach and coming home. You are not welcome at the abbey until I say you are."

No servants meant a cold and lonely house. Freddie's mind scattered in a thousand different directions. How was he to keep his rooms warm? Who was going to clean his clothes? And, most importantly, who was going to feed him?

His father walked toward the door. "I won't be staying here. Friends have invited me over for dinner and I shall stay with them overnight. Oh, and don't bother to write to your mother expecting to find sympathy. She refuses to even hear your name mentioned in her company. In fact, it was her idea to cut you off."

"But why?"

His father walked over to where Freddie stood and put a hand firmly on his shoulder.

"You are not a wicked man, but from the rumors I have heard about London you have allowed yourself to be led astray. The Frederick Rosemount I know would never have treated a young woman the way you did Evelyn Saunders. He most certainly would not have brought the shame you have on our family." His grip on Freddie's shoulder hardened. "You were not there the morning Adelaide Saunders and her daughter left. You were not even man enough to face her and see the pain you had inflicted upon that girl. She was absolutely heartbroken over you. I am ashamed to be your father at this moment. No son of mine would ever be so cruel as to hold out hope of love to a girl and then crush it so mercilessly. But you did. I can only hope that the misery you are about to go through will give you some time to find yourself once more. At this moment I do not know you, Frederick."

He walked from the room and left Freddie standing in shock. All his plans to celebrate his great victory went with his father.

He turned and took several steps toward the door. For a fleeting moment of madness, he thought to catch up to his father and beg for mercy, to promise whatever it took to stop his father from leaving him destitute.

The echo of his father's final words stopped him in his tracks.

I do not know you.

Hot tears come to his eyes. His family were not proud of him and all that he had achieved. Instead, they were ashamed.

All the puff and bravado that had filled him the past few weeks went out of him like air from a pair of bellows. His father's words made him a lesser man.

Freddie stayed in his father's study for several hours, too ashamed to go out and face the servants who were busy packing up the house. It was only when the sounds of the house fell silent that he finally ventured out.

As he stepped from his father's study, he immediately noticed the eerie silence.

"Hello?" he called.

A deafening silence responded. His father had been true to his word. All the servants were gone.

"Bollocks," he muttered.

A scattering of claws on the tiled floor signaled the arrival of Saintspreserveus. The dog scampered up to Freddie and eagerly accepted his master's vigorous scratch behind his ear.

"At least someone is still in a good mood," he said.

The dog tilted his head to one side and looked up at Freddie. Their gazes met and the dog whimpered. Freddie snorted. He could swear at times the dog had more intelligence than he was given credit for. "I'm sorry, boy. It's not your fault we are in this mess."

And a right mess it was. With the servants gone, there was the immediate and pressing problem of what food had been left behind.

With Saintspreserveus following behind, Freddie ventured down into the household kitchen. He was pleasantly surprised to find a fresh loaf of bread, a small wheel of Stilton cheese, and some carrots on the pantry shelves. Up high on the meat shelf he found a juicy bone, which he pulled down and handed to the dog.

Saintspreserveus snapped up the bone and wandered over to his bed in the corner where he proceeded to give the bone his full attention. At least the dog was happy for the moment.

In the pantry, Freddie located a few bottles of wine. Alcohol was not going to be a problem in the house as Thomas had shown him how to pick the lock on the door of their father's wine cellar at a young age. His father could cut Freddie off for several years and the extensive wine supply would last. The cheese and bread would suffice for the rest of the day, but after that he had no idea what he'd do.

"The money!" He raced back upstairs and into his father's study. He snatched up the small bag of coins and held it in his hand.

"Please, *please* let there be enough for me to dine out each day," he muttered.

Opening the bag, he tipped its contents onto the desk. Then he slumped down into the chair and stared at the meagre amount of money.

He picked up the bag again and stuffed his hand inside, hoping to find at least a one- pound note. The bag, however, was empty.

He slowly sorted the coins into piles as the sickening feeling in his stomach continued to whirl round and round. Some of the coins were of such little value he couldn't remember having ever possessed one before. What the devil would a chap do with a handful of farthings? The piles of farthings, groats, and sixpence amounted to less than what Freddie would normally have spent in a week on pies and other snacks at university. He was going to have to budget very carefully over the next few weeks, all the while praying his parents would have a change of heart.

"Well that is going to make paying for my seat on the board a little difficult," he muttered bitterly.

The contents of the sack could be ten times what it held, and he would still be a long way short on the money to pay Osmont.

"Ah!"

His father might refuse to give him any money, but he had friends. Godwin might claim his father cared little for him, but he never went without. Godwin wouldn't need to know exactly what Freddie wanted the money for, instead a small white lie would have to do. He just needed to get Godwin to ask the Duke of Mewburton for an advance on his yearly allowance, and then lend it to him.

Freddie vowed to pay Godwin back ten- fold on the loan when he made his first successful investment.

He scooped up most of the coins and put them back in the bag, tucking a few of the sixpence into his pocket. With a hopeful smile, he rose from the chair.

It was early enough in the day that he knew Godwin would still be at home. His love of the green weed from India and the dens where he could smoke it ensured Godwin would not have made it home until the early hours of the morning.

Putting on his coat, Freddie gave his dog a cheerful farewell.

"Wait there for me, boy. I shall be home soon enough and we shall have servants and food again before you can say snap."

The Duke of Mewburton's magnificent mansion was a short distance from Grosvenor Square. Freddie made it in quick time, the spring in his step returned.

Reaching the house on Mount Street, he bounded up the front steps and confidently knocked on the front door.

"Good morning. Lord Godwin, if you please," he said to the butler who opened the door.

The butler hesitated for a moment, then screwed up his face. "I am afraid Lord Godwin is indisposed to all visitors this morning."

Freddie huffed. He had lost count of the number of times he had arrived at Mewburton House and dragged his drug-addled friend from his bed. This morning he expected things to be no different.

He was about to remonstrate with the butler when the door was opened wide. A man who Freddie guessed would have been in his early thirties stood before him. From the manner of his dress and the color of his hair, Freddie supposed him to be one of Godwin's older brothers. "And who are you?"

Freddie stuck out a hand. "Frederick Rosemount, son of Viscount Rosemount. How do you do?"

The other man looked at Freddie's outstretched hand and shook his head. Freddie's good humor dimmed.

"Come inside. I don't want this conversation to be had on the doorstep in front of the help," said Godwin's brother.

Freddie stepped into the magnificent foyer of Mewburton House. After slipping off his hat, he handed it to the butler. The butler stood in the foyer holding the hat, a clear indication that Freddie's stay was not going to be a long one. He was ushered into a nearby drawing room and offered a seat.

While he sat down, Godwin's brother remained standing. Then he cleared his throat. "You and I have never met, but I was at school with your brother, Thomas. Decent chap, married a lovely girl. He seems to have his head on straight. Which I am afraid, from what my brother has told me, cannot be said of you."

Freddie sat forward in the chair as a burning sense of déjà vu hit him. "I'm sorry, sir, but you have me at the disadvantage. I don't know you who you are," replied Freddie.

"I am the Marquis of Copeland. Godwin is my youngest brother. I am here to tell you, you are to stay away from my brother from this day forward. You may not care for his health and heart, but our family does, and we shall not stand idly by while he whores and drugs himself into an early grave. He is coming home to Mewburton Castle with me today, and he will not be returning to London anytime soon. He needs to get his life and health in order. Good day to you, Rosemount. Give your brother my best regards."

Freddie was handed his hat and shown the door in quick time.

As he headed back toward Grosvenor Place, he dejectedly stuffed his hands in his coat pocket. This was fast becoming the worst day of his life. The day he had overslept a major exam at Oxford paled into insignificance at the disaster he was currently facing.

"Think, Freddie. There must be a way," he muttered.

Having spent his childhood in the countryside and then years as a social recluse at Oxford, he didn't have a wide group of friends in London on whom he could call for assistance. Trenton Embry was one of the few people Freddie knew beyond a casual hello, but he knew Trenton well enough not to even consider asking him for money. Who else in London did he know that he could call upon to assist him in his financial crisis?

He slowed his pace and instead of going home, he turned around and headed toward the Thames. It was a wild throw of the dice, but he was fast running out of options. Osmont Firebrace knew how wealthy Viscount Rosemount was; while it would take some clever words, Freddie felt confident he could convince Osmont to let him join the board and then pay his membership dues once his father had put him back in funds.

"Yes, that's it. Well done. Third time is the charm."

Chapter Twenty-Seven

F or the first time since he had known Osmont, Freddie was made
to wait for an audience. He sat on the hard bench outside
Osmont's office and silently prepared his speech.

It was close to an hour before the door to Osmont's office opened. A
young man appeared in the doorway. His faced was flushed and he
appeared to be most ill at ease. When he saw Freddie, he flinched. The
young man made a dash for the front door and was gone.

"Ah, Rosemount. That was quick. I take it you have come to bring
your admission fee?"

Freddie turned to see Osmont with one hand on the door. For an
instant, Freddie could have sworn his mentor was a little flushed in the
face, but as soon as he blinked the color of Osmont's face returned to
its normal pale shade.

"Actually no, but I would rather we spoke in your office if you
don't mind," replied Freddie.

Osmont stood back and uncharacteristically bowed to Freddie as he
entered his office. Freddie's skin crawled at the odd gesture. He took a
seat in one of the deep burgundy leather couches, but rather than
lounging back on it as was his usual habit, Freddie sat upright.

On the table in front of him was a half empty wine glass, which

Osmont picked up and placed near the fireplace. "Now, why haven't you come to pay your membership fee? Don't tell me after our discussion and my cognac that you have changed your mind. That little filly hasn't got a hold of your cock, has she? It would be disappointing to have to rescind the membership offer," said Osmont. The sneer of disdain in his voice could not be missed, but Freddie ignored it. He was not about to tempt the temper of the man he was hoping would give him money.

"No, no, I still intend to take my seat on the board. It's just that I have had a small setback, and require your temporary assistance," he replied.

A sly smile drifted across Osmont's face as he turned away and went to his desk. Freddie swallowed. Something was not right about the situation. He began to question the wisdom of his decision to come and ask for money.

"Go on," replied Osmont.

"Well, my father has decided he needs to teach me a lesson for a few weeks and so has restricted my line of credit. I was thinking since this is a temporary situation, you would consider lending me the money for my membership, along with a few extra pounds to tide me over."

This is not a good idea.

"Hmm," replied Osmont. He opened a small cupboard and took out a glass, and a half empty bottle of wine. After pouring some wine into the glass, he set it down in front of Freddie.

To Freddie's growing discomfort, he took a seat on the couch next to him. He reached out and patted Freddie on the shoulder where his hand lingered. "You are in a spot of bother, young man. I am glad you trusted me to help you."

Osmont's hand slowly worked its way down Freddie's arm and settled on his leg. Freddie's heart began to thump loudly in his chest.

"While I cannot help you in your hour of need due to my own financial obligations, I do know of other members of the Bachelor Board who would be willing. They wouldn't charge you interest on the loan."

Freddie's mood lifted at the unexpected good news. There were obviously decent chaps on the board who understood the situations young men sometimes found themselves facing.

"Excellent," he replied.

Osmont patted Freddie's leg. "A fine young man such as yourself could do many favors for fellow members of the board. It all depends on how much you want them to help you." He picked up the glass of wine and handed it to Freddie. "Drink. It's a good burgundy. I have a whole new shipment in my wine cellar if it takes your fancy."

Freddie took the glass and held it for a moment. He was caught somewhere between not wanting to take the wine and also not wanting to cause offence. Osmont hadn't done anything, nor had he actually said anything untoward.

Freddie had taken a mouthful of the wine before the notion that it might be drugged crossed his mind. He set the glass down and closed his eyes. *You fool.*

The face of the young man who had left Osmont's office shortly before reappeared in his memory. A cold, hard reality began to slowly settle on Freddie's shoulders as Osmont moved his hand up Freddie's leg and rested it within a matter of inches of Freddie's manhood.

"Tell me, Frederick. Did you ever have to suck the cock of a professor at Oxford to get him to give you a good mark on a final exam? If you did, you wouldn't be the first or the last lad to do so. There is nothing to be ashamed of in the mutual exchange of favors."

"No. I … I …" stammered Freddie. His brain was screaming for him to get up and leave the room, all the while his lips were speaking words that made no sense. He froze as Osmont placed his hand on his cock and squeezed hard.

"There is a lot of money which could be gifted to you from the members. It just depends on how much of a good boy you are willing to be. There are some members with very deep pockets. You could offer yourself and that nice tight arse of yours to them and make yourself a very pretty penny," purred Osmont.

I am ashamed to be your father.

The words of rebuke from his father broke through Freddie's tainted wine haze. He pushed Osmont's hand away and struggled to his feet. "No."

He staggered to the door and fumbled with the handle. By sheer force of willpower, he made it outside and into the street. As soon as he got out of sight of the building, he ran to a small tree in a nearby garden and slumped down under it. He prayed Osmont would not follow him or dare to risk a scene in public.

With his head and back against the tree, he tried in vain to focus. Finally, he gave up the struggle and closed his eyes. The powerful narcotic Osmont must have put in the wine overcame him.

❧

When Freddie woke, it was late afternoon. How many hours he had lain unconscious under the tree, he couldn't tell. A light rain was falling. A throbbing headache sat in the front of his brain and his mouth was as parched as a desert.

"Ooh. What was in that bloody wine?" He struggled to his feet, using the tree to help him balance. Eventually, he was able to walk out into the main street.

He was about to hail a hack to take him home when he remembered why he was at Barton Street in the first place. The handful of coins in his pocket would not cover the cost of the short trip home. "This is officially the worst day of my life," he growled.

He ambled home, stopping several times in St James's Park to throw up. When a group of well-dressed people passed him by, he heard them slyly remark about his inability to hold his alcohol. He ignored them, his sole interest being in putting one foot in front of the other and making it safely back to Grosvenor Place.

When it began to rain more heavily, he looked up. The dark grey skies overhead matched his miserable mood. He had gone from thinking he was king of the world to discovering just how insignificant he truly was.

The best-laid schemes of mice and men, go often askew.

By the time he finally staggered home, he was wet through. He banged on the front door several times before remembering his father had ordered the household servants away. Rummaging around in his pocket, he found his front door key, and slipped it into the lock.

As the door closed behind him, the echo of the thud rang out in the empty foyer. His clothes were soaked through, and his hair was stuck flat to his head. He looked and felt like something the cat had dragged in.

"Can this day get any worse?"

He went upstairs to his cold bedroom and stripped off his wet clothes before putting on dry ones. He needed to light a fire somewhere in the house to get his clothes dry, but heating his bedroom was a luxury he would not be able to afford for the foreseeable future. The kitchen had a large fireplace and stove, it would be much easier to keep himself warm if he kept to the downstairs kitchen.

Fortunately, the household cook had stored new firewood inside the kitchen earlier that morning, and there was a basket of kindling ready to set a fire.

"Right. This should be simple enough," he said. Taking the tinderbox down from a nearby shelf, he emptied its contents and set them out on the table. Tinder, flint, and steel. Placing the tinder into the box, he held the steel in his right hand and the flint in his left. He struck it against the steel.

Sparks flew, but the tinder failed to ignite. He tried a second time. And a third. He was well into a litany of foul language when a stray spark finally ignited.

He blew gently on it, relieved when a flame appeared. Hurrying to the fireplace, he grabbed a handful of kindling and stood it on end. He finally got a small pile in place, just as the tinder flame went out. "Bloody hell."

He searched the cupboards, looking for more tinder, but found none. With a grim mood taking hold, he marched back upstairs and spent the next hour going from room to room in search of another tinderbox. Saintspreserveus shadowed his every step.

It was dark by the time he finally managed to get a fire lit. It had taken him nearly two miserable hours. As the flames took hold of the small logs, he slumped onto the cold hard floor.

"All this to get a cup of tea," he muttered.

The dog wandered over from where he had been sitting observing Freddie's efforts, and nuzzled up against his master. Freddie gave him a good rub behind the ears. "Well at least someone is not angry with me, are you, boy?"

The dog nudged him and gave a small whimper. Freddie was clearly not getting the message.

"You want food, don't you? That makes two of us."

He hadn't eaten since breakfast. A quick check of the kitchen pantry shelves yielded the small wheel of cheese, the remainder of the loaf of bread from the morning, and some apples which he had missed earlier. As he regularly dined out there was little need for the house cook to keep a stock of supplies in the kitchen.

He cut the cheese and some of the apples up into dog-sized pieces and placed them on the floor. Saintspreserveus sniffed at the odd food combination but chewed it down in quick time. He came back for more, leaving Freddie with no option but to feed him the food he had intended to eat himself.

As he sat and watched the dog finish off the rest of his supper, Freddie cut a large chunk off the loaf of bread and chewed it.

From king to pauper in one day was a long, hard fall.

Chapter Twenty-Eight

F reddie woke in the early hours of the morning with a start. He had slumped down over the kitchen table and woke to Saintspreserveus licking his face. As he lifted his head, his back muscles immediately protested at having been held in such an uncomfortable position.

"Oh," he groaned.

He climbed up from the table and stretched his arms above his head. His neck was stiff and tight, and it barely yielded at his attempts to loosen his muscles.

The first sign of morning light shone through the kitchen window. There was no point in him going to bed now. His stomach rumbled. The bread was mostly gone, and there was nothing to feed the dog.

"Come on then, lad. Let's go and see if we can find a pork pie. My coins should extend to a couple of those for us."

By the third day of living on cold pork pies and over-salted roast beef from a nearby tavern, Freddie knew something had to change. He sat at the table in the downstairs kitchen and counted out his rapidly depleting coins. His money wouldn't last forever, and Saintspreserveus ate enough food for two people.

He had to find another solution to the problem of staying alive and not ending up being found half eaten by a giant Irish wolfhound. Why couldn't Eve have chosen a small dog for their game, something that did not threaten to eat him out of house and home?

The sudden thought of her pulled him up short. He had been so caught up in his own predicament that he had quite forgotten about Eve.

Perhaps Osmont had read him right. He was a cold-hearted brute capable of breaking a young woman's heart without mercy.

From out of his jacket he pulled the final challenge letter Osmont had given him. It had become habit to carry it with him. He read it once more, knowing if he were asked he could cite it word for bitter word.

Wherever she was, he knew Eve hated him. When she eventually found out about his reduced circumstances he hoped she would gain some satisfaction in knowing he too was in pain.

Yes, but you brought this on your yourself. She didn't deserve what you did.

He folded the letter back up and put it in his pocket.

With Saintspreserveus on a tight lead, Freddie headed out to the market just after six o'clock in the morning. He was back to keeping country hours again.

The area around Covent Garden was home to many of London's ladies of the night. Brothels operated in elegant houses in nearby Fleet Lane and Long Acre. He chuckled as an elegantly dressed gentleman, who was leaving one of the houses, quickly turned on his heel and went back inside as soon as Freddie caught his gaze. *Who am I to judge?*

In the market, Freddie was pleased to find good quality, sensibly priced apples and pears. He bought some, placing them in the basket he had found in the kitchen at Rosemount House. A well-dressed young man like himself carrying a basket naturally attracted a few enquiring stares. He ignored them, too concerned with filling his empty stomach to worry about the opinions of others.

At another stall he purchased some eggs and cheese, and a small loaf of bread. With the fire now being kept burning in the downstairs kitchen at home, he could cook up some fried eggs and serve them with bread and butter. A hot breakfast was especially appealing.

He was leaning over the counter of a market stall, about to enquire of the price of a pat of butter, when he caught sight of a familiar face passing through the early morning crowd.

Harriet Saunders, Eve's sister-in-law, was headed his way. She had two strapping footmen trailing behind her, each carrying a heavily laden sack.

He tried to hurry and complete his purchases, intending to make good his escape, but Hattie had already seen him.

"Freddie. Hello, fancy meeting you at the market."

He swallowed a lump of shame and turned to her. "Mrs. Saunders. A pleasure to see you," he replied. He managed a half-bow with the basket in one hand, and the lead of his dog in the other.

She turned from him, before stopping and smiling. "I forget that is who I am now. When I hear that name, I keep expecting to see Adelaide standing behind me. Please call me Hattie. So, what brings you out into the market at this hour of the morning?"

He gritted his teeth. Word would eventually come out about the second son of Viscount Rosemount being cut off by his family. Hattie no doubt would also know that he and Eve had broken off their friendship.

He looked at the two footmen standing behind her and winced. If he was to reveal his current circumstances, he would much prefer it not be in front of servants and market stall holders.

Hattie handed one of the footmen a few coins. "Could you please go to the stall nearest to the bookshop and ask if they have any fresh carrots this morning? Tell them I don't want the soggy old ones they tried to sell me on Tuesday. Not unless they are very cheap."

Once the footmen had gone, Hattie pointed in the direction of a nearby set of tables and chairs. "They serve a decent cheese bun and weak coffee. Let's you and I talk there."

Once seated, Hattie ordered. The proprietor of the makeshift café knew her by name and greeted her warmly.

"I find it odd someone of your station would have friends in the market," Freddie remarked.

Hattie picked at her freshly baked bun. "Well I have been coming to the market for the past few years. I'm not sure if Eve ever told you, but I run a soup kitchen out of St John's Parish near the rookery of St Giles."

Freddie nodded, reliving the embarrassing memory of how horrid he had been to Hattie at Vauxhall when he'd refused to take her hand. He hadn't expected Will Saunders would permit his new bride to continue her work with the poor once they were married.

She looked at him and he sensed she was quietly reading his mind. "The two footmen are part of the agreement I have with Will so I can continue my ministry with the poor. I made some enemies in the gangs of the rookery a little while back. Things have quietened down since then, but he insists I have them with me at all times. But enough about me."

The storekeeper placed two large cups of muddy coffee on the table, then bent down and proceeded to give Saintspreserveus a friendly pat. "What's your dog's name?"

"Saintspreserveus. It's a joke," replied Freddie, feeling foolish.

Saintspreserveus growled. The man screwed up his face and went back to serving other customers, the joke clearly lost on both man and hound.

"You do know that is a ridiculous name for a dog. Even he doesn't like it, from the way he growled. Poor thing. Fancy being saddled with that for all your days," said Hattie.

"I think perhaps I should consider changing it. He is my one true friend at the moment, so he does deserve better."

"You have no disagreement from me on that count. But tell me, why are you here at the market at this hour?" Hattie's gaze locked on Freddie's basket of goods.

He gritted his teeth. There was no point lying to her. "My father has cut me off. I am in disgrace over the way I treated Eve. I have a few coins to live by, but other than that, I am on my own. No servants; no credit. And I thoroughly deserve it. I am nothing more than a black-guard of the lowest ilk."

Hattie frowned. "Don't say that," she replied.

Freddie picked up his coffee and took a hesitant sip. It looked the same color as the murky waters of the River Thames. He took a second sip. He had been served coffee in some of the finest restaurants and clubs in London, but nothing tasted as good as the coffee made by the market stall holder in Covent Garden.

Hattie smiled at him. "Will discovered our coffee man. He was like an excited child when he finally found someone in London who could grind and brew the beans just the way he likes them. He comes here quite regularly."

The smile disappeared from Freddie's lips. Kind, religious Hattie was one thing, but Eve's older brother was not someone he was in any particular hurry to encounter. He looked over her shoulder, ready to beat a hasty retreat if Will suddenly appeared from out of the throng.

"He is still abed. My husband is not an early riser," she said.

Freddie relaxed. "I came here this morning, because I cannot live forever on pork pies. There are several cookbooks in the kitchen at Rosemount House; I thought I could attempt some recipes. I'm going to try cooking eggs today as a start and then see where that takes me."

Hattie nodded, after which they sat in silence and finished their coffees. As Freddie drained the last of his cup, he silently hoped for a second one.

Hattie pulled out a small notebook and pencil from her coat pocket. She didn't carry a reticule or bag like other women. She began to cross a few things off a long shopping list. Then, turning to another page, she wrote down an address before pulling the page out of her notebook and handing it to Freddie.

"That's the address of St John's Parish. If you feel the need for a warm bowl of soup you are most welcome. We usually serve soup from around late afternoon to the end of evensong."

A lump formed in his throat. He was being offered charity.

His earlier encounters with Hattie had been shameful. He had mocked her work with the poor, even made note of her dowdy clothes. What had seemed a fun part of the Rude Rules now revealed itself to be the cruel and heartless jest it truly was. Yet here she was, showing him compassion.

"Thank you. I don't deserve your kindness. Not after all the horrid things I have said and done to your family," he replied.

"I am sure we will all survive. I put your unkind remarks to me down to the folly of youth. Besides, at the time, I had much bigger issues to deal with in my life. To tell you the truth, you were an odd and amusing distraction during a difficult time for me. Will and I did not have an easy start to our relationship; the trip to Vauxhall was a peace offering on his part. As for Eve, she is a strong girl. In time, she will give her heart over to someone else and find love again."

He had thought of Eve increasingly over the past few days, wondering how she was, and hoping she was not sitting at home alone crying over him. She deserved to be happy. "How is Eve?"

"She is fine. The Saunders family are made from tough material. She had one or two days at home keeping indoors, but she is back out circulating in society once again. While I am unsure as to the exact reason for you calling things off with her, rest assured there are plenty of other fine young men more than willing to take your place." Hattie finished her coffee but left the rest of her bun untouched. She pulled a handful of coins from out of her pocket and handed them to the coffee stall holder. Freddie reached for his pocket, but she waved him away. "Keep your money. Use it to buy yourself fresh carrots; they are good to eat raw if you cannot get the fire hot enough in the kitchen to cook. The offer to come to St John's is always open to you, Freddie. You would be most welcome."

She gathered up her things and headed over to where her two footmen were now waiting on the other side of the cafe. Freddie watched as they walked away.

Eve was already back in circulation. He should be pleased. But that piece of news was a double-edged sword. It was heartening to think her heart had only been bruised by his betrayal. Less comforting was the thought she hadn't loved him as much as his ego had led him to believe. He shouldn't care, but the sting in his heart told him otherwise.

As he rose from the chair, Saintspreserveus stood next to the table. Spying Hattie's unfinished bun, Freddie reached out a hand to take it, but the quick dog beat him and gulped it down in one go. The gods were still not done with punishing Freddie.

"Come on, lad. Let's get you some bones and then head home. These eggs won't cook themselves," Freddie said with a sigh.

The eggs burnt in the bottom of the overheated frying pan and he eventually gave the whole mess to Saintspreserveus who ate it all in one gulp. Freddie didn't particularly mind, he wasn't that hungry anyway. Hattie's news about Eve had stolen his appetite.

Chapter Twenty-Nine

Passing through the front of the house later that morning, Freddie found a letter slipped under the door. He picked it up and turned it over.

Lord and Lady Pole.

He eagerly tore it open. The Poles were regular entertainers in their Mayfair mansion. Entertainment meant a break from the monotony of living alone with a dog. It also meant a warm house and servants bearing platters of hot food.

A relieved smile found its way to his lips. It was an invitation to an informal gathering of friends and family for later in the week. An informal gathering for Lord and Lady Pole meant several hundred guests. He would make a brief appearance, eat, and then leave before he encountered anyone he knew.

Inside his father's study, he found paper and pen and wrote a note of acceptance. Without thinking, he picked up his father's bell and rang it. The ring resounded in the empty house.

"Fool. No one is going to take your note to them." He would have to walk over to Mount Street and hand-deliver it himself. "Damn."

Getting back into society in order to get a hot meal also meant skirting around its edges to keep news of his current financial situation a secret for as long as possible. His pride had taken enough of a battering. "Well if I am to play postmaster general, I may as well get a few other letters out," he said.

He picked up a fresh piece of paper and set to work. It was a short note—there didn't seem much point in going into too much detail. Osmont Firebrace would know the exact reason for Freddie's resignation. When he was finished writing the letter he folded and sealed it.

"Well, that is one first I can lay claim to for myself. I am the first Rosemount to work at the House of Commons, and the first one to resign."

Eve was not going to sit at home and pine over Freddie. As far as she and Caroline were concerned, the sooner she got back on the proverbial horse, the better.

"There are thousands of other fish in the sea," said Eve.

Caroline handed Eve her cloak and patted her sister on the arm. "Absolutely, and you shall dance with every single one of those fish tonight."

Eve looked at her sister and swallowed back the lump in her throat. It was odd that it had taken a broken heart for her to realize the pain she had caused her sister. Eve rejoiced in the rediscovery of her close friendship with her younger sister. The hours they spent together, talking, shopping, and laughing, were the well-needed balm to her soul.

Arriving inside the grand mansion in Mount Street, Eve and Caroline took their time to check their cloaks and make certain their gowns had not creased during the short trip from Dover Street. Francis took Eve's arm and, as had become customary, Harry offered Caroline his. Eve and Caroline shared an encouraging smile. It was good to be out and socializing again as both sisters and friends.

Once inside the main ballroom, Francis wasted little time in finding an excuse to leave the girls. As he and Harry headed off to find the nearest cluster of unmarried young ladies, Caroline turned her back on them. "Thank the heavens they have gone. If Harry looks at me one more time tonight with those puppy-dog eyes I shall scream," she said.

Eve was surprised to hear her sister speak in such a harsh way about their friend. Everyone knew Harry carried a flame for Caroline, but she had assumed Caroline was kind enough to tolerate him.

"Oh, don't look at me like that, Eve. Harry is constantly lurking around me. I was a fool to spend time with his mother and sister. He now thinks he has a real chance of making me his wife."

"You have told Francis to have a word with him, have you not?" replied Eve.

Caroline flipped out her fan and held it in front of her face. Eve leant in close. "I told him myself. He was making all manner of silly remarks at Will and Hattie's wedding about me being the next one to be married. I took him aside and spoke plainly but carefully to him. I told him there was no chance for us. That if I hadn't fallen in love with him by now, it was never going to happen."

"And what did he say?"

"He said, time wore down even the largest of stones," replied Caroline.

It was obvious there was nothing Caroline could say that would deter Harry. He had set his heart and mind on marrying her.

"Anyway, it doesn't matter. I shouldn't be talking about messy relationships considering how things—" Caroline stopped mid-sentence and gripped Eve's arm. She raised a pointed finger toward a space over the other side of the ballroom. A space which was currently inhabited by the not so Honorable Frederick Rosemount.

Caroline drew in a haughty breath. "The cheek of that man showing himself in public so soon after what he did to you."

Eve's gaze settled on Freddie, and there it remained. "Yes, well, his misdeeds are not well known in society, so I expect he feels he can still attend social gatherings."

Eve's heart began to race. It felt like a lifetime since he had stood over her in the barn and told her he didn't want her. A lifetime since he had ripped her heart to shreds.

She began to walk toward the dance floor, her gaze still locked on him. He turned and caught sight of her. She saw him flinch. His discomfort was deeply satisfying to her.

"What are you doing, Eve?" whispered Caroline beside her.

"Nothing. Just toying with a mouse," came the reply.

As she moved in a clockwise fashion around the edge of the dance floor, heading for six o'clock, Freddie moved toward midnight. He was rising to the next hour as she moved down the other side of the clock face. Her gaze never once left Freddie and his remained fixed on her.

"Ah, there you are, Caroline. Harry wants to put his name on your dance card."

The girls ignored Francis. He fell in beside them and was soon appraised of why they were slowly circling the dance floor. "The cheeky blighter. Must be out seeking a free feed," muttered Francis.

His words broke the spell that held Eve within its power. She stopped and turned to Francis. "What do you mean?"

There were rumors that Freddie returned to London only a day or so after her, but until tonight he had managed to keep a low profile. For someone who had been living large on the London social landscape only a matter of weeks before, Freddie had suddenly turned into a ghost.

Francis raised an eyebrow and leant in close. "There is a reason he has been keeping a low profile. A rumor is spreading like wildfire that his father has cut him off. Word is, he and that large, mangy dog are the only ones in residence at Lord Rosemount's townhouse. All the servants were called back to Rosemount Abbey. Freddie is having to make do for himself."

"The perfect punishment," said Caroline, chuckling with delight.

Eve, meanwhile, had other concerns. If it was common knowledge that Freddie was being punished by his father, there would be questions asked as to the reason why. The last thing she wanted was for her name to be caught in the mix. Her reputation would be in ruins.

"So, what is the story about why his father cut him off?" replied Eve.

"A friend of a friend spoke to him earlier tonight and asked about the story. He was none too pleased word had got out. He told this friend he had gambled heavily and his father is determined to make him pay back all the money he lost. But there are others who are beginning to whisper otherwise," replied Francis.

She turned to her brother. "Who else and what are they saying?" A cold shiver of dread chilled her body. Was someone playing games?

Francis pointed toward another young gentleman standing a few feet away from them. As Eve looked at him, the young man bowed.

"He is the Honorable Trenton Embry, second son of Viscount Embry. He is another of the young men who are cadets at the House of Commons with Freddie. He would like to have a private word with you."

She feared whatever news Trenton Embry had to impart would be bad, but still, she had to know.

Trenton Embry stepped forward at Francis's beckon and offered her a formal bow.

"Miss Saunders."

"My brother tells me you wish to speak with me," she said.

He looked over to where Freddie had been, and then nodded. "I take it you are aware Freddie Rosemount is here this evening?"

Eve nodded.

"I know something of matters which transpired between the two of you, having also been a cadet at the House of Commons this year," he said.

Eve waited. Trenton met her worried gaze, then leant in close. "What I really wanted to tell you was that Freddie is not a bad chap. I know by throwing you over he behaved abominably, but he did so because he is under the influence of a very evil gentleman named Osmont Firebrace. I don't know if you are particularly interested, considering all that has happened, but Freddie is in a bad place at present. His life is a disaster and he has much of the blame to wear himself. That said, if you do still hold any sort of affection for him, I would counsel you to find it in your heart to forgive him," he said.

Her mouth dropped open with shock. She had no intention of ever speaking to Freddie again, let alone forgiving him. "Thank you, Mr. Embry. Your words bring comfort to me. To know Freddie Rosemount's life is in complete shambles truly gladdens my heart. Feel free to convey those same sentiments to him when next you speak."

She turned and left Trenton Embry alone.

Francis took hold of Eve's arm. "Bloody coward. Fancy sending a friend over to talk to you in the vain hope you would feel sorry for him."

"Yes, well, it's all over with now. Whatever mess Freddie has gone and got himself into is none of my concern," she replied.

Freddie may have given up on any pretense of shame, but her pride had been somewhat restored. However, the sight of Freddie and her conversation with Trenton had rattled her nerves. She needed time alone to gather her composure.

"I might just go outside for a moment and get a spot of fresh air."

A reluctant Caroline let Francis accompany her to find Harry and give him the dance he had requested. Eve accepted Francis's condition he would come and find her after a short while and that she was not to wander off anywhere on her own.

§&

As soon as she stepped out into the cold night air, Eve felt relief. The heat in the large, crowded ballroom had been stifling. The night garden afforded her the peace and quiet her rattled brain so desperately craved.

She found a small stone bench in a quiet corner and sat down. A footman offered her a glass of wine and she took it. The cool, sweet wine helped her to focus on the here and now.

A shadow crossed the light from the house, leaving her in darkness. She looked up, squinting as her eyes tried to find focus.

Her gaze found Freddie standing over her.

"Eve."

A sickening flash of memory hit her brain. The last time she had seen him, he had been standing over her in very much the same fashion, telling her that she didn't love him and that they would never marry.

The one saving grace on this particular occasion was that she wasn't lying partially clothed in a horse stable, having just offered him her virginity.

"I have nothing to say to you, Freddie. Your friend Trenton Embry has already spoken for you. Please go away." She looked past him as she took a slow slip of her wine.

"Yes, I saw you and Trenton Embry greet one another in the ballroom. Though I wouldn't say he and I were friends, more acquaintances. What did he say about me?" he asked.

Eve's blood began to boil. Freddie was far more self-centered than she had fooled herself into believing. She got to her feet. "Something or other about you keeping the company of evil men. I can't remember all that he said, because I wasn't really paying attention. My mind tends to go blank whenever it registers mention of your name."

He nodded. "I deserve that and much more. I just want to say I was ..." Freddie didn't get the chance to finish the rest of the sentence. Francis had arrived and immediately grabbed a hold of him, spinning Freddie around to face him.

"You bloody bastard. You broke my sister's heart. Well, here is something for you to go and get fixed!" His fist landed in the middle of Freddie's face with a sickening thwack.

Freddie staggered back, his hands held to his face. When he took his hand away, blood streamed from his freshly broken nose. Francis shaped up to hit him a second time, but several other male guests rushed forward and restrained him.

"There are plenty more where that came from, Rosemount. The next time I see you, I shall add a couple of broken teeth to your collection," growled Francis.

Chapter Thirty

F reddie managed to find a servant who brought him a large
handkerchief with which to stem the blood. With the handkerchief covering his broken face, he left the party via a side entrance, and
staggered the short distance home to Grosvenor Square.

He found his way into the kitchen, and after grabbing a jug, filled it
with cold water from the pump outside. He rinsed the handkerchief
out several times before finally managing to stem the flow of blood
from his nose. Saintspreserveus stayed uncharacteristically on his bed
in the corner, watching Freddie's every move.

Freddie ran his finger tentatively along the length of his nose,
flinching when it got to the break at the bridge. For all his foppishness,
Francis was possessed with a hell of a punch.

When he had seen Trenton greet the Saunders siblings at the ball,
he had been filled with fear. He had intended to find Trenton and ask
what the devil he was up to, but Francis Saunders's fist had inter-
rupted his plans.

Dealing with Trenton would have to wait. Freddie's nose needed
attention.

Saintspreserveus finally rose from his bed and wandered over to
Freddie. He nuzzled Freddie's leg.

"Always my loyal boy," he said, giving him a pat.

The dog pushed harder against his leg, before finally wandering over to his food bowl and standing beside it.

Freddie groaned. He had been so wrapped up in his worries about feeding himself, he had forgotten about the dog. On the high shelf about the stove, a dog bone was wrapped up in cloth.

"Here you are, lad," he said, retrieving the bone and placing it on the floor.

As the dog leapt upon the bone with unrestrained relish, Freddie remembered he had not made it as far as the supper table at the ball. The meat on the dog bone looked more appealing than it should.

"Looks like bread and cheese again tonight for me. Enjoy your meat," he muttered.

Setting his nose again could not wait. Once it became swollen, he would not be able to do it properly.

Using a stack of books, he stood a small hand mirror up on the kitchen table, then took a seat and made himself as comfortable as he could. Having played rugby at school, he had seen plenty of others take a broken nose in hand and set it straight. The thought of moving his bones back into place made his stomach turn.

"Come on, get it done," he urged himself.

Placing his hands either side of the bridge of his nose, he felt where the nasal bones were out of alignment. He held his breath and pushed hard to the left. Pain shot through his brain.

"Ooh," he winced.

He sat back and waited for the pain to subside, then leant forward and inspected his face in the mirror once more. His nose looked a lot straighter than it had been a moment earlier. He took a deep breath of relief, then sighed. He could breathe properly once more.

At least I have been able to fix something this evening.

With his face sorted, Freddie could consider the other problem this evening had created.

Eve.

He had only seen her briefly exchange greetings with Trenton, but he doubted Trenton was simply making small talk.

He washed his face and topped up Saintspreserveus's water bowl. For a moment he stood and looked at the dog as it lapped at the water.

"Hattie was right. You have a ridiculous name."

With his membership of the Bachelor Board no longer an issue, he didn't have to inflict such a foolish name on the loyal beast. He bent down beside the dog.

"I think it's time you and I agreed on a new name. How about Zeus? While you won't ever be an ancient god, I do think it adds a certain level of gravitas to your impressive size."

The dog's ears pricked up. Freddie walked out of the kitchen before stopping at the bottom of the stairs.

"Zeus! Come on, boy," he called.

The sound of paws and claws scattering on the stone floor came from the kitchen, followed by the appearance of a large head in the doorway. Zeus had a huge grin on his face.

With Zeus by his side, Freddie went in search of a bottle of his father's good wine. He would need to numb himself to the pain of his bruised and battered face if he was to stand any chance of getting sleep this night.

જ

The following morning, he paid Trenton Embry a visit.

"I was wondering when you would darken my doorstep," said Trenton, ushering Freddie into a drawing room.

He walked up to Freddie, then stopped. He let out a disapproving "tut" as his gaze ran over Freddie's face. The force of Francis's punch had resulted in a pair of black eyes as well as a broken nose. The two bottles of wine he had polished off the previous night had at least given him a decent night's sleep, but Freddie knew his face was a mess.

"No need to ask who gave you that," said Trenton, pointing at Freddie's face.

Freddie straightened his back. He had never taken to the dour Embry. "Since you already know full well whose handiwork is reflected on my visage, I came to ask you why you felt the need to seek out Evelyn Saunders last night. Eve and I were finished the moment she left Rosemount Abbey, so why would you feel the need to stir the pot?"

Trenton snorted. "As usual, you have it all wrong. I spoke to Miss Saunders and told her you were under the influence of Osmont Firebrace, and that at some point in the future she may wish to hear you out and possibly forgive you for being a complete ass. If there is one thing I know about women, it is they don't suddenly fall out of love with a chap. You no doubt broke her heart, but I would wager a guinea on the fact she still lies in bed at night and cries over you. She, of course, told me otherwise. The girl does have a strong spirit about her."

"And that is all you told her?"

Trenton pointed toward the door. "Yes. The rest of it is of no interest to me, nor of my concern. You made this mess; I suggest you either set about cleaning it up or accept you are going to be lying in it for a very long time."

Freddie pushed past him and headed for the front door. Trenton followed. As they entered the front foyer of the elegant townhouse, Freddie noticed several large travel trunks.

"Going somewhere?" he asked.

Trenton nodded toward the trunks. "Home to Somerset. I'm getting married at the end of the month. This London trip was my final fling before leaping into the arms of wedded bliss. Truth be told, I cannot wait to get out of this god-forsaken city. The stench is bad enough, but the people within it are rotten to the core. If I never set foot within its boundaries again, I shall die a happy man." He held out a hand to Freddie. "Second sons like you and I can live perfectly happy, purposeful lives, without having to make naked grabs for power and ill-gained wealth. I hope someday you come to that realization. I think deep down you are a better man than your actions have reflected. You need to search for the truth of who you really are."

A reluctant Freddie shook his hand. He now understood Trenton's indifference to the Bachelor Board challenges. He had never intended to win a seat on the board.

Freddie headed for the front door.

As the butler opened it, Trenton hurried to Freddie's side. He took him by the arm and pulled him into a nearby room. "If there is one final piece of advice I would be keen for you to hear, it is that Osmont Firebrace is not a man to be trusted. He and the other members of the Bachelor Board are no friends to you. Firebrace is not the man you think he is—he is pure evil. He will bring you down to a level where you will lose yourself forever."

Freddie met his gaze. "I know."

Chapter Thirty-One

Freddie made it back to Grosvenor Square and proceeded to lay low for the next few days. The swelling around his nose and eyes made it difficult to see.

He finally made it out of the house and to Covent Garden late in the morning some two days after Francis had done his best to rearrange his face. Being the hour, it was, he knew Hattie and her bodyguards would have come and gone some hours earlier. He made his purchases and headed home.

After putting his shopping away and feeding Zeus, he emptied his coat pockets of coins and deposited them onto the kitchen table. Among the coins he found a small folded up piece of paper.

He frowned, unable to recall where the paper had come from. He unfolded it and let out a small. "Ah."

St John's Church, High Street, Holborn

Hattie Saunders's soup kitchen was based out of the church. He read the address a second time. It wasn't too far a walk to High Street, similar to the distance he had regularly walked to the House of Commons.

She was the one person in London he did know who might give him a fair hearing. Hattie had offered for him to come to the church. To share a meal with her and the parishioners. She was someone who had changed her life, and now led an existence with meaning and purpose.

Trenton's words rang in his ears. *You need to search for the truth of who you really are.*

It was a humbling thought that the two people he had ridiculed the most were the very same people who seemed to know him best.

His face was still a bruised mess, but no doubt Hattie would already know the cause of his injuries when she saw him. He closed his eyes, sending out a silent prayer. If he was to seek a way back to the Freddie he had once been, he would have to find a new path to tread.

"Sorry, Zeus. I don't think they would appreciate you coming in and trying to eat their supper. You shall have to stay here," he said.

He jammed a chair against the door to keep Zeus from going upstairs while he was gone. He put his coat on, ruing the fact Eve had bought him a dog who could open doors.

"Try to be good. If you cannot, I would appreciate you don't start chewing on any new pieces of my mother's furnishings. You have made a mess of enough of them already."

He closed the door behind him, in the full knowledge Zeus would have the door open by the time he got to the garden gate. His mother would kill him when she found out what the dog had done to her favourite couch.

❧

The church was not as easy to find as he had thought it would be. Freddie walked past it before he realized the simple stone-fronted building was in fact a house of worship. He stood outside for a short while, unsure whether he should go inside.

The thought that going home would only give more credence to Trenton's opinion of him being a coward kept him from turning on his heel and leaving. Finally, he mustered up enough courage and pulled on the brass handle of the solid oak front door.

Once inside he found himself standing in a simple, but well-kept church. He had been half expecting to find beggars on the front steps and homeless families asleep inside. There were little of the trappings of the wealthier churches such as St George's, Hanover Square, where his parents attended when they were in town. The windows were plain glass, with no expensive leadlight to add color to the room. Two small vases with red roses were the only sign of decoration. A fire burnt in a nearby hearth, adding a little warmth to the place. While it lacked the towering gilt-edged columns and highly polished wood of St George's, St John's still had a dignity about it.

He walked farther inside, unsure of himself. He wasn't certain as to why he was there; what he did know was that he had been drawn by the promise of change.

The door to the right of the chapel opened, and Hattie stepped inside. She had a basket filled with vegetables in her hands, which was clearly heavy from the way she struggled to carry it. Freddie hurried to her side and quickly relieved her of the heavy burden.

"Thank you. I am very pleased to see you," she said, wiping sweat from her brow. Her gaze fell on his bruised face, and a flush of red burnt on his cheeks. "Oh dear, it's as ugly as I thought it might be. How is the face healing?"

"The swelling has gone down, and I can sleep on my back once more. Other than that, it is as well as can be expected. Not that I deserve anything less than what Francis dished out," he replied.

She shook her head and tut-tutted softly.

"If you would be so kind as to bring the basket, I will show you the kitchen," she said.

He followed her out to a room that ran off the side of the church. It was very similar to the kitchen at his home, but with a much bigger fireplace. Over the fireplace hung two large pots, the contents of which were giving off a heady aroma. *Soup.*

His stomach growled loudly.

Hattie chuckled. "Here, put the basket down and grab a bowl. The afternoon meal will be served in an hour so you have time to eat before the hungry hordes from the St Giles rookery arrive on our doorstep."

When he hesitated with embarrassment, Hattie took a ladle and filled up a bowl before handing it to him. "Go on. You look like you could do with a hot meal."

Freddie sat down at the table, and she took a seat opposite where she began to peel onions.

"I find if I get a head start on the evensong meal about now, we can get everyone fed and out of the church by just after nine o'clock. Will gets impatient with me if I come home any time after ten," she said.

Freddie nodded as he put his spoon to his mouth and tasted the soup. A hot meal was something he had not enjoyed for some time. The moment the soup touched his tongue he felt his mood lift.

"This is really good," he remarked.

Hattie looked at him from over her pile of onions. "I've been making it for quite some time now—I've lost count of the number of batches. Though, I must confess, it has risen substantially in quality since Will began supporting the soup kitchen. We now have barley, meat, and herbs in it. The old mix was rather watery."

Freddie took a second mouthful. The comforting warmth seeped deep into his bones.

"I see you didn't bring your dog with you," she said.

"No. Zeus is at home probably destroying something else with those sharp teeth of his," he replied.

Hattie nodded.

"Zeus? So, you took my words to heart about the dog's name being ridiculous. I think this new name suits him much better. I expect he is grateful. Well done, Freddie."

He smiled. It was strangely comforting to sit with a friendly person and talk. He missed the simple pleasure of being with friends and family.

Hattie sat back from the onions and puffed out her cheeks. She sucked in a deep breath before rising quickly from the table and dashing outside. When she returned a few minutes later, her face was flushed and she was wiping tears from her eyes.

Freddie said nothing but having been at home during the early stages of both of Cecily's pregnancies, he knew the signs of morning sickness only too well. He pushed his bowl to one side and picked up the knife. He was surprisingly adept at peeling and chopping onions and soon had the pile reduced and sitting on a plate.

"What else have you got for me to cut and peel?" he asked.

Hattie pointed to a large basket by the door piled high with carrots and turnips. He lugged the basket over and between the two of them they made short work of the rest of the vegetables.

The simple action of chopping vegetables brought a rhythmic calm to his troubled mind. By the time they were finished, he was prepared to admit he was actually enjoying himself.

"I should get the bowls ready," said Hattie. She went to a nearby cupboard and picked up a pile of wooden bowls, which she brought over to the table.

Freddie followed suit. "Where did you get all these bowls?" he asked.

"Will managed to source two hundred for us from the army stores. Before that we had to manage with a lot fewer and people usually had to share. Some of these saw service with the troops on the battlefield at Waterloo … as did he," she said.

Freddie stopped momentarily piling bowls on the table. He knew Will had been an agent for the crown in Paris during the war, but it had never occurred to him that Eve's brother would have actually been in the midst of the final fight to topple Napoleon. "Will fought at Waterloo?"

"He didn't actually draw his sword. He wasn't stationed with any of the regular regiments; he was a special operative. He brought news to the allied command of Napoleon's troop movements and suspected battle plans," she replied.

Eve had said little of Will's role during the war. Will Saunders had risked his life for his country, and an ass such as Freddie Rosemount had had the cheek to play the fool in front of him. He took a slow, deep breath in as a powerful sense of shame filled his heart.

Hattie hummed a happy tune to herself as she worked, leaving Freddie to make yet another promise that his selfish, self-centered days were a thing of the past. Trenton Embry had been right about second sons being able to live useful and purpose-filled lives. He needed to find his true path forward.

They had just finished piling the bowls and spoons onto the table when the first of the local parishioners arrived for their supper. Hattie and Freddie stationed themselves near the large pots of soup and soon had an orderly procession of hungry people rotating through the church.

A young lad no older than five held up his bowl and smiled a toothless grin. Freddie leant over and gave his dark brown hair a friendly ruffle while Hattie filled the boy's bowl with soup. Freddie picked up a large piece of bread and handed it to the boy, whose eyes lit up at the unexpected bounty.

"You need a big piece so you can grow tall and strong," he said.

The lad headed over to a nearby table with his soup and bread in hand, and Freddie stood and watched for a moment as he tucked eagerly into his meal.

This is worth more than all the finest houses and horses.

As soon as the first pot of soup was finished, Freddie cleaned it out and filled it with vegetables and barley to begin cooking for the later sitting. When the last of the vegetables went into the pot, he stood back and took in the humbling sight of fifty hungry people all quietly eating soup.

Hattie came and stood next to him. She reached out and gave him a gentle pat on the back. "Well done, Freddie. You helped to feed all these people. The children will sleep with full bellies tonight because of you."

He was humbled by the simple goodness of Hattie Saunders and her selfless endeavors to help strangers. Once he would have dismissed her efforts as being that of a religious zealot, but at no time during the evening had she pressed anyone on the matter of God.

As she went about her work, he remembered the story of the Good Samaritan. What someone did in their life was the most important thing of all, not what they said they should do. All his puff and bluster about wanting to be a member of the Bachelor Board meant little when it had been about himself. Shame was one thing but knowing the pain he had caused his family—and especially Eve—stung him hard. The poor of London seated at the tables eating a meal made with honesty and love had more honor than him.

"I would like to come here every day and help, if you will have me," he said. The lump in his throat made speaking difficult, while the tears in his eyes had him blinking hard.

"Of course, we will have you. No one is ever turned away from St John's; this is a house of God. We accept all those in need, not just the hungry," she replied.

He turned to her, and it finally dawned on him why he had come. He was in need. In need of a way to find himself again. To earn forgiveness from his family. To find the strength to face Eve once more.

"Can I go to the market for you in the mornings? I can meet your footmen there and have the fresh supplies here by the time you arrive." It would not be polite to mention Hattie's delicate condition. If he went to the market early in the morning and got supplies, Hattie would be able to rest at home until later.

"It is an early start, and I have to admit it is becoming a bit of a struggle at the moment. An extra hour or so of sleep would be wonderful but are you sure you want to take on such a responsibility?" she replied.

"Yes, I am certain. Though, I think …" He stopped for a moment, unsure of himself. This was about more than just himself. He was re-forging his connection with the Saunders family. While Hattie may have been able to forgive his transgressions, there were others who may not. "I think … I mean, I would like to have Will's blessing about this matter as well. I know this is your soup kitchen, but he is Eve's brother and I behaved terribly toward her. It would mean a lot to me to know he approves of our arrangement or is at least aware of it."

Hattie looked at Freddie, her face a study in seriousness. "Of course. If there is one thing Will and I completely agree on, it's that we do not have secrets we withhold from one another. It took us long enough to come to that realization when we first met, and I would never do anything to give him cause to doubt me now."

Her words took him by surprise. He had assumed that Will and Hattie were a simple enough love story, but it would appear that they too had not had an easy journey into wedded bliss.

She read the look on his face. "One day, I shall tell you the story of Will and I. It began far from London. Make enough pots of soup and you will earn it. In the meantime, we had better get ready for the next group of hungry mouths."

"Thank you. I promise I won't let you down," he replied.

Hattie went over to the large pot of soup and stirred in some more herbs. Freddie headed out to the tables and began to make his way around, collecting bowls and talking to the parishioners.

Late that evening, he finally dried the last of the clean soup bowls and closed the door of the church behind them, then helped Hattie to her waiting carriage. He politely refused her offer of a ride home, knowing he needed the walk.

Every step he made helped to clear his mind. Unlike the last time he had travelled along Oxford Street, he now knew he wouldn't find his next victory on the back of a speeding horse. His road to redemption and his new life lay in the honest toil of cutting vegetables and making soup.

Chapter Thirty-Two

E ve was excited over the event which lay ahead. Will and Hattie, the newlyweds, were coming to the Saunders home for a family dinner. With Freddie no longer in her life, she could enjoy evenings of social interaction without the worry of offending anyone under the Rude Rules.

Will had finally found contentment and peace back in England. Hattie had captured his heart, and he had freed hers to love again. Theirs was a union which offered hope for all.

Her own relationship with Freddie may have ended in disaster but knowing love existed between other couples gave Eve the comfort her wounded heart sorely needed. Somewhere, someone was waiting to capture her heart and hold it for himself.

She finished dressing and was downstairs waiting when her brother and his new bride arrived.

"Eve, my sister, how lovely to see you," said Hattie.

Eve smiled and hugged her.

Will handed their coats and hats to a footman and escorted his wife into the family drawing room. The look of contentment on his face stirred Eve's heart. She had never seen her brother so happy. He almost glowed.

"Ah, there you are. My two favorite newlyweds," announced Charles. With arms open wide, he embraced Will and Hattie as one. Adelaide and Caroline soon joined the happy gathering.

"Where is that snow-haired lump of my brother?" asked Will, when Francis did not make an appearance.

"Francis sends his apologies. He and Harry received last-minute invitations to a party at Carlton House, and they felt it would not be good form to refuse an invite from the Prince Regent," said Charles.

Eve was proud of her younger brother. He was starting to make a name for himself as a canny businessman; the receipt of invitations from select parts of London society were becoming a regular occurrence. There was never a shortage of others seeking to add to the coins in the bottom of their pockets, by seeking the advice of someone on their way up in the world.

The family gathered around the couches and chairs, which were set out in a semi-circle. Will and Hattie sat hand in hand, close to one another on one of the smaller couches. Every time Hattie looked up at her husband, he squeezed his wife's hand gently.

Two footmen entered the room. One was carrying a tray laden with champagne glasses, which he set down on the table in the middle of the arranged furniture. A second footman placed two bottles of champagne on the table, before the two men quietly left the room.

Will rose from the couch and picked up one of the bottles of champagne and worked at freeing the cork. Eve recognized it as being a particular and expensive French brand.

Charles and Adelaide looked at one another and rose from their seats.

"Gosset. Is there a special occasion?" asked Charles.

A loud bang echoed around the room as Will finally managed to free the cork from the bottle. With champagne bubbling out, he hurriedly filled the glasses.

Hattie rose from the couch and picked up two of the filled glasses. She handed one each to Adelaide and Charles. "We have news."

It didn't take more than a second for the look on Adelaide's face to change from one of slight interest to tearful joy. She flustered around for a moment, before thrusting her champagne glass into the hands of her husband. She pulled Hattie into her embrace. "Oh, that is magnificent. You have no idea how long I have wanted to be a grandmother. You are a wonderful girl."

Will turned to Eve and Caroline, who were also standing and handed them both a glass of champagne. "I am going to be a father," he said.

Caroline promptly burst into tears, while beside her, Eve did some rough calculations in her head. Will and Hattie had not been married that long.

She made a mental note to interrogate Hattie further at some point. She suspected the relationship between Hattie and Will may have begun some time before they went public with their courtship.

"Congratulations. That is wonderful news. I promise that Caroline and I shall endeavor to be the absolute best aunts we can be, and if we fail terribly we shall make certain to spoil your progeny and therefore keep our failures hidden," said Eve.

Caroline laughed through her tears and nodded. "Yes, our corruption of your offspring shall be subtle but irrevocable."

Eve gave her sister a friendly pat on the back.

Hattie moved closer to Will who put an arm around her, pulling her in close. He kissed her fair hair and said, "I told you they would be excited."

The joy on Hattie's face made Eve's heart flutter. Hattie deserved all the happiness in the world. She had brought a light back into Will's life that Eve had feared would never return after the death of his first wife. With a baby now on the way, a new happiness would fill their lives.

❧

Eve yawned. The champagne and supper of roast beef and vegetables had left her sated, but tired.

The evening had been filled with laughter and unrestrained joy. Adelaide and Charles spent the best part of the night teasingly calling one another Grandma and Grandpa. The glint in her mother's eye had shone bright all throughout dinner.

Eve excused herself from the table. "I shall take a walk in the garden and get some fresh air to restore my energy. I won't be long."

Hattie leant over to Will, and a whispered exchange took place between them. Will nodded.

"I shall come with you," offered Hattie.

Arm in arm, they walked from the room and out into the rear garden.

As soon as she set foot into the chill night air, Eve felt refreshed. "I am surprised you are not flagging. I heard women in your condition are often tired," she said.

Hattie chuckled. "I spent nearly all the afternoon in bed. And that was after having risen well past the hour of nine this morning. I swear I am beginning to develop Will's habit of sleeping late every day."

"But what about the soup kitchen? I thought you attended the market in the morning and then headed over to St. John's?" replied Eve.

They wandered over to a nearby garden bench and took a seat. Francis had convinced his father to install one of the new-fangled gas lamps, and so they were offered the rare luxury of a well-lit garden at night.

Hattie sat forward on the bench and turned to face Eve. "I haven't had to do the early morning market visit for a little while as I have a new assistant. He attends the market for me and then begins to prepare the vegetables before I arrive. He also cooks a rather delicious pasty that can be taken home by those parishioners with sick family members who cannot attend the church," she explained.

The door to the garden opened and Will stepped out. "Have you told her?"

Hattie shook her head. "I was about to. You were a second too early."

"Told me what?" asked Eve.

"Freddie Rosemount is my new assistant. I met him at Covent Garden one morning, and after he visited St John's he offered to help," said Hattie.

If Eve had been asked to put together a list of a thousand things that Hattie could possibly have said at that moment, Freddie working at St John's church would not have been one of them. After all the hurtful things he had said to Hattie about her work, Eve could not conceive of Freddie having the nerve to turn up on the doorstep of St John's.

"What do you mean he offered to help?" asked Eve.

Will walked closer. "He has seen the error of his ways."

Eve snorted. The only way Freddie would have seen the error of his ways was if someone hit him over the head with a large blunt object. Even then he would find a way to blame someone else.

"You mean he came to you for sympathy after his father cut him off and you shamed him into helping. Don't tell me he had the cheek to ask for handouts at your soup kitchen."

"No. He was shopping for food at the market early one morning and I saw him. To be fair to him, he tried to avoid me. He was too ashamed to face me after all that had transpired between him and the Saunders family. I was the one who held out a hand to him," replied Hattie.

Hattie's ability to see the good in everyone was beyond Eve. "So why did he come to St John's?"

"He wanted what we all want: to belong to something. From the little that he has said, I know he is deeply ashamed of what he did. He is unsure of how he can approach you," replied Hattie.

"Why would he want to approach me? He told me he didn't want me. What else is there to say?"

Will placed a hand on Eve's shoulder. "I think you might find he loves you. And until you tell him otherwise, he will continue to hold onto the slender piece of hope that he could find his way back into your life."

Eve studied her brother for a moment. He was a different man from the brash young Will who had left the family five years ago, chasing the heady danger of life as a spy. Hattie had brought out the softer, more even-tempered side of him.

Doubt crept into Eve's mind. She had convinced herself Freddie didn't love her, that he had only at best held a passing interest. She had been a pawn in his game of winning a seat on the Bachelor Board and she had been blinded to reality until it was too late. Why then would Freddie be holding onto any sort of hope of love from Eve?

Eve reluctantly let Hattie take a hold of her hand. "And what do you want me to do?"

"Nothing. Will and I have agreed we shall stay out of this matter unless you wish us to speak to Freddie on your behalf. He asked that we tell you of his presence at St John's just in case you happen to visit and find him unexpectedly there. He is most anxious to avoid any further unpleasantness between you and him," replied Hattie.

Eve rose from the bench and headed toward the doorway that led back inside the house. Before she reached the first step, she stopped. "I'm not sure what to say to this unexpected piece of news but thank you both for being honest with me. It would have been a huge shock to have visited the church and discovered Freddie working there. I promise to let you know before I visit next time. As Freddie said, we would all like to avoid any further unpleasantness."

She went back inside but decided not to go back into the dining room. It would be impossible to make small talk with her family with thoughts of Freddie now whirling around her mind. Will and Hattie would understand her reasons for not staying to bid them farewell.

Once inside her bedroom, Eve quickly undressed and dismissed her maid for the evening. With her warm robe wrapped around her, she took a seat in the bay window of her bedroom. She opened the curtains and looked out onto the street below.

A steady stream of carriages and people passed by the house. The social set of London were moving to their next place of entertainment for the evening. Many a night, she herself would be getting ready to join the throng of late-night partygoers, but tonight she was glad to be staying home.

Her mood had shifted from one of light-hearted frivolity over the news of Hattie and Will's baby to that of deep reflection.

Freddie's move in the world was most unexpected. She thought he would continue to remain outside her sphere until at least his father restored him to favor.

While Hattie did see the good in all, and held a life mission in saving others, she was not blind. If Freddie had thought to pull the wool over Hattie's eyes, he would have discovered by now that she was no man's fool. Will, too, had a sharp mind. If he thought Freddie was attempting any sort of play in regard to his sister, he would have added to Francis's facial handiwork and swiftly shown Freddie the door.

What are you playing at?

She wiped away a tear, disappointed to discover he could still make her cry. There was only one thing she was sure of at this moment, and that was that she had to move on from him. To find a way to accept the scars which were now imprinted on her heart and find new love.

She had learned some hard lessons from having her heart so cruelly broken, lessons she intended to put to good use. But before she could seek out a new life partner, there was still the question of Freddie.

They had not crossed paths since the night Francis had taken to Freddie with his fists. At the time, her anger toward him had been too raw for her to consider how future encounters would go. Membership of the *ton* wasn't so large that she could spend the rest of her life moving within its circles and be assured never to set eyes on him again.

She let out a soft sigh of resignation. There was only one thing to do. Hard as it might be, she had to meet with Freddie. She still didn't understand why he had thrown her over. If he had never wanted to marry her, then why had he toyed with her so cruelly?

"And why would you have told Hattie that you loved me?" she whispered.

If nothing else came from seeing Freddie she could at least have some of the questions in her mind answered. An understanding of his actions would allow her to begin to heal the hurt.

If he didn't want her, she could close that chapter of her life and begin again.

But what if he does? Can I risk my heart once more?

Chapter Thirty-Three

F reddie was up and planning his day by five-thirty the next morning. He had never been an early riser, but it was becoming a habit he enjoyed.

Before heading out to Covent Garden market, he went through his cookbook and checked the ingredients needed for a fruit version of his pastry parcel. His vegetable pasty was most popular with visitors to the soup kitchen, but he wanted to give his friends at St John's a new experience. Something to tantalize their tongues once their bellies were full.

"Apples with spices. Hmm, I don't think the church coffers will extend to spices," he said.

But, he was not to be defeated in his efforts. At the back of a high shelf in the kitchen he came across a small jar of preserved orange peel.

"You might just do the trick," he said, dusting off the lid.

The aroma of oranges filled his nose as he opened the jar and breathed in. With excitement now bubbling in his mind, he hurried back to the cookbook and flipped the pages until he found a recipe for preserving oranges. He could use the jar of preserved oranges to make some test pasties, but he would need fresh fruit to make them in bulk. "Apples and oranges, it is."

He grabbed his coat and gave Zeus a friendly pat goodbye.

"If my new recipe works, I promise to make you a special dog-sized apple pasty. In the meantime, if you could try to stay out of the rest of the house or at least not chew anything new today, I would be most grateful."

Closing the kitchen door behind him, he stood in the rear garden, enjoying the first rays of sun as he buttoned up his long warm coat.

"It's going to be a good day. I can feel it," he said, heading out into the rear laneway.

Walking the streets of London in the hour before dawn gave him a different perspective on the world's greatest city. There was an energy in the hurried movement of the many delivery carts and household servants which he found fascinating. The rich and powerful of London would soon wake to hot breakfasts and fresh flowers, all of which had been sourced in the early hours at the city's markets.

He met up with two of the footmen from Will and Hattie's house. While Hattie was not currently making the trip to the market each morning, and therefore not needing protection, he still availed himself of the extra pairs of hands to help bring the fresh produce back to St John's.

"Morning, chaps. We need some extra ingredients today," he said.

They made short work of their time at the market. The local traders now had Freddie's order ready when he arrived. By nine o'clock, he was at St John's with most of the day's vegetables peeled, chopped, and ready to go into the soup. He was seated at the table calculating how much flour he would need for his first batch of fruit pasties.

"Parsnips look a little sad this morning.'

Freddie looked up from his work at the kitchen table and saw Hattie standing in the doorway. She had managed to make it to the soup kitchen before ten, but her face was pale and drawn.

"Yes, they didn't have many of them. I bought some extra potatoes to bulk up the soup. Today, I'm going to try to make a fruit pasty and ask what the folk think of it. If they like it, I will make a bigger batch tomorrow. There is hot water on the stove if you would like a cup of tea," he replied.

Hattie took off her cloak and hat and hung them on a nearby hook, but instead of following her usual routine of making herself a weak cup of tea, she came and stood next to him. "We have a visitor. She is waiting outside in the garden if you agree to seeing her."

Hattie didn't need to mention their visitor by name. He knew. Freddie gritted his teeth as his self-confidence faltered. "You told her I was here?"

Hattie nodded. "As we agreed, this way we can avoid any unpleasantness. Neither of you deserve to have your private pain on display for all to see."

Freddie took a hold of Hattie's hand and raised it to his lips. She was a wonderful woman. She could make him feel so small at times, yet every day he still came to work at St John's because she made him want to do good. To be a better man.

"Go and talk to her. Tell her you are sorry for how things ended. If nothing else comes of seeing her, you will at least have managed to offer up an apology," she counselled.

He made to remove his apron, then stopped. It wasn't that he didn't expect Eve to remain long at the church, rather that he needed her to see him in his true light. To see the real Freddie Rosemount, not the pompous dandy she had set her heart on marrying.

"She likes her tea sweet with a little honey in it," said Hattie.

Freddie took the hint. It would be hard enough to face Eve—a peace offering in the form of tea might help the situation.

With cups in hand, he stepped out into the warm sunlit garden. Eve turned from examining the herb garden, and the moment her gaze fell upon him, all the bravery he had hastily mustered fled.

Eve straightened her back and confidently stepped forward. Coming to a halt just in front of him, she cleared her throat.

"Freddie."

He had forgotten how beautiful she was, how the mere sight of her stirred his soul to life. How he had come so close to winning the greatest prize of his life, only to throw it away in a moment of rash selfishness.

If he hadn't been so damn foolish, right now he would be able to pull her into his arms and she would let him kiss her. Eve would be his; they would have a future.

Instead, she was little more than a stranger. A stranger who still held his heart.

"Tea?" he finally managed, offering her the cup.

She took it, and to his surprise took a seat on an upturned box next to the steps. He watched for a moment, unsure of himself, then decided he had better follow suit. He sat on the edge of the nearby step and took a tentative sip of his tea.

"Beautiful morning to be out. This must be the first real day of sunshine we have had in weeks," she said. Eve closed her eyes and leant back against the grey, stone wall of the church. She lifted her cup to her lips and slowly sipped her hot tea.

Freddie watched with endless fascination as the sunlight shone on her face. She was so unlike the other young women of London high society. She was comfortable sitting in the sun in the tiny, shabby garden of one of the capital's poorest churches.

He tore his gaze away and stared at the nearby garden beds, reminding himself to do something about digging up the soil, and making a bigger herb garden for the kitchen.

"Nice tea. The honey seems to have a particular spice to it. Who made it?"

He stirred from his musings and chanced another look at Eve. "I did. I like to put a sprinkle or two of ground cinnamon into the honey. It adds an interesting tone."

She chuckled softly. "Does it now? You sound like a true connoisseur of the art of tea-making. I would never have thought you to be a man capable of brewing a good pot of tea."

He saw the glint of humor in her eyes. The Eve he once knew, the girl full of life and laughter, was still there. He hadn't crushed her completely.

"I've had to learn to make do. I expect you know, as does the rest of London, that my father has cut me off," he replied.

"Yes. I am aware he has done so. He was very angry with you the last time I saw him at Rosemount Abbey. He didn't take kindly to you throwing me over. Nor, for that matter, did I."

Freddie sucked in a deep breath. He had been such a selfish, self-centered blackguard in tossing her aside to win his seat on the Bachelor

Board. Now when he thought about the Bachelor Board, the mere memory of that den of sickening corruption made his stomach turn.

"I must confess to being a little more than surprised to discover you are working at the soup kitchen. It doesn't strike me as somewhere you would find yourself very comfortable," Eve continued.

Eve was right in one regard. A simple church on the edge of London's biggest slum was not the place you would normally expect to find the son of a viscount. Yet, she was wrong in thinking Freddie didn't belong here.

Among the people of the parish he had found meaning in his life. In the words and kind actions of Hattie and Will he had also found some forgiveness for his misdeeds.

The gulf between him and Eve however, was still as wide as the sea.

The final note from Osmont Firebrace sat in his pocket. Every morning when he rose, he pulled it out and reread it. It reminded him of why he was living this new life, and that he had much to atone for in the world. It was also a bitter reminder of the love he had lost.

"Why have you come?" he asked.

When she looked at him, he caught a wariness in her eyes. Of course, she didn't trust him, and after what he had done it was little wonder.

"I came here today because I wanted to see you. I need to understand what you did to me and why you did it. Only then can I begin to move on with my life. But the first thing I should be asking however, is why are you here and not home in Peterborough trying to curry favor with your parents?"

He drained his cup of tea and set it down on the step next to him. There were many different versions of the truth he could give her. How much of the truth she was willing to hear was something he would have to take a risk on.

"I am here because I have done many things over the past few months, especially during the Bachelor Board challenges, of which I am deeply ashamed. I am not here simply because I was cut off by my father. I have caused the people closest to me great pain and brought shame upon my family. I also treated you far worse than the lowest rakehell would ever do. If you are asking what I should tell you of that last day at Rosemount Abbey, what would you have me say?"

She rose from the upturned box and stood before him, her cup of tea cradled in her hands. He saw the stiffness of her posture, the tightness of her shoulders. His heart went out to her. It was obvious it had taken a great deal for her to see him this morning to seek out the truth.

"I want to know it all. Leave nothing out. No matter how horrid it is, you have to tell me. You have smashed my heart to a thousand pieces already—there is nothing left for you to break," said Eve.

Freddie reached into his jacket pocket and pulled out the note from Osmont. It was only fair she got to read it, having lived through the execution of its cold and clear instructions. Without a word, he handed the note to Eve.

She opened the paper, and he held his breath as she slowly read the words. When she was finished, she folded the note back up and stuffed it into her reticule. "Thank you for the tea. It was delicious. Please tell Hattie I had to leave. My carriage is outside waiting."

With that, she turned on her heel and walked out of the garden.

Freddie finished his work at the church. He didn't bother with the new recipe for the apple pasty, deciding it would have to wait until the next day when hopefully his mind had settled. He barely spoke to any of the parishioners as he served them their food.

Hattie offered for him to leave earlier than usual. "I'm sorry. I should have given you prior warning Eve may visit this week. I didn't realize it would rattle you so much," she said.

"It is not your fault; Eve and I were bound to meet one another at some point. But yes, I think it best that I go home," he replied.

Freddie's mind was singularly focused during the walk home to Grosvenor Square. Had he made a grave mistake in giving Eve the note from Osmont Firebrace? Her face as she had read the note had shown no emotion. He had expected tears, or at least a mouthful of Eve-quality abuse, but she had given nothing away.

Upon reaching home, he let himself in through the kitchen door.

Zeus welcomed him with a cheerfully wagging tail and what Freddie surmised to be the remains of one of his mother's hand-embroidered cushions from the upstairs sitting room. The dead cushion was added to the growing list of items the dog had chewed or slobbered to death over the past few weeks. Even after his father eventually returned him to funds, he would be poorer than a church mouse. It would take months to replace all the damaged and broken household items.

He had done everything he thought possible to keep Zeus below the stairs during the day, but the dog was far smarter than his awkward lopsided face gave away. It was a pity his father had taken some of the household keys home, leaving Freddie unable to ensure Zeus stayed out of particular rooms in the house.

He opened the bag of dog meat he had bought at the market that morning and deposited it into Zeus's bowl. Claws scattered on the stone floor as Zeus pushed Freddie to one side in his haste to get to the food.

"Steady on, boy," Freddie muttered.

While Zeus wolfed down his dinner, Freddie pulled some small logs from the fireside stack and arranged them over the embers of the fire he had lit earlier that morning. Using the set of bellows, he managed to give enough air to the fire to soon have a small flame licking at the edge of the wood. He brushed the wood dust from his hands, then hung the kettle over the flames.

In a short while he had hot water, and he settled down at the kitchen table to drink a cup of tea. He lifted the lid of the honey jar and scooped a spoonful of honey in. He was about to grate a small piece of cinnamon into his cup when he remembered Eve's words.

You have smashed my heart to a thousand pieces.

He put the stick of cinnamon down on the table and stared at it.

His mother's fine things could be replaced. Even his well-chewed boots could be repaired, but there was nothing he could do to undo what he had done to Eve. He would be forever the man who had crushed her heart. Another of his firsts that held no honor.

And now she was ready to move on and find love with someone else. He should be glad she was over him, that he was simply a cautionary tale in her past.

Someone else.

Someone else who would hold her in his arms and kiss those wickedly soft lips. Another man who would know the soul-deep sound she made when she came to completion. Another who would …

"Damn."

He had been naïve to think Eve would never visit St John's. His one place of sanctuary from his misdeeds was a sanctuary no more. Every day he would be looking up from the kitchen table waiting to see if she reappeared in the doorway. She had never truly left him. His erotic dreams of her continued every night. He had worked hard to put another face to the woman he dreamed of making love to, but Eve steadfastly refused to give up her hold on him. Night after night he saw her beneath him, her lips parted as she gave a soft cry as he claimed her love.

Seeing her in the flesh this morning had only reinforced her grip. He knew it was more than lust. The whole time she had been in the garden at St John's he had wanted to reach out and take her in his arms. To hold her and beg for forgiveness. To offer whatever it would take to have her gift him with her smile once more.

"Yes, well you made doubly sure she will never give you a minute of her time again," he muttered.

He wondered how many times she would read Osmont's note. Had she torn it into a thousand pieces like he had done with her heart? Or was it already a small pile of cold ashes in her bedroom fireplace? He prayed she had destroyed it the instant she returned home. The last thing he wished was for her to sit and stare at that damned piece of paper, mulling over all that had been so cruelly taken from her.

Not for the first time since he fled into the woods at Rosemount Abbey did Freddie rue his fateful decision. There had been far too many *if only* moments for him to have made any headway in the war with his conscience.

He picked up the cinnamon stick and broke off a small piece, stirring it into his tea. The damage was done. At least Eve would now know the whole truth of what had happened at Rosemount Abbey: that she had not in any way been the one at fault. He would have to accept that small grace and move on.

Chapter Thirty-Four

E ve was proud of herself. She didn't cry in the carriage on the way home to Dover Street. She made it through dinner with her parents and still managed to smile. By the time she, Francis, and Caroline headed out to a late evening party she was positively beaming.

From the moment she had left Freddie sitting alone in the garden at St John's, an old biblical quote from the book of John had been rolling around in her head.

Then you will know the truth, and the truth will set you free.

Her uncle Hugh, the Bishop of London, would be proud of her. She had had a life-changing revelation in the middle of a church garden.

The note had not contained the heartbreak she had so feared when Freddie first handed it to her. It had given her the gift of knowledge she so desperately craved. She understood why Freddie had ended their relationship. She should be thanking him for having spared her the rest of her life with him.

Yet, for all her self-reassurance, she could not escape the undeniable fact Freddie's unexpected honesty had cut her to the core. *Damn you, Freddie Rosemount. You couldn't make it simple, could you?*

After a restless night, she rose early the following morning. She was dressed and ready to leave the house long before anyone else from the family had come into the breakfast room. She downed a hurried cup of coffee and half a piece of toast before calling for the family town carriage. She had considered walking, but the streets that led to St Giles passed by Will and Hattie's house, and she couldn't risk bumping into either of them.

Her mother would have a fit when she discovered Eve had left home without a maid or footman. Eve was in too much of a hurry this morning to bother with the niceties; she had to see Freddie.

She cursed him for his honesty. It would have made things so much easier if he had simply lied to her or kept the whole of the truth to himself. Instead, he had opened a Pandora's box of questions, all of which she badly needed answered.

After reaching St John's Parish, she made her way in through the garden gate. She found Freddie in the kitchen, busy washing potatoes.

"Good morning."

He looked up. She quickly stifled her enjoyment at the look of shock on his face.

I don't expect you ever thought to see me again.

"Eve?"

She pulled the note he had given her the previous day from her reticule and waved it in front of her. "I think it is time you and I had an honest conversation about the Bachelor Board. After what you did to me, I would suggest you owe me that much."

He stopped washing the potatoes and wiped his hands on his apron. His movements were slow, guarded. She sensed he was trying to control his emotions. "Very well. Though I must say I am surprised to see you here today. After you read that note, I didn't expect to see you again. I *did* half expect to see Francis, mind you."

They stepped back out into the garden and resumed the same seats as the previous morning. When Freddie offered to make Eve another cup of tea, she waved him away. "If I don't throttle you after we have talked, then perhaps you can make me a cup of tea. I understand the *what* of Osmont Firebrace's letter, but I don't under the *why*. I thought perhaps you might be able to shed some light on the subject," she said.

He nodded. "Yes, of course. I should have expected you would have questions. Where to begin? Well, firstly can I say it was never my intention for things to end the way they did. I didn't set out to hurt you. You played the game brilliantly. Even before we left for Rosemount Abbey, I was well ahead of Mewburton and Embry."

She ignored the remark about the other players. She couldn't care less about the result of the game.

"You always knew that the aim of the game was to secure a seat on the Bachelor Board. What you didn't know, was that the Bachelor Board is a secret society of men who hold great power in London. The reason why someone like me would want to join, is because as a second son I will never inherit a title or lands from my father. I will be gifted a small living, nothing more. The Bachelor Board offered me a priceless opportunity to be something more than merely my father's second son."

His words made sense. A position among men of power and influence was one worth winning. But the one thing that had kept her up most of the previous night was the question of why the game included having to break the heart of a woman who loved you. All the rest of the challenges were foolish pranks; breaking someone's heart spoke of an evil agenda. "Why the need for you to break my heart? What could that possibly achieve?"

He closed his eyes and sighed. "It achieved exactly what it was meant to. It showed them I would do anything to gain a seat on the Bachelor Board—that I had no scruples. It was only after I returned to London that I began to discover the price of your broken heart was only a down payment on what they wanted from me. Even if I had possessed the money to buy my way onto the board, they would have had me in their web. Suffice to say, Osmont Firebrace is an evil man who enjoys destroying the lives of others. The price to join the board is far more than simply money. As the gatekeeper to the board, he demands not just your dignity, but your very soul."

"And you decided you were not prepared to pay that?"

"Yes, but too late to realize I had already paid a heavy price by jilting you. I just wish I could do something to stop the likes of Osmont from continuing with their twisted corruption of young men. I am certain I am not the first, nor the last, man they will ruin."

Eve got to her feet and began to pace up and down the garden path. She was oddly proud of Freddie. He was now looking beyond himself and thinking of how he could set a better future for others. When she walked back to where he sat, she stopped. "What about Will? Have you considered talking to my brother? He might be able to give you some advice in your quest to bring down Osmont. He may tell you to leave it well enough alone but knowing him, I doubt it. At least this way you won't spend the rest of your life wondering what you could have done about saving other men from a fate similar to yours," she said.

Freddie met her gaze. It was so typical of their relationship, that while Eve was thinking clearly about trying to deal with the Bachelor Board, his own mind was focused on wanting to pull her into his arms.

He rose from the step. "Excuse me for a moment. I need to check on the soup."

Freddie walked back inside the kitchen, his heart racing. Dealing with Osmont Firebrace was something he hadn't truly considered until now, but Eve's words rang true. What if he could do something to stop Osmont?

He walked over to the large pot of soup, simmering over a low heat. He picked up a wooden spoon and was about to plunge it into the liquid when he stopped.

Osmont and his cronies could wait.

Of more pressing urgency was the matter of Eve. She was waiting for him outside in the garden. He had broken her heart, and she claimed to want to move on with her life, yet she was here.

Was there a remote chance he had not burnt all his bridges with her?

"She is here. Don't waste this opportunity," he whispered as he began to stir the soup.

She may never come here again, never be alone with him again.

This may be the only chance he would ever get to speak the words his heart was demanding of him.

He watched as the vegetables and grains swirled around in the gently bubbling soup, then turned and looked to the door leading back outside.

For heaven's sake, go to her. Tell her your heart.

He had already lost her. There was only a small hope, but he had to risk it. He put the spoon down, summoned all his courage and walked back out into the garden.

Eve was leaning against the high, stone garden wall, not far from the gate. The gate which she had walked out of the previous morning, one he had not expected her to ever walk through again.

With slow hesitant steps he came to her and took her gently by the hand. He lifted it to his lips and placed a tender kiss on her fingertips. He heard her soft sigh and looked up to see her eyes shining with tears. He brushed his hand on her cheek, thumbing one of the tears from her face. "I could spend an eternity telling you how deeply sorry I am for all I have done. That deceiving and betraying you is the very worst thing I have ever done in my life. I could tell you a thousand times I know I have lost the greatest love of my life. But I know none of it will ever wipe the memory from my mind of the look on your face that afternoon in the stables."

"Freddie," she murmured.

He slipped his hand under her chin and lifted her face so she was looking directly into his eyes. His gaze fell upon her soft rose lips. Lips he knew were meant to be his for all time.

"I love you," he said. His lips descended, but a hand came between them and gently pushed his face away.

"Not yet."

He searched her gaze. "When?"

"*If* is more the question that needs to be answered. There is still much I need to think about. So many things of which I am uncertain," she replied.

Disappointment burnt his heart, but along with it was a spark of hope. Hope, which until now, he had thought was stone dead. "Can you answer me one question?"

"Yes."

"Are you done with me?"

She walked toward the garden gate, stopping a few feet from the entrance. She turned and looked at him. "No, I'm not done with you, Freddie Rosemount. Of that I am certain."

Chapter Thirty-Five

F reddie stood outside the house in Newport Street and waited. He had left a note there earlier that morning that he wished to see Will Saunders. He was continually being reminded as to how much he had previously relied upon the use of servants in the day-to-day running of his life.

When he checked his pocket watch for the fourth time and saw it was close to eleven o'clock, he opened the front gate and headed up to the door. A sprightly, old butler answered and after Freddie had shown him his card, he ushered him into an elegant drawing room on the second floor.

"I shall let Mr. Saunders know you have arrived," he said.

Freddie was busy examining an odd collection of glass eyes when he heard the door to the drawing room open. He put down a large, red eye and turned to see Will Saunders enter the room.

"Good morning, Will. I hope I am not disturbing you at this hour." Freddie held out his hand and was relieved when Will took it.

Will looked to the bowl of glass eyes and raised an eyebrow. "I hope you are planning on stealing a few of those. I promise I will make every effort to forget how many of them are in that bowl. They belong to Hattie's father. This is his house. We are renting it while he is in Africa. The man has terrible taste in decorating," said Will.

Freddie's gaze fell on the elegant chairs that sat about the room. There was nothing terrible about them. They spoke of a keen sense of taste and wealth.

"Those are mine. I brought them back with me from France," said Will.

Freddie felt sick. While playing the Rude Rules with Eve he had made fun of Will and his time in France. "I cannot begin to tell you how sorry I am for all the foolish things I said to you. How I could have dared to mock you when you had served our country so bravely."

He had a good many other people in London and at home to apologize to, but it felt right to attempt to make amends with Will Saunders. Freddie held him in high regard. Many other men of London high society would not permit their wives to work with the downtrodden, indigent population of the slums. Will was a special breed of man. The fact he was Eve's brother added a special significance to their relationship.

The butler who had answered the door entered the room carrying a tray with a teapot and cups balanced somewhat precariously upon it. Will walked over and took the tray.

"Thank you, Mr. Little. I shall take it from here". Will placed the tray on a nearby coffee table and offered Freddie a seat. "I expect you miss having servants. I must admit the first time I had to light a fire it took me over an hour."

Freddie raised an eyebrow. It had never occurred to him that anyone else in his acquaintance would have had to do the domestic chores he was currently undertaking.

Will looked up from pouring the tea. "I was supposed to be a lowly shipping clerk during my time in Paris. I couldn't exactly maintain a house, let alone a retinue of servants. I was a bachelor for the first few months I was in France. But enough about me. What can I do for you?"

Freddie sat forward on the finely handcrafted French chair and clasped his hands. He had practiced his speech for the best part of the previous evening, but when it came time to make his case, he feared his nerves would fail him. He cleared his throat. "Have you ever heard of the Bachelor Board?"

Will fixed him with a steely glare. "I had heard rumors of it when I was a young man, but never paid much attention. I was busy with other matters. Why?"

"Eve and I were playing in a series of challenges in order for me to gain entry to the board. Though, at the time we were playing, she did not know the true purpose of the game. She simply thought it was a silly game and that we were having a spot of fun."

"Go on," replied Will.

"I won the right to join the Bachelor Board. But with my father having cut me off after I had jilted Eve, I couldn't stump up the blunt for my membership. That's when Osmont Firebrace made me an offer to rent my body out to other members of the board. Before I had a chance to refuse him, he drugged me. I expect it was in order to rape me and then force me into doing his bidding in exchange for keeping silent. Fortunately, I was able to escape his office before the drugs took a complete hold." Hot tears came to his eyes. He had buried the memory of that afternoon deep in his mind, refusing to allow it to resurface. He knew, however, that if he was to get Will's support, he would have to tell him the truth.

Will sat silent, watching him, then rose from his chair and headed over to a small cabinet. When he returned, he was bearing a large glass near filled to the brim with whisky.

"Forget the tea. Get this down you. I promise to send you home in my carriage," he said.

"Thank you."

The hour that followed was the longest and hardest of Freddie's life. By the end of it, Will Saunders knew the whole sordid story. When Freddie finished relating the events at Rosemount Abbey, he sat with his head bowed. He had never felt so ashamed of himself in his life. His father had been right; he had brought disgrace on their family.

"Well that explains the outrageously stupid name you gave your dog. I am sure he is grateful you decided to give him something more suitable. Which now brings me to the question of what you want *me* to do to about Osmont Firebrace?" said Will.

"I need to do something about Firebrace and his friends. You are the one person who I feel I can come to for advice," replied Freddie.

Will sat back in his chair and looked at Freddie over his steepled fingers. The room was so quiet, Freddie could have sworn he could hear Will's brain as it churned over the ugly revelations.

"Tell me this: are you doing this out of some sense of civic duty or is it purely revenge?" asked Will.

Freddie considered the question for a moment. He hadn't expected such a forthright discussion, and now he was silently kicking himself for having underestimated Will. *He was a spy, you bloody fool.*

"To be honest, there is a little revenge included in the piece. The game cost me the love of a wonderful, spirited girl. And yes, I was the one who made the choice between Eve and the board—that failure is completely my own. But the members of the Bachelor Board are predators who prey on the insecurities of younger sons. I was a fool to be blind to their real motives. I also have no doubt that if Lord Godwin's family had not stepped in, the board would have offered him a seat and he would be caught up in their web. These men have to be stopped. I just don't know how. Eve suggested I speak to you."

He finished the last of his whisky, wondering where it had gone as he set the glass on the table. It was a surprisingly cathartic experience to finally speak to someone about his experience at the hands of the board. While he could tell Eve about what happened, he felt only another man could truly understand his position.

"Alright. Let me sleep on this news. Firebrace has been in power at the House of Commons for over twenty years. His network of friends will be extensive. I will need you to give me a full list of those whom you met during the challenges. If we are to move on them, we will need to be sure of whom we trust. If he gets a sniff of anything untoward coming his way, you can be certain he will come after you," replied Will.

Freddie got to his feet. He would go home and wait for Will to contact him. In the meantime, he would go back to baking his pasties, cooking soup, and catching the occasional treasured moment with Eve.

Will shook his head. "Sit down, lad. You and I are not finished."

A perplexed Freddie resumed his seat and met Will's stern gaze.

"My sister may be displaying her best social face whenever you meet her, but I know full well a river of tears has been shed over you. She is wounded, but she has her pride. And with that pride comes the Saunders family stubborn streak. It wouldn't surprise me in the least if she up and did something rash like eloping with the next chap who is half pleasant to her. Someone entirely unsuitable. Someone who is not you," said Will.

Freddie silently chastised himself. Of course, Eve's brother would want to dig over the ground of what he had done to Eve. After his encounter with Eve at St John's, he wasn't completely certain where he stood with her. In the deep recesses of his mind was the nagging worry Eve was toying with him simply to exact her revenge when the time suited her.

She had said she was not done with him but knowing Eve that could mean anything.

"Eve and I have spoken. She appears to understand. As for forgiveness or any other matter of the heart, only time will tell," he replied.

Will sat quiet for a moment. It was the longest of moments. "I would give you this advice: listen to what Eve has to say. She is an intelligent girl, but headstrong at times. There have been long heart-searching and character rebuilding moments for her as a result of what happened at Rosemount Abbey. She has seen the folly of some of her headstrong ways, but she is still attracted to scandalous behavior and the taste of danger. The problem I see with her is that she has never had to face real danger. Until she does, she will think it is exciting but not understand the risk. As someone who learnt the hard way about having a taste for danger, I would caution you to be careful where you tread," said Will.

"I will be careful with Eve. I am well aware she has her own mind; it is one of the things that I love about her. I also know I am going to have to give over the reins of our relationship until she starts to trust me again. But, if we ever get to a point of being together again, I know I shall have to address her thirst for risky endeavors."

Will chuckled. "You have no idea what you are letting yourself in for if you allow her to set the rules. It is going to take a lot to win her back, and even then, it won't be an easy path to the altar for the pair of you. But I can guarantee you this much: if she doesn't kill you before she forgives you, Eve will certainly make the rest of your life interesting."

Chapter Thirty-Six

Two days later, Freddie stood inside the foyer of Strathmore House nervously fiddling with his hat. He hadn't expected Will to take his story about the Bachelor Board with more than a grain of salt. How many other young men had offered up tall stories to explain their way out of poor behavior? Yet here he was, summoned to the home of the Duke of Strathmore, one of the most powerful men in the country.

He gritted his teeth. The duke was Will and Eve's uncle, and no doubt had heard enough of what Viscount Rosemount's second son had done to his niece to have formed a poor opinion of Freddie. Freddie was not looking forward to this particular meeting.

The footman took his hat. Freddie was adjusting his jacket for the third time when the Strathmore House butler opened the front door and Charles Saunders stepped across the threshold. Freddie's breath caught in his throat.

"Rosemount," said Charles.

Freddie bowed.

"Have you seen Will?"

"I have just arrived myself. I haven't seen anyone as yet," replied Freddie.

A nearby door opened and out stepped a well-dressed young man with fair hair. Freddie immediately recognized him as the Marquis of Brooke. He crossed the floor to Charles and held out his hand.

"Uncle Charles, good to see you. I hope you and Aunt Adelaide are well." He then turned to Freddie. "And you must be Freddie Rose-mount. Alex Radley. Good to finally meet you, though I wish it were under more pleasant circumstances. You were a year or so ahead of me at Eton, as I recall. I never made it to university," he said.

Freddie shook Alex's hand. "Yes, I was. I remember you and your older brother David very well."

What he really meant was the Marquis of Brooke and his illegitimate older brother were legendary for their exploits at the school. The Radley brothers had their places firmly cemented in the history of Eton.

With the brief greetings over, they were ushered into a nearby room. As soon as Freddie stepped inside his heart began to race.

Seated at the head of an elegant mahogany table on one side of the room was Ewan Radley, the Duke of Strathmore. Also present was Will Saunders. It was the third man who had Freddie's pulse racing.

Hugh Radley, the Bishop of London.

While all the men present held various levels of power and influence, it was the Bishop of London who had the Prince Regent's ear. If anyone could strike a blow against Osmont Firebrace and the Bachelor Board, it was Hugh Radley.

To Freddie's surprise he was warmly greeted by all those at the table and offered a chair beside Will. The bishop sat directly across from him.

As a footman poured them each a glass of wine, a slow trickle of sweat worked its way down Freddie's back. Exams at Oxford had been nerve-wracking enough, but they paled into insignificance against this moment.

"Now I know most of you have a good idea about what has happened to young Frederick here, but I think it is time you all understood how serious the situation is with regard to these chaps," announced the duke. He looked in the direction of his brother and the bishop cleared his throat.

"The goings on of the Bachelor Board are not a secret among the men of the *ton*. At some point or another in our lives, most of us have had a friend suddenly elevated into a position of power and the Bachelor Board has been behind it. As with Freddie here, the younger sons of families have been the prime target for membership for a number of years. Once a chap joins them, it becomes his duty to ensure he does everything to assist other members, and so on," explained the bishop.

There was a collective nodding of heads from the others seated at the table.

"What you do not know, and what has been kept from all but a few, is the members of this secret society are behind some of the recent social upheavals we have experienced in England. They are actually one of the main reasons why the rule of habeas corpus has been suspended since February of this year. There is a growing body of evidence they are plotting to overthrow the crown."

Freddie's blood turned to ice. In his small world, it had all been about righting wrongs. He had hoped to have Osmont Firebrace relieved from his role at the House of Commons—that was the size of the victory he had in mind. Never once had he thought the Bachelor Board was more than a group of self-serving libertines. That they could actually attempt to seize power was an immense shock.

Will placed a reassuring hand on Freddie's shoulder. "We know you had no idea of the depth of their treachery. We have been secretly investigating them and their dubious business affairs for some time. It is one of the reasons why I came back to England. They don't know me well enough to see me as a potential threat."

The bishop nodded. "Yes, the evidence Will and other government agents have been collecting all year is now enough for laying charges under the Treason Act. There is going to be a number of arrests over the next few weeks. Several members of the Bachelor Board were arrested last week as they attempted to flee England. They are currently being held in prison without trial, though of course everyone thinks they are travelling abroad. This country is going to be rocked to its very foundations when the names of those being brought before the courts are made public."

He turned to Freddie, who was feeling nauseous at this point. He was just starting out in life. If he was swept up in the trials of those charged with treason he was finished in England.

The bishop leant over the table and met his gaze. "Fear not, young Rosemount. Since your role in this has only been as a minor player, you will not be asked to give evidence in court. I have spoken with his Royal Highness, Prince George, and he has agreed you have done enough to help bring these men down. Several names you gave Will have been added to the list of people to be questioned and likely charged. Your name will have to appear in the court transcripts, so you may wish to speak to your father once the arrests begin."

Freddie sat back in his chair and closed his eyes. Tears threatened. He had brought shame upon his family already. He had no idea how he would face his father once the Bachelor Board and all its depravity became public. The fact he would play a hand in bringing down Osmont Firebrace was only a minor comfort at this moment.

He chanced a look at Charles Saunders, who was seated with his arms crossed at the end of the table.

"If you have any problems with your father, I am willing to speak to him. As a Frenchman I have an understanding of the havoc that secret societies of powerful men can inflict on a country," said Charles.

"Thank you, sir," replied Freddie. The lump in his throat made his words barely decipherable.

He left a short time later and stepped out into the mid-morning sunshine. He looked up at the pale grey clouds sitting above London. In the distance, a darker rain band threatened.

The day matched his life. Eve was the glimpse of sunshine which occasionally managed to poke through the grey. Yet even as he savored the warmth, he knew a tempest was brewing.

Will came and stood next to him at the top of the steps. "My father and uncles have asked I give you reassurance you will be protected. The Prince Regent himself will be at great pains to ensure only the guilty have their names tarnished by this scandal. He cannot afford to have young men like yourself destroyed. You represent the future of this country. A country he will be king of within a few years."

Freddie mustered an encouraging smile for Will's benefit. He would be spared from much of the fall of the Bachelor Board, and he had to be grateful for such mercy in his life. But once the arrests and subsequent trials began, he doubted Eve and her family would stand by him.

Only a fool could think that the innocent would be spared when England began to clean its house of traitors. Freddie Rosemount would pay in one way or another for having tried to be someone he was not.

Chapter Thirty-Seven

E ve tried to speak to her father when he returned home. She knew from snatches of conversation between Charles and Adelaide that a meeting had been conducted at Strathmore House that morning. As she left the breakfast room, she heard Freddie's name mentioned but thought better of trying to press her father for more information. Her quiet encouragement of Freddie to seek Will's advice about the Bachelor Board appeared to have borne fruit.

Not long after Charles arrived home from the meeting, he headed into his study. Adelaide soon joined him, and the door was closed behind them.

The only person who could give Eve further information on the secret meeting was the very person she had plans to go and see.

A modiste fitting for Caroline gave Eve the perfect opportunity to be out of the house. Caroline was delighted when Eve offered to come with her in place of their mother. Her humor was tested though when Eve asked she drop her off in Grosvenor Square and then pick her up on the way home.

"Are you sure about this? I know he has been doing good work with Hattie at the soup kitchen, but you mustn't forget this is the man who broke your heart," cautioned Caroline.

The Saunders town carriage was making the short journey up New Bond Street to Oxford Street where the family dressmaker was situated. It was a quick side trip to Grosvenor Square.

Rather than start another of their old arguments, Eve found herself comforted by Caroline's advice. In putting aside their many differences they had discovered the other was not so different from them self.

"I visited him at St John's with Hattie. He told me things that made sense of a lot of what happened between us. He truly regrets what he did to me," replied Eve.

"And you still love him," said Caroline.

Eve had mulled that very same notion over and over in her head since she had heard of Freddie's work with the poor. After their first meeting, and reading the note from Osmont Firebrace, she had done her best to convince herself she was well and truly over Freddie.

"Yes, I think I do. Lord knows I have tried to hate him, but to no avail. The fact is I cannot move on with my life until I know he does not want me. I went to St John's alone and spoke with him," said Eve.

Caroline nodded. "What did he say?"

"That he is sorry for what he did, and he knows he has lost the greatest love of his life."

Caroline's eyes grew wide. She leant across the short space between the seats of the carriage and took a hold of Eve's hand. "He really told you that he loved you? Oh, Eve. What can I do to help?"

Eve hadn't considered that anyone, apart from perhaps Hattie and Will, would want to help her and Freddie reunite. She had expected to be on her own when it came to winning over her parents, Caroline, and Francis.

"If you can keep my secret for a little while longer that would be lovely. I want to be able to spend time with Freddie and get to know the real man. The whole time we were together before, he was playing a game to join a secret society. He is no longer in the game," replied Eve.

She wanted to confide in Caroline about the Bachelor Board but Caroline had her limits. Star-crossed lovers she could understand and place her heart and soul behind. But Eve did not want to expose Caroline to the truth of what men such as Osmont Firebrace did in the shadows of society. If the *ton* had to have darkness, then it also needed the light beautiful girls such as Caroline gave it.

Her sister kept her word, and Eve was soon standing out the front of Rosemount House watching as the Saunders town carriage turned the corner into Duke Street.

She nervously bit down on her bottom lip as she walked up the steps which led to the front door. Rosemount House was a classic Portland stone mansion. There were at least three others in Grosvenor Square that had the same portico front, and color scheme. The only feature to distinguish it from the other houses was the Rosemount family crest, which sat in gold and black above the door. A single black boar on a gold shield with a series of small black stars around the outside proclaimed the Rosemount family heritage.

She remembered imagining how the crest would look on the hem of her wedding gown when she was certain Freddie was about to propose. How once she had been so certain her future place was secure within the Rosemount family.

Her hand was reaching out for the door knocker when she suddenly remembered she was an unmarried miss who was about to enter the house of a young man whom she knew full well had no servants. A ripple of thrill raced down her spine.

"You are a wicked girl, Evelyn Saunders," she muttered.

Quickly leaving the front of the house, she made for the servants' entrance. She knocked on the door and waited.

The sound of a dog barking within was quickly drowned out by the call of its master. "Zeus, silence!"

She held her breath.

Freddie opened the door, his hand firmly gripping the collar of the giant Irish wolfhound. "Eve?"

"The one and only," she replied.

Upon seeing Eve, the dog leapt high, and Freddie lost his grip. Zeus bounded over to his former mistress and placed some worshipful slobber all over her gloves. Eve gave him a welcoming rub behind the ears while Freddie stood close by with hands on hips.

"Who is Zeus?" she asked.

Zeus wagged his tail hard against her skirts.

"The dog. He didn't deserve to be saddled with that other foolish name. He never answered to it anyway. He seems to like his new name much better," replied Freddie.

A frown appeared on his face, and Eve silently guessed what the next words out of his mouth would be.

"Are you alone?"

She chuckled, having won the wager against herself. "Yes. Caroline is in Oxford Street at an appointment. She will call by and collect me on the way home in an hour or so. I thought we might take the time to talk to one another in private," she replied.

"Will you allow me to say you should not be visiting a young man at his home without a chaperone? I need to say it in case I get asked by your father or one of your brothers," he said.

Eve smiled and nodded.

"Then you had better come inside."

She followed him into the house. Entering the kitchen, she discovered Freddie had made quite a comfortable home for himself. There was a fire burning in the hearth. Pots were cooking over the flames, and she caught the scent of fresh pastry baking in the oven.

"Got yourself a housekeeper?" she teased.

Freddie laughed and shook his head. "No. I was left to fend for myself and that is exactly what I have done. I taught myself to cook."

There was pride in his voice and a sparkle in his eyes. He was happy. "It smells good, whatever it is that you are baking,' she replied.

He opened one of the kitchen cupboards and pulled out a plate covered in cloth. He placed the plate on the kitchen table and unwrapped it. The heady smell of recently baked pie filled her nostrils. Her stomach promptly rumbled in anticipation.

"This came out about an hour ago. I have to put it on a high shelf otherwise Zeus will get to it. I didn't think dogs ate pie, but after twice having come home to the remains of crumbs for my supper I realized they did."

He set about the kitchen with a comfortable familiarity, and soon had plates and a pot of hot coffee on the table. Taking a large knife, Freddie cut into the pie and placed a piece on one of the plates. He handed it to an eager Eve. "I am doing some experimenting with my pies. This one has leek, potato, and chicken in it. Tell me what you think."

Eve slipped her gloves from her fingers and broke off a piece of the pie. Zeus scuttled under the table and made himself at home. As soon as she took her first bite, Zeus whimpered.

"Do not let him give you that sob story. I fed him not an hour ago. That dog is a bottomless pit when it comes to food," said Freddie.

Eve broke off another piece of the pie and conveniently dropped it onto the floor. Looking under the table, she watched as Zeus made short work of her offering.

Freddie shook his head. Eve took another bite of the pie and sat working it thoughtfully around her mouth for a minute.

Freddie laughed. "That is exactly the same face our family cook at Rosemount Abbey pulls when she makes something new." He pulled a notebook and pencil out of his jacket pocket, then proceeded to thumb through the pages until he got to a clean page. "So, would you say it needs more pepper?"

Eve took a second bite and let it sit in her mouth for moment before chewing. Her tongue tasted chicken and leek mostly but only a hint of pepper. She chewed the bite down and swallowed. "A little more pepper, perhaps. Have you considered some parsley or thyme? Our family cook often adds them to roast chicken," she replied.

Eve saw him make a note of her suggestions in his book, and then added in rosemary and tarragon.

"Thank you. Constructive criticism is most welcome. I don't get a lot of it at the soup kitchen. The parishioners are usually too busy filling their empty bellies to give me their opinions of my cooking." He put his pencil down and gently clasped his hands together. The mood in the kitchen changed, and Eve felt tension in the air. "I am very pleased to see you, even though we both know you should not have come alone."

She waved his concerns away. "I came because I realized the conversation we had at the church was the first honest one you and I have ever had. Every one before that had been clouded with either the game, or our own private agendas."

"I suppose you are right. We never did get off to an even start," he replied.

"Which is why I am sitting in your kitchen. I don't want to go through all the whys and wherefores of what happened before. I need to know just one thing. Do you want me?"

He took hold of her hand and brought it to his lips. She smiled as he kissed the last of the pie from her fingertips. He continued to kiss her fingers long after the last trace of the pie had gone. Eve felt heat stir in her body remembering what else his fingers had done to her.

"Yes. I do want you. Trust me, the one thing this whole disaster has taught me is that you and I are meant for one another," he said.

Eve fought to hold back sudden tears. "I am not so sure about the trust part. I have discovered you can love someone, but not trust them. It will take time for you to win back my faith in you. I want to know the real Freddie Rosemount and if he truly feels life's passion the way I do."

He went quiet. She watched with interest, having never seen this side of him before. It felt like she was seeing him for the very first time.

"If you give me a second chance, I will do all I can to win your trust. To have you offer up your love to me once more. Just tell me what I need to do," he replied.

She let out a long slow breath and met his gaze. "When the time comes you will know."

Chapter Thirty-Eight

F reddie's surprise over the sudden reappearance of Eve Saunders in his life was now accompanied by a sense of calm, and what he guessed must be the first stirrings of happiness.

He had forgotten how good it was to be with her, how unpredictable she could be when it took her fancy. He still couldn't believe she could be so daring as to come to his house unaccompanied, knowing he would be home alone. She was risking a great deal in doing so. Will had been right about his sister's lust for scandalous behavior.

After dragging a half-asleep Zeus down the stairs to the lower kitchen the next morning and jamming the door closed as best as he could, he threw on his overcoat and headed out the door.

The chilly morning wind had him quickly working on the buttons of his coat and pulling his hat down over his ears. He shivered as he turned the corner into New Bond Street on his way to Covent Gardens market.

The thirty-minute walk had become more than simply habit. He enjoyed strolling through the predawn streets of London. The weather in late October was still somewhat kind; how he would feel about making the trip in the dead of winter he didn't want to consider. With luck, his father would have restored him to favor by then and he would be able to take a hack, if not the family carriage.

He crossed St Martins Lane. Covent Garden was close. He darted down a small laneway, which connected through to Bedfordbury Street, and was busy with his own thoughts when he spied a woman standing on the corner of a small close. Her head was wrapped up against the chill of the morning with a dark green shawl.

The streets around the market were where the local prostitutes plied their trade. They were all looking to relieve the market traders of their coin.

Freddie had no inclination for using the woman's services. He had vegetables, meat, and fruit to procure.

As he passed her by, he gave a nod in her direction. It would be rude to completely ignore a person.

"Hello darlin'," she said.

"Morning," he replied, and kept going. He was a good half-dozen steps past her when he heard a loud huff.

"Freddie," she said.

He stopped mid-stride as his blood turned to ice. He swung round on his left foot and turned to face her.

The woman dropped the shawl from her head.

"Bloody hell," he exclaimed.

Standing before him, dressed in clothes he knew did not come from the salon of her mother's modiste, stood Eve.

She chuckled. "Nice to see I can still shock you," she said.

He looked around. She was alone. "Please tell me you have a lumbering and large footman concealed in one of those doorways."

She shook her head. "No, where would the fun be in that? I left the house alone. No one but you knows that I am here. I took a hack from Dover Street and got him to let me out at St Martins Lane. I couldn't risk bumping into Will in Newport Street—not that he is ever up and about this early."

She curled her finger and beckoned him over. As soon as he reached her side, she stepped forward and placed a hot kiss on his lips.

He was powerless to refuse. His mouth opened and his lips quickly responded to her. Their tongues tangled deep and hard. The depth of

Eve's hunger for him was etched in her kiss. His own unspoken need for her took hold and he pulled her hard against him.

Grabbing his hand, she placed it on the buttons of her coat. When he didn't begin to undo the buttons, she took on the task herself. The folds of her coat opened.

Encouraged by her actions, he slipped a hand inside her coat, gasping as his fingers touched warm naked flesh. His fingertips brushed over her hard nipples.

He pulled out of the kiss and stood for a moment, staring in disbelief, as she pulled the lapels of her coat open wide and revealed her breasts. His manhood twitched at the breathtaking vision. "What?"

A sly smile appeared on her lips. When she ran her tongue along her bottom lip he felt himself go hard. "You might be done with playing games, but I am just beginning. You asked how you could prove yourself. To win me back, you need to play the game of Eve. That is, of course, if you want to play. If not, I can go home and you will never see me again," she purred.

Freddie had sworn off games for the rest of his life, but this was something else—a powerful force pulling him back into a new connection with her. Saying no to Eve and her new game was impossible. "Alright, yes, I will play. But you need to lace up the front of your gown. You can't be in public like this. People will see," he replied.

Eve shook her head. "The only time my gown is getting laced up is when you and I are finished. I know how the local street ladies work. I've seen them out late at night enough times to know how this plays out. You need to prove to me you can still play dangerously."

He frowned, unsure of exactly what Eve meant by her words. Her intentions were made clear when he saw her begin to hoist up her skirt. He grabbed a hold of her hands. "Not here, Eve. Plenty of people use this as a thoroughfare to the market. Anyone could see us," he cautioned.

She leant forward and captured his lips once more. Her kiss showed she had no intention of taking no for an answer.

"Then you had better hurry up and get busy," she replied.

Realization finally dawned on him. Eve was not going to leave the dirty laneway until he had pleasured her.

His fingers closed about her right nipple and squeezed. She rewarded him with a soft gasp of delight.

His mind began to work fast. A quick grope of her breasts was never going to suffice. If he was to get through this particular challenge he would have to step up the tempo. "I will pleasure you, but you must conceal your face. If, on the off chance, someone who knows either of us passes through here, we cannot run the risk of you being seen. You will be utterly ruined," he said.

He wasn't going to mention he would likely be thrown in chains and sent on the first ship to the far-flung colonies if his father found out what he was about to do to the girl who he had so badly mistreated. The girl he had steadfastly refused to marry was the girl he was about to set his hands to in the middle of a grimy, London laneway.

There were few other things that could be more scandalous.

"Ruin me," she whispered.

Freddie bent down and took her nipple into his mouth. He suckled hard. Then, as he savored the sounds of her soft cries, he slid a hand up her skirt. His fingers touched the soft, delicate skin of the inside of her leg.

As his erection hardened further, he knew it would be impossible for him to shop at the market in such a highly aroused state. He would have to go home and attend to himself before going on to St John's to make the soup.

Eve's hands settled on his shoulders. She tightened her grip, silently urging him on.

When his fingers reached the top of her leg he looked up at her. There was still time to stop, to call off this moment of rash behavior, and let her skirts drop.

Her half-closed eyes and soft, heavy breathing told him otherwise. Eve was fully in the moment of passion. Gentleman or not, he knew she was desperate for him to give her sexual release.

He felt the soft curls at the entrance to her womanhood before he pushed a finger inside of her. He swallowed when his finger slipped into her slick, wet heat. She was more aroused than she had been in the stables that night, and she had been prepared to give him her all in that moment.

"Freddie," she murmured.

He began to stroke. Long, deep strokes which settled into a rhythm matched by Eve's labored breathing.

She was a passionate woman. He had always loved that about her. If he could win back her heart and get her inside a church, he knew he would have a minx in his bed for the rest of his life.

"Harder, deeper," she pleaded.

He felt her muscles begin to tighten. She was close to climax. Pulling his finger from her heat, he quickly replaced it with his thumb.

Eve gasped and her grip on his shoulders became tight. She was close. He just needed to push her over the edge. He rolled his thumb over the nib of her clitoris and she whimpered.

He slid a finger into her as his thumb continued to massage her sensitive nib.

"Come for me," he commanded. A satisfied smile found its way to his lips as she cried out at her release. The pulsating spasm of the muscles in her core gave him the satisfaction of having done the job right.

Her grip on his shoulders loosened. "Thank you," she whispered.

Her words were all the reward he needed. He withdrew his hand and let her skirts fall. As he did, she mewled. He frowned. Had he not just given her a deep pleasuring? His pride wouldn't stand for a woman to think him not capable of meeting her sexual needs.

"What's wrong?" he carefully ventured.

"What about you?" she replied.

She began to lift her skirts once more. Freddie caught sight of her knees and then the white of her thighs. If Eve kept going he knew he would get a glimpse of the Promised Land.

He shook his head, grateful that at least his brain was trying to keep control of the situation. He reached out and took a hold of her skirts. They wrestled over the layers of fabric.

"You are playing safe again, Freddie. I don't want to play safe. I want you inside me," she said.

The struggle over her skirts and his rock-hard arousal was bad enough, but her demand for him to ruin her was a step beyond. "I am not deflowering you against a brick wall. Your first time should at least be in a private place. Your first time should be memorable," he ground out.

She huffed in disgust, leaving him to wonder how many other men would be arguing the point rather than taking what was being so openly offered. "But if you fuck me hard against this wall, I assure you I shall remember every second of it," she replied.

He was stunned for a moment. He had never heard such language from a woman of his social class before, let alone a young, unmarried miss such as Eve. He was shocked she even knew such a word. "No."

He heard the sound of boots on stone and turned to see a group of young men appear in the laneway. As they passed by Freddie and Eve, they exchanged knowing grins.

"Good luck to you, sir," said one of them.

Freddie and Eve watched as the group disappeared around the corner at the end of the laneway. Turning to Eve, Freddie was about to mention they were still in a public place, but the look on her face stopped him in his tracks.

"If you won't take me here, then let me attend to you. I am supposed to be a lady with skills of a particular nature. Let me practice them," she said.

His hard arousal twitched its single-minded approval.

She stepped forward and took hold of Freddie's coat, pulling him toward her. She placed an enticing kiss on his mouth and he was powerless to stop her. The kiss quickly escalated into a fiery, passionate encounter.

"I want you against the wall, now," she commanded, when they finally let go of the kiss.

He was losing the battle of wills. When Eve took a hold of the placket of his trousers and loosened the first button, he made only a half attempt to stop her.

"Good boy. Let me do my work. If you don't then I shall scream, and that will bring people running. You wouldn't want that now, would you, Freddie?" she asked.

With his back against the brick wall, Freddie watched in disbelief as

Eve went to her knees before him. When the last button of his trousers was open, she pulled back the fabric and released his manhood.

She took hold of his hard, swollen shaft and wrapped her fingers around it. The last sensible thing he was able to do before he was lost in passion was to pull her shawl farther over her head. Any passers-by would know exactly what she was doing; he could only pray they didn't see her face. "Now let me remember how you like to be serviced."

Freddie placed his hand gently on her head and closed his eyes. "I am sure whatever you do, will be ... *oh* ... sweet heaven, Eve."

Her lips closed over the tip of his cock and his heart stopped. Her mouth was a hot, wet Eden of pleasure.

With a hand placed either side of his hips, she soon settled into a long rhythm of inflicting tortuous pleasure upon him. Slowly in, slowly out.

When a second group of market workers walked into the laneway, Eve did not falter at her work. She was a fast learner. Soon she was taking him deep into her mouth, her lips forming hard ridges which his manhood rubbed against.

Freddie ignored the snorts and soft chuckles of the men as they passed by. He was too deep in mindless pleasure to even open his eyes. He was completely at her mercy.

She built up the tempo. His breath grew shorter and more labored. His fingers speared into her hair. The shawl covering her face fell back, but he was powerless to do anything. The fingertips of his other hand were dug into the cracks of the brick wall, desperately seeking purchase.

The thought he should stop her before he came flashed for an instant in his mind, but it was too late. With a rush that had him stuffing his fist in his mouth to stifle a roar, he came in her mouth. He slowly stroked her hair as he came back to earth.

To his satisfaction, Eve continued to tenderly minister to him. She sucked the last of him before releasing him from her care. Sitting back on her haunches, a soft smile crossed her lips.

He adjusted his clothing and buttoned up his trousers, then reached down and pulled Eve to her feet. Their lips met once more.

"Thank you," he said.

She laughed softly. "I'm not sure how much to charge you but knowing your circumstances, I don't expect you could pay it anyway."

Freddie chuckled and pulled her into his embrace. As his arms wrapped around her, he sent a silent prayer to the heavens that she was the more stubborn of the pair of them. By rights, he should have sent Eve home in a carriage the moment he saw her. But being Eve, she had made certain he delivered on her wish to have a heated sexual encounter in a public place.

He would never forget this moment as long as he lived.

Eve stole back into her family home a short while later. She hurried up the stairs and into her bedroom, locking the door behind her.

She had done it. Freddie was now the other player in a sexy new game of her making. They were playing by her rules, and if Freddie kept to them, they would both be victors.

She had kept some of the Bachelor Board rules. Activities were to be in public wherever possible. It was disappointing that Freddie hadn't taken her virginity in the laneway, but she was prepared to give herself game points for improvisation, and the knowledge she had brought him to climax with her lips.

The look on his face when she had demanded he deflower her there and then was priceless. So was the look when he pulled her to her feet after she had pleasured him.

She had no idea such things were possible, but a recent afternoon of illicit reading of the Karma Sutra, courtesy of the India-born Marchioness of Brooke, had opened her eyes to a whole new world of possibilities. Alex's wife, Millie, was slowly but surely educating all the unwed women of the Duke of Strathmore's family in how they should seduce their intended husbands.

She was going to marry him, but first, he had to prove to her he was more than the bookish young man his mother had claimed. An intelligent and educated husband was desirable, but with those traits also had to come fire and passion. Their union could never be allowed to become dull and comfortable.

When her maid knocked on her door an hour or so later, she was surprised to find Eve awake and partly dressed, seated at her writing desk. The working-class clothes Eve had worn on her secret mission were well hidden in the back of her wardrobe. If the game continued, she intended to use them again.

She closed the pages of her diary and locked it in her writing desk drawer. The plans for the next part of the game were written within its pages.

Chapter Thirty-Nine

As soon as Zeus began to bark late in the evening, Freddie knew who was about to knock on the kitchen door. The only thing he found slightly odd was that Eve had waited for almost a week after their encounter in the laneway to finally pay him a visit.

He opened the door and pulled her roughly to him, kicking the door closed behind them. "You took your time," he said, before kissing her hard.

Eve reached out and pulled on the fabric of Freddie's linen shirt. He came closer and wrapped his arms about her waist. She fitted to him like a glove. "I told you I was setting the rules of the game," she purred.

He went hard. He prayed she still wanted him. If she did, he would not refuse her. "Can I assume you are not here to sample the pasties?" he replied.

She placed a hand on his chest, over his heart. How he could ever have been such a fool to willingly break her heart he would never understand. She was worth all the riches in the land.

"I am here because I am certain I shall go mad unless you strip me naked and claim me with your body. I need you to take all I have to offer, and then demand more. When you are done with making me yours, I need you to do it again. Only then will I know you are truly mine."

෫

Eve had practiced her speech all the way over from Dover Street. Standing in front of Freddie, she prayed it was enough. To finally have him claim her as his woman.

"As long as you understand once I have made you mine, there is no going back," he replied.

She let a long sigh escape her lips. Her blood was heated and pumping hard through her body. Tonight, she would burn all the bridges behind her. There was only one path that lay before her now— a life with him. "Take me."

"Wait here," he replied.

Releasing her from his embrace, Freddie opened the door which led to the upper floors and walked out of the kitchen. Zeus followed.

A moment later, he returned without the dog.

"Zeus normally sleeps on the end of my bed. You and I shall stay in the warmth down here. I don't normally heat my bedroom; firewood is too expensive and we need warmth for what we are about to do."

He dragged the kitchen table across the floor and placed it in front of the door. Zeus would not be returning tonight. "I told you your first time should be in private. After that we can negotiate new rules to the game. Now come here."

He held out his hand, and Eve went to him. Nimble fingers quickly had the buttons of her cloak undone. He laid it over a chair.

When he went to untie the ribbons on her gown, she stopped him. It was time for her to take back control.

"Sit," she said, pointing to the bench next to the table.

Freddie did as instructed.

She licked her lips. She had been rehearsing this moment all afternoon in the privacy of her bedroom. Slowly, she worked at the top of her gown, opening it and revealing her breasts to him. An appreciative sigh escaped his lips.

She kicked off her slippers and slid her stockings from her legs.

When she looked up, she was greeted with the vision of Freddie's hungry gaze.

Perfect.

She approached him.

"Take it off. Strip me," she commanded him.

Eager hands grabbed hold of her gown and pulled it over her head. "Oh, Eve."

Her plans had been to lean down at this point and kiss him, but Freddie had other ideas. Standing, he lifted her and spun her around.

She found herself lying naked on her back on the table, Freddie leaning over her.

"I have never stopped thinking about you. I dream of you every night. Heated dreams of what should have happened between us long ago. Of what I am going to do to you tonight." He pushed her legs apart and set his lips to her heated flesh. When she buckled as his tongue touched her clitoris he pushed a hand down on her hips, holding her in place.

"You will suffer my torture until you scream," he murmured.

Her eyes opened and she stared up at the ceiling as he slaved at her with his tongue. On and on his tongue worked over her. Every ounce of her strength went into trying to control her response, a whimper the only thing she could manage. She was utterly at his mercy.

Her orgasm slowly built. She was completely under Freddie's masterful control.

He pulled away. With hungry fascination, she watched as he rid himself of his shirt and trousers. He lifted her from the table onto her feet and pulled her into his naked embrace. She reached down and took a hold of his engorged manhood, slowly stroking him.

"You said you wanted your first time to be memorable," he said.

"Yes," she whispered.

He turned her and laid her over the table. She held her breath as he pushed her legs apart. The tip of his cock parted her wet, slick folds, and she felt him enter her.

A small burning sensation which quickly passed, confirmed she was no longer an innocent.

"Are you alright?" he asked.

She nodded.

He slowly began to push deeper into her body, long slow strokes in and out. She sobbed as his hands reached around and took hold of her nipples. He gripped them hard.

She closed her eyes and let the rhythm of his strokes take over her mind. Her orgasm began to build once more. When he tweaked her hardened nipples, she whimpered softly. He groaned with pleasure as he thrust harder into her.

"Freddie," she moaned.

"Freddie what?" he growled.

"Harder, please, Freddie. I need you to take me harder."

His hands released her breasts and settled on the sides of her hips. The tempo of his strokes increased. He thrust deeper and harder.

He pulled her away from the table and slipped his hand around Eve's hip. As his fingers found her sensitive nub, he continued to pound into her willing body.

When a wave of blinding pleasure finally crashed over her, she was left breathless in its wake.

Freddie slowed his strokes.

"Good girl, now you are ready for me," he said.

Moving her forward, he lay Eve over the table once more. A firm hand pushed Eve down onto the table, her breasts flat against its surface. The tempo of his strokes began to build again.

As her mind cleared from the haze of her sexual release, she enjoyed the primal sensation of him pounding deep into her. His gruff groans of pleasure getting louder and louder, until he finally let out a howl and collapsed over her.

"Oh Eve, I love you," he murmured.

When the heat of their encounter began to cool, Freddie pulled Eve into his arms. He kissed her tenderly and held her close. Their naked bodies touching. "Now that is why I didn't take you against the wall in the laneway. I wanted to be the only one to hear you come as I made you mine," he said.

She wrapped her arms around him. Her first time had been better than she could have ever imagined. She was sexually sated, but best of all, he was finally hers.

"I love you Freddie," she said.

෪

"You really do make decent scrambled eggs," said Eve.

Freddie smiled. Aside from his pastries, he had also mastered a number of recipes with eggs.

"My culinary skills are coming along nicely. I'm considering opening a bakery and employing a baker who can take on some of the young men from the church as apprentices. Will has offered to help me get started," he said.

Eve held out her hand to him. "I could come and work for you. You know how easy I am to get along with," replied Eve.

He raised an eyebrow. Eve was many things, but easy was not one of them. He was too busy counting his lucky stars to quibble with her.

Their first time together had been exactly how he had hoped it would be. Eve had relaxed into the sexual act, making his taking of her virginity an easy and simple matter. Hearing her come to climax as he thrust into her willing body was truly a gift he had been humbled to receive.

The grandfather clock upstairs struck the hour of two.

"I had better get you home. It won't do for your maid to be wondering why she cannot rouse you in the morning," he said.

Knowing Eve, she would gladly sleep beside him in his bed, but after all he had done, he was not foolish enough to tempt the wrath of her parents.

The fact they would wed was no longer in doubt; it was the manner of how they went about it that held his mind. He had been to enough weddings in his lifetime to know society would expect a formal church service, followed by a wedding breakfast and a glittering ball. After all, he had put their families through, his mother and Adelaide Saunders deserved nothing less.

"Or you could have me a second time," she said. Her hand settled on his thigh. He gently removed her hand from his leg.

"I think you have had enough of me for your first night. You will be sore in the morning," he said.

She mewled with disappointment and Freddie laughed.

"So, can I come and visit you again tomorrow night? We could discuss your new business proposal a little more. My dowry could be put to good use in securing a suitable shop for your bakery," she said.

"I am working late at the church tomorrow. After we have served supper, Will and I are going to move some new large tables into the middle of the church. Reverend Brown is happy for the parishioners to sit at tables during the services, which will mean we can get more people fed when the soup kitchen is open. I won't be home until very late."

She frowned at him. "I can slip in here early and wait for you. Even if we get caught, there is nothing anyone can do about it. I'm already yours. Though you seem a little unsure. Why?"

While Eve was under the impression she had the run of the situation, Freddie knew he had to take command. He had to take effective control of their relationship and future without her realizing it.

Eve's taste for danger could pose a real threat to them and their combined future. The *ton* would only forgive so much. She had to learn there were boundaries that could not be crossed. They would need the support of their families and friends to make their future together a success. He would have to gamble on her love for him one last time. Then she would know that he truly loved her.

A lie formed in his mind; pulling her into it was a risk he would have to take.

"Osmont Firebrace has gone missing. The authorities are keeping quiet about his disappearance, as they think he may have been tipped off. If that is the case, then he may also know I had a hand in his downfall. I don't want you alone in this house without my protection," he said.

She huffed with frustration. "He couldn't be that foolish as to try something. He must know people are looking for him."

"Yes, well, you never know. He knows there are no servants here, and I am alone at night. If I finish early on Thursday, I shall send word to you. But until all of the Bachelor Board members have been arrested, you have to promise me you will be careful. I don't want you in this house alone. I don't want you put in danger."

"So, Thursday it is," she replied.

"Did you hear what I just said?"

She moved to sit on his lap. He sucked in air, trying to keep his erection from getting the better of the situation. Her lips came to within an inch of his.

"Yes, I heard you. Now tell me you love me, kiss me, and take me home."

He slipped a hand around her head and drew her to him. "I love you."

Chapter Forty

Freddie arrived home late as usual the following night. As he entered through the rear garden, the sight that greeted him had him swearing in frustration. Eve had ignored his instructions.

"Bloody woman. How am I supposed to protect you?" he muttered.

The golden glow of flames from the fireplace could be seen through the upper windows of the kitchen. Eve had arrived early and built up the fire awaiting his return. He opened the door, words of rebuke ready on his lips.

"I thought we agreed you would wait until I sent word on Thursday," he said.

"And a warm hello to you too," came the sardonic reply.

He turned to see Thomas seated at the kitchen table. By his feet lay Zeus, fast asleep. Freddie scowled. He had never managed to get Zeus to sit quietly for him.

The smile on his brother's lips made Freddie immediately forgive Thomas yet another first.

"Ah, brother mine. I was wondering when you would make it home. I have been keeping your pup company for several hours. Still keeping late hours at the soup kitchen?" asked Thomas.

"You know about St John's?" replied Freddie.

Thomas handed him a letter. It bore the mark of the Duke of Strathmore. "This arrived late last week at home. It tells of your good charitable deeds, among other news."

Freddie hesitated. "What other news?"

Thomas rose from the table and pulled his brother into a heartfelt embrace. "The letter said enough for me to be able to put two and two together. I cannot begin to tell you how terrible I felt when I heard you had got mixed up with the Bachelor Board. I should have warned you about them. I failed you. I am relieved beyond words that you did better than I in escaping from their vile sexual abuse," said Thomas.

Freddie pulled out of his brother's hug and stared at Thomas. Thomas was tall and strong; it would take a lot to bring him down.

Thomas nodded at the unspoken question. "I wasn't always a big lad. There were members of the Bachelor Board in residence at Oxford. I needed some extra tutelage to pass a particularly hard exam in my final year. One of the professors offered to help me. I went to his study night after night to work with him. The night after I had sat the exam, he asked me to share a celebratory drink with him in his private chambers. I, being a naïve fool, trusted him. The next thing I knew I was lying semi-naked on a couch and he was climbing off me."

Freddie began to shake, and he feared he would be sick. "I don't know what to say. I had no idea," he stammered.

"I have never told a soul until this night. Not even Cecily knows. I love my wife and I couldn't bear to have her see me as anything but a strong and capable man. It took me a long time to understand rape is not so much about sex. It is about power and control."

Freddie had a sudden vision of his brother being alone and scared. It had been hard enough for him to confess his own narrow escape; he doubted he could have told anyone if the drugs had rendered him unconscious and he too had become another victim. Staring at his brother, he finally understood the true power that the Bachelor Board held. It wasn't money or influence; it was silence.

"I have been in London for the past few days, staying at Mivart's Hotel. Father read the duke's letter but he still doesn't quite understand exactly what it means. I don't plan to tell him the worst of it— that is your business. Though, from the rumors swirling around the city, it won't be long before he does comprehend, and you may be forced to have a difficult private conversation with him," said Thomas.

The first public arrests of members of the board had been made late the previous day. While Freddie and Eve had been together at Rosemount House, the authorities had raided more than a dozen homes in the central London area. The military had been dispatched to a number of country estates. The downfall of a dangerous secret society had begun.

Zeus stirred from under the table and lumbered out into the kitchen proper. He settled into a long stretch of his limbs before loping over to where Freddie stood. His master gave him a playful scratch behind the ear. "Good boy, Zeus."

"Glad to hear you changed that poor animal's name. I take it the foolish moniker you gave him was part of the game," said Thomas. He reached into his pocket and pulled out a set of keys, then handed them to Freddie. "It might be a little late in giving these to you, I see from the damage upstairs you have not been able to keep that beast from the rest of the house. Father will have to take responsibility for that oversight. Though you might want to have repairs made before he and Mama next venture to town, you are still not exactly popular at home."

Freddie gave a weak smile. He had a matter of a handful of coins in his possession. The only way his mother's cushions were going to be repaired would be if he took up needle and thread himself. His domestic skills started and ended with food.

"Be a good lad and make me a coffee, and then come and tell me what else has been happening in your life, Frederick."

Freddie snorted with laughter. Thomas had an uncanny ability to take on their father's voice and mannerisms. "Yes, Papa." He chuckled.

Over a cup of hot coffee and some of Freddie's pasties, the brothers settled down at the table.

"I am hoping you will be pleased to hear Eve and I have become reacquainted. She understands all of what happened with the Bachelor Board, including the incident with the drugged wine," said Freddie.

Thomas raised an eyebrow. Sexual assault of men was not something most women were even aware of in London high society. Especially not unwed, young women.

"If she was ever going to consider forgiving me and taking me back, I had to tell her everything. She is the one who suggested I go to William Saunders about Osmont Firebrace. That is when I discovered the Bachelor Board posed a threat to the crown."

"And will Eve, have you?" asked Thomas.

A flutter of happiness rippled through Freddie's stomach. For all his foolish and selfish endeavors, against all hope, Eve had taken him back. But nothing was certain as yet. He still had to prove himself worthy. To show her he was the man who deserved her love.

"We are still negotiating how we move forward as a couple, but yes, we have a future together," he said.

Thomas sat back, chewing on his pasty. He smiled at Freddie, pride in his eyes.

"These are good. You could always consider opening a small chain of bakeries. I'm sure Papa could help to get you started with money. Something to consider now you are about to get married."

"A chain of bakeries?" replied Freddie. His initial plans had been for a single shop. His brother now had him rethinking his goals. Thomas dusted off his hands. "Well, I had better be off. I have a late dinner appointment with friends, then in the morning, I have to buy a few things for Cecily before I leave for home. One must never disappoint one's bride."

Freddie noted the subtle hint.

The brothers embraced once more. Freddie sighed with relief. It was good to be with Thomas again, to know there was a way back to being a part of the Rosemount family. His parents might be some way still from forgiving him, but he could trust Thomas to help clear the path.

After Thomas left, Freddie went back into the warmth of the kitchen. Zeus sniffed at his feet, then gave a less-than-subtle push against Freddie's leg.

"Alright, boy. I haven't forgotten your suppertime," he said.

He went to the high cupboard where he kept the dog bones out of dog-reach, and as he opened the cupboard he found a small, leather wallet sitting at the front of the shelf. He picked it up. Under it was a folded piece of paper. He stared at the wallet, which he held in one hand, and the note, which he held in the other.

He opened the note first.

> *I was handed this as I left the abbey. Father is still angry with you, but after he received the letter from the Duke of Strathmore he decided it was important to ensure you are not left exposed and without means of financial support. You have been punished enough. You will be relieved to know that the servants will return to the house by the end of the week.*
>
> *Mama's favourite cushions have been sent to the menders and should be back to you by early next week. I trust you to keep them from the dog in the future. Be a good lad.*
>
> *Thomas*

Freddie's heart began to race as he looked at the wallet.

"Please let there be enough for a bag of coffee beans. Please," he prayed.

As soon as he opened the wallet, he knew his family were on their way to forgiving him. There was enough money to buy a dozen bags of coffee beans. There was also enough to buy a new pair of boots, a hat, and a deposit on a good horse. He punched the air with delight. He would be able to afford a decent hot meal that he didn't have to cook from scratch.

With the household servants returning in a matter of days, he would have to press ahead quickly with his other plans. The first of which involved making a private appointment to see Charles Saunders.

Chapter Forty-One

"There are going to be some very difficult conversations in the House of Commons over this scandal. The prime minister is threatening to call a general election if the two members of the house named so far do not stand down."

Eve was seated at the breakfast table next to Caroline while their father held up that morning's copy of *The Times* and showed it to the rest of his family. Across the front page was an article detailing the names of the members of the Bachelor Board who had thus far been charged with treason. Five men were currently being held in the Tower of London. Osmont Firebrace was not among their number.

"Yes, from what Hattie tells me, Will has been working late most nights with the prosecution helping with putting the evidence together. She says she has barely seen him for the past week," replied Adelaide.

"Absolutely appalling. *The Times* says the prosecution will have enough evidence to see all of them hang," added Charles.

Eve took a bite of her toast. The press was mainly concerned with the charges of treason, but she knew enough from Freddie that the corrupting influence of the Bachelor Board had gone far deeper into English society. Lives of young men had been ruined. Futures had been corrupted because of the secrets the board held over its members. Once a man joined the Bachelor Board, his life was bound tight by its rules.

Freddie had so narrowly avoided the same fate.

"Oh, and Freddie's name has now made the papers. It was to be expected. Have you spoken to him of late?" continued Charles.

Eve put down her toast as her appetite evaporated. Wherever he was, Osmont Firebrace would now know Freddie had played a part in his downfall. "I saw him at St John's last week," she replied.

Her parents would find out soon enough that matters between her and Freddie had moved to a point where marriage would naturally follow. But in the meantime, she would continue to indulge in the thrill of stealing out of the house late at night to secretly visit him. The danger of being caught added to the heady pleasure of being a sexually active unmarried woman.

In her reticule was the note she had received late the previous day from Freddie, informing her that his role as a witness for the crown prosecution was about to be made public. She was anxious to see him as soon as possible.

"So, what do you two young ladies have planned for the day?" asked Adelaide.

"Hatchards have a new book of poems by Shelley in stock this week. It includes his latest work, *A Hymn to Intellectual Beauty*. Eve and I are going to buy a copy. After that, I expect we shall find a nice cake shop and stuff our faces while we read our new book," replied Caroline.

She and Eve had been writing their own humorous version of the poem and were keen to see how badly they had insulted the famed poet's work. Adelaide picked up her cup of coffee and smiled as she took a sip.

"Yes, well next time you girls are finished writing your naughty poetry you might want to make sure you put them away. We found them in the sitting room last night. After having read your efforts, I think we can safely say Mr. Shelley would not be amused."

Charles Saunders chuckled from behind his newspaper.

Eve and Caroline both finished their breakfast and shortly after ten o'clock climbed into the family carriage in the rear courtyard of their home. As the carriage turned out of sight into Piccadilly, Freddie Rosemount arrived in a hack at the front door of Dover Street.

Chapter Forty-Two

E ve was hungry when she returned home from a long afternoon of shopping with Caroline, but her need was not for food. Having given herself to Freddie, the hunger to lay with him again burned constant.

It was Thursday, and the evensong usually ran late. Freddie wouldn't be home until close to midnight. He hadn't sent word, but she couldn't deny her need for him any longer.

She would visit him and discuss plans to move their relationship to a more socially acceptable state. Her thoughts ran to the obvious conclusion that once Viscount Rosemount discovered Freddie had openly declared himself as being her future husband, he would restore his son to favor and funds. She would let Freddie govern when he felt the time was right for him to inform their parents of the impending wedding.

She spent a pleasant evening with Caroline and Adelaide discussing family plans for Christmas at Strathmore Castle in Scotland. With the three oldest Radley cousins all recently married, the castle would be even more full of noise and merriment than it had been in previous years.

A little after eleven, Eve bade her sister and mother good night and headed to her room.

She changed into a dark, woolen gown and waited until she heard the other members of the family turn in for bed. After throwing on a heavy cloak, she silently stole downstairs and out through the rear garden.

She hailed a hack around the corner in Old Bond Street and was soon on her way to Grosvenor Square. After searching through various flower pots, she found the key to the rear door of Rosemount House.

"So much for keeping your house safe from wicked men," she muttered.

Inside the kitchen, she lit a candle and made her way upstairs.

"Zeus," she called out.

The dog was nowhere to be seen.

"That's odd," she murmured. Freddie was sometimes able to keep Zeus bailed up in the kitchen, but most times the dog had the run of the house. The silence was eerie.

She shrugged it off. Perhaps Freddie had decided Zeus needed the exercise and had taken him to St John's for the day. She chuckled at the thought of the mess the giant Irish wolfhound would make of Hattie's soup kitchen.

The clock in the downstairs hall chimed half past the hour of eleven. Taking the tinderbox and some of the kindling from the kitchen, she hurried upstairs to Freddie's bedroom. If she lit the fire now, it would take the chill off the room before he arrived home. Tonight, she intended to share his bed.

She placed a handful of coins on the top of the mantelpiece. "There. That should cover the cost of the wood," she said.

Taking the tinderbox, she struck at it a couple of times before succeeding in getting a spark. The dry kindling in the fireplace caught alight and soon a fire had taken hold. She shifted a few small logs into place and sat back on her haunches, watching with satisfied pride as the fire began to build.

She had just put the tinderbox back on the shelf when she heard noises downstairs. With a smile on her lips, she headed to the bedroom door. Freddie's early arrival home meant they would have more time together. Stepping out onto the landing, she heard unfamiliar voices.

"Where did you say he kept the gold?"

"I don't bloody know. Anyway, we didn't come here for that; we came for young Rosemount. He is about to get a nasty lesson in not crossing powerful people," replied a second man.

Eve stilled. Her heart began to thump loudly in her chest. She hadn't taken Freddie's warnings about not being in the house alone seriously. No one knew she was there; no one could help her. *Think, Eve, think.*

She crept back into Freddie's bedroom and softly closed the door. "Oh no," she whispered, noting the lack of a key in the lock.

She had just decided his bedroom might not be the best place to hide after all when she heard the sound of heavy boots on the stairs. Her heart was racing, her mouth dry. Fear of the strangers and what they would do if they discovered her, had Eve trembling.

What am I to do?

Voices outside the bedroom door told her she had little time. Racing across the floor, she grabbed her cloak, and dropped to her knees. She slid under the bed and did her best to throw the cloak over her head.

As the door opened, she silently rued the fact she had managed to light the fire.

"Looks like someone is at home. Nice of them to have lit the fire for us. Pity we won't be here long enough to enjoy the comforts of home."

The other intruder gave a guttural laugh.

Eve lay under the bed and listened as the intruders went through all the cupboards. Drawers and clothes were tossed about onto the floor.

Her hands began to shake uncontrollably and her bottom lip quivered. If those men had been sent by the Bachelor Board she would be in grave danger if they discovered her.

The men left the room but stood outside in the hallway. Eve prayed they would leave the house. She had to escape and warn Freddie.

There was silence for a short time. All she could hear was the sound of her heart beating loudly in her ears.

The fabric on the edge of her cloak was roughly pulled away and right in front of her appeared an ugly grinning face.

"'Ello darlin'. Didn't think we'd find you, did ya?" the man said.

Eve tried to move to the other side, but the second man was there waiting for her. He grabbed hold of her skirts and dragged her from under the bed.

"Stand up," he ordered.

Eve got to her feet. She was about to make a grand statement about her uncle being the Duke of Strathmore, and her other uncle being the Bishop of London, but the shiny blade in the intruder's hand put paid to that notion.

He looked her up and down. As he did, his companion came around to the same side of the bed.

"I know her. She is Freddie's fancy woman. I reckon if we take her, he will come out of hiding. We won't have to go looking for him."

"I don't know who you are, but my family has money. I am certain whatever your employer is paying you, my father will double it to see me safely returned home," she said. Her father had always taught her money spoke a language everyone understood. All men could be bought—you just needed to establish the right price.

The two intruders exchanged a knowing look.

"Sorry, love. There is nothing your family could give us that would make us betray our masters. After you and your sweetheart's sudden disappearance, other people will think twice about testifying against members of the board and the crown's case will collapse. We will be rewarded with a king's ransom of jewels and all the whores we can use." He reached out and took a rough hold of Eve. From out of his jacket pocket he pulled a length of rope.

Eve screamed.

A hand came over her mouth. The soft cotton of a handkerchief soaked in ether pressed against her face. She held her breath for as long as she could, but it was no use. Her knees buckled from under her. She silently screamed as the ether took her under and rendered her unconscious.

Chapter Forty-Three

E ve awoke to find herself lying bound on the floor of a moving carriage. Her hands were tied in front of her and her legs were secured tightly together.

The effects of the drug took a little while to wear off, and she passed out several times more. When her head finally cleared and she was able to remain conscious, she remembered the events of the previous night.

She had been kidnapped.

The jolting of the carriage made it impossible for her sit up. After several attempts to gain purchase on the floor, she lay down, sobbing in desperation and fear.

"Oh, Freddie, I am so sorry. I should have listened to you. Now I am going to get us both killed," she muttered.

She struggled in vain against the ties that bound her hands. They had been expertly applied. No matter how hard she tried to pull her hands free from the bindings she couldn't make headway.

Her feet were a slightly better option. She managed to loosen the rope around her left ankle. She was close to getting the rope to move down her foot when the carriage began to slow.

It moved to one side of the road and came to halt. She listened to the jingle of the reins, bridle, and bit as the driver settled the horses. A sharp whistle rang out, followed by the sound of several pairs of boots on loose stone.

The door of the carriage opened.

She squinted in the bright morning light, catching a glimpse of brown, curly hair before a sack was thrown over her head. Strong, but surprisingly gentle, arms pulled her from the carriage and helped her find her feet.

"Time to attend to your needs. You have five minutes, so make it fast," spoke a gruff voice.

She recognized the voice as belonging to one of the men who had taken her from Rosemount House during the night.

"Take my arm."

"I can't see, and I can't really hold onto you. My hands are tied," she replied.

The man swore. Then took hold of her hands and removed the ties around her wrists. Eve rubbed them, glad to be free of the tight bindings.

She was sorely tempted to lift the sack, but a rough slap on her back gave her pause. The sack was made of heavy cloth, and it effectively cut out all but a tiny amount of light. Eve was blind.

"Hold my arm tight then, and don't try anything clever. I've had no sleep and I'm not in the mood for any games," he said.

He guided her from the roadside and she felt the soft spongy texture of grass beneath her feet. When they had gone a short way, he stopped.

With both hands on her shoulders, the kidnapper stood behind her. "Now, this is how it's going to work. I take the sack off so you can do your business. You keep your back to me. If you try to turn around things will go badly for you," he said.

He pulled the sack from Eve's head and she stood blinking in the bright sunlight. Without thinking, she began to turn, but the sound of a pistol being cocked stopped her. Neither of her kidnappers had done anything to harm her up to this point, but until she understood a little more of their plans, she would be foolish to risk incurring their wrath.

She turned her back fully to him. It was not the privacy she was used to when it came to her toilette, but with a full bladder she had little option. Lifting her skirts, she squatted down and relieved herself on the grass.

When she was done, the sack was put back over her head and she was guided back to the carriage.

"Turn your hands over, palms upward."

A small bread roll and a piece of cheese were placed into her hands. With some difficulty she managed to get the food under the sack and to her mouth. Hunger stopped her from complaining about the pitiful size of her meal. A flask was pushed into her hand, and without a word she took it and drained it of the lukewarm tea inside.

"Thank you," she said, waving the empty flask out in front of her.

It was snatched from her hands.

"Please, you don't have to do this. I haven't seen your faces. You could just leave me here by the roadside," she pleaded.

There was no reply.

With her head covered by the sack, she was reliant upon her hearing to gather any further information about her kidnappers. A second pair of boots scraped on the roadside.

"Is she done?"

The good news was that they seemed to want her not only alive, but in good health. She knew that was a blessing not to take for granted. If they wanted her dead, she would not have made it out of Rosemount House alive.

The penny had dropped not long after she had first regained consciousness. She was being used as bait to get to their real target: Freddie.

What happened to him? Was he still alive, and if so, where was he? Did he even know what had happened to her? She rued her impetuous nature. It was morning, so her family would only now be discovering her disappearance. Even with Caroline telling them of Eve's secret visits to Rosemount House, they would have little to go on as to her actual whereabouts.

"Where are we going?" she asked.

A guttural laugh beside her was the only response. She was pushed against the side of the carriage and her hands were tied tightly once more. Rope was tied about her waist, holding the sack in place, but at least her feet were left free.

She heard the sound of the carriage door being opened once more and she was lifted inside and deposited without ceremony onto the long leather bench. She held her breath, hoping they were not going to tie her feet and make her lie on the floor once more.

The door was closed and she heard the sound of a key in the lock. There would be no sudden bolting from the carriage even if she managed to get her hands free.

The carriage pulled away from the roadside and continued on.

Eve sat back against the seat and tried to settle her worried mind. She took long, deep breaths. It would be easy enough to let her fears overcome her and give in to the tears, but she was determined to do everything in her power to survive. The one lesson Will had told her from his experience as a spy, was to keep a clear mind. She cursed herself for not having listened to his other advice about avoiding dangerous situations. If she ever saw him again, she would listen.

She came to the conclusion the best thing she could do was to comply with their commands. Soon enough, she would find out who was behind her abduction and no doubt what plans they had for her. Only then could she attempt to do something about trying to escape.

Later that afternoon, the carriage pulled over once more and she went through the same routine with the kidnappers. When night fell, she curled up as best she could on the carriage bench and snatched a few hours of fitful sleep.

On the second morning of her ordeal, she was woken by the sensation of the carriage coming to a sudden halt. There came loud shouting. She froze with fear as the sound of a pistol shot rang out.

"I've been shot. I'm done for, oh god!" came the cry of one of her kidnappers.

Eve began to sob. Whomever else was outside on the road meant business.

"Get down!" a familiar voice bellowed.

She pressed her ear to the side of the window and prayed her salvation was at hand.

The loud bang of a body being pushed against the outside of the carriage had her fearing the rescue attempt had gone awry. There was silence for a time. She put her ear tentatively to the window one more and listened.

A key was placed into the lock of the door, and fresh air hit her skin as the door opened. Hands worked at the ropes around her waist and the sack was pulled from her head.

"Oh, sweet Jesus," she whispered as she caught sight of her rescuer.

"No, just Freddie," he replied.

He made quick work of the bindings around her hands. The second her hands were free, she threw her arms around him and promptly burst into tears. He held her tight.

"Oh, Freddie. I've never been so frightened. I thought they had killed you, and they were going to shoot me in some lonely field and leave my body for the crows!"

Her imagination had had several days to come up with all manner of explanation as to what the kidnappers had had in mind for her. She had managed to keep the worst of her fears at bay until now, but no longer.

"It is alright. You are safe now. I found you," he said.

The wave of relief which washed over her made her feel light-headed. She lay her head against his shoulder and closed her eyes. She had barely slept for two days.

"What about the men?" she asked.

Freddie kissed her forehead. "One of them bolted as soon as I arrived. I did manage to get a pistol shot in his direction, I think I hit him. The other I gave a crack over the head," he replied. Taking Eve by the hand, he helped her to climb out of the carriage. She kept a tight hold of his arm as she swayed with giddiness once she was fully on her feet. There was no sign of the kidnappers.

"Either I didn't hit him hard enough or his accomplice came back for him," said Freddie.

Eve was too overcome with relief and sudden fatigue to discuss the merits of Freddie's rescue attempt. She was free from her bonds and safe with him. Nothing else mattered.

"Come on, let's get as far away from here as we can. Who is to say they don't have other accomplices who could come to their aid?" asked Freddie.

Eve squeezed his hand. Freddie led her over to his horse that was tethered to a nearby tree. He soon had both of them on the horse's back and riding away from the carriage.

As they rode, Eve let her head fall forward. With her arms wrapped around Freddie's waist she let more tears fall.

A few miles down the road, they came across a small farming village. In the middle of the village was a coaching inn. Freddie rode into the yard. A stable hand took the reins of Freddie's horse and they both dismounted.

"We shall stay here for tonight. I expect you could do with some sleep and to wash the dust from the road out of your hair," he said.

As they reached the door of the inn, Eve pulled back on Freddie's hand. She ushered him to one side. "I don't have any money. They took me from your bedroom. All I have is the clothes I am standing in.

I doubt that the innkeeper will extend us credit," she said.

Freddie smiled. He leant forward, and for a moment she thought he was going to kiss her. She wished desperately that he would. After all that she had endured, she ached for him to take her in his arms.

"I have money. Thomas came to see me in London the day before you disappeared. I am back somewhat in favor with my parents. I am flush again with funds. Fear not, my love. You shall eat within the hour and sleep in a proper bed with me tonight. I shall have word sent to your family."

The innkeeper was more than happy to accommodate the young wedded couple who arrived on his doorstep asking for a room. His son, a strapping big lad, brought a metal bath up to Eve and Freddie's room and soon had it filled with warm water. Eve looked longingly at the tub and the small bar of soap which sat on a nearby table. She couldn't wait to bathe.

After he was gone, Freddie took an exhausted Eve and stripped her naked. He helped her to stand in the bath and with a fresh cloth began to wash her. "Let me attend to your needs, my love. I have a particular gift for the lady's toilette," he said.

His hands tenderly washed the grime and fear from her body.

Butterfly kisses were trailed up the back of her leg and along the small of her back.

It was late autumn, but she shivered not from the cold. She was alive. She had never felt so much alive. Her hero had rescued her from an uncertain fate. And now she was standing before him while he tended to her needs. The only need he had not met was the slowly building sexual heat within her body. Every stroke of the washcloth sent tremors of expectation through her.

When she was clean, he helped her from the bath. He slowly began to dry her damp body. He wiped her face, then wrapped the towel around her, and pulled her to him. He held her face in his hands and their gazes met.

'I am sorry I didn't listen to you. I put us both in danger," she said.

"We will talk later. Just know that I would die before I let anything happen to you. You are my world," he said.

His lips descended upon hers in a fiery kiss that confirmed his words. No man would ever kiss her like Freddie did. She belonged to him. Only him.

He pulled her roughly against him. Through the thin towel she could feel the hardness of his erection.

Her fingers slipped down to touch the front of his trousers. She gave a gentle squeeze of his manhood, his appreciative groan telling her his mind and hers were as one.

He released her from the kiss and stepped back, taking the towel with him. "Let me finish attending to your needs, my lady."

The gruff edge to his voice matched the passion shining in his eyes. Freddie knelt before her and once more placed butterfly kisses on her body. When his tongue touched the outside of her mound, Eve gasped. His fingers gently opened her to him, and his tongue swept inside. Her breath shuddered as he speared into her with strong, deep strokes. Her hands rested on his head, his hair entangled in her fingers.

When he teased her to the point she now knew so well, Eve pushed him back onto his heels. "Your lady commands you take her to bed and show her how good you really are at serving her."

He needed no further instruction.

Chapter Forty-Four

The following morning, Eve and Freddie slept late. They made love a second time in the early hours before the dawn, after which Freddie wrapped his arms and legs around her and held her close.

A hearty breakfast of eggs, bacon, and kippers replenished the energy levels that Freddie's lustful attentions to her body had depleted. Eve sat with a cup of coffee in her hand and looked at him over the rim.

"So, what do you intend to do about the blackguards who kidnapped me? I am surprised you didn't ride to find the local militia once we got here," she asked.

Freddie looked up from his breakfast. "The nearest militia post is a good twenty miles away. I reasoned by the time I managed to get there, find someone who would listen to my story, and have them return with me, it would be too late. I am sure once we return to London, we shall gain a better understanding of who exactly had you kidnapped," he replied.

"So how was it that you found me?"

He put down his knife and fork and cleared his throat. Eve sensed something was off by the way he wouldn't meet her gaze. "They left a note," he finally replied.

She was about to question him further when the innkeeper arrived at their table.

"Begging your pardon, sir, but I have not been able to find a small carriage for your use. The only thing I have is a cart. If you wish to take that, you could change it over for something more suitable at the next major town," he said.

Freddie wiped his lips with his napkin and got to his feet. "Excuse me, my love, I must go and attend to the matter of our transport. If you would finish your breakfast and then gather anything you have in our room, I shall meet you out at the stables shortly."

He followed the innkeeper out the door, leaving Eve to ponder his sudden evasive manner.

She went back upstairs and made herself ready to leave. She wrapped her cloak around herself ready for the long journey home.

The inn was situated at the front of the yard, with the stables at the rear. As she stepped out, Eve saw the various carriages and travel coaches of the other guests who were staying at the inn. She was walking slowly toward the stables when she passed by a carriage that nearly made her heart stop.

It was a black carriage, like hundreds of others that travelled the roads of England, but it was the man who was seated up on the driver's seat which had her hastening her steps.

She rounded the corner and was relieved to see Freddie talking to the innkeeper. She kept her stride even as she walked, resisting the urge to run to him. Will had taught his siblings never to show when they had uncovered a secret—it gave too much power away.

The innkeeper's son was busy loading a small trunk into the back of the cart to which Freddie's horse had been harnessed. She ignored their odd mode of transport, her mind solely focused on her need to speak to Freddie.

To warn him.

As soon as she reached his side, she took a hold of his arm, and pulled him in close. "The men who took me are here! I saw the man who grabbed me at your house on top of a black carriage in the front yard," she said.

Freddie frowned. He looked to where the carriages were lined up in the front yard.

"Which one?"

She followed his gaze, then shook her head.

"It's the third or fourth as you go back around the corner. You can't see it from here. Thank god. It means they cannot see us."

He told a hold of the reins of the cart and spoke to his horse. He ran his fingers up and down its forehead. "I know it's a small cart and it is beneath you, but beggars cannot be choosers."

With a loud huff, Eve grabbed hold of Freddie's arm. He was taking the situation far too lightly for her liking. "What are you going to do about them? If the militia are as far away as you say they are, then what is to stop them from assailing us on the road and taking both of us captive?"

Her words seem to have the desired effect. Freddie stopped tending to his horse and turned to her. "This is what we are going to do. We are going to get in the cart. You are going to cover yourself with your cloak and we are going to pray to the heavens they don't get a good look at us," he replied.

Without further ado, Freddie put his hands around Eve's waist and lifted her into the passenger seat of the cart. He climbed up beside her and gave the whip a crack.

Eve put the hood of her cloak up and covered her head. As they passed by the row of carriages, she turned her head away from them. Freddie gave a crack of the small whip, and the horse picked up the pace.

He turned the horse's head to the north as soon as they cleared the inn. A mile or so outside the village, he turned to her. "You can take your hood off now. We are well out onto the road, you can relax" he said.

Eve threw back the hood and glared at him. When he refused to meet her gaze, she gave him a hard thump on the arm. "Relax, are you mad? What is to stop them from coming after us? I am sure that they

SASHA COTTMAN

must know who we are, and this cart is not exactly built for speed. What are we going to do?" she asked.

Freddie pulled the horse and cart over to the side of the road. He jumped down and tied the horse to a nearby tree.

A fuming Eve sat in the cart, arms folded.

He rounded to her side of the cart and put up his hands. She refused to take them. When he began to laugh, she wished she could beat him with her fists.

"They are not coming after us. I promise you that," he said.

"And how can you tell? Can you read the minds of evil men? What is to stop Osmont Firebrace from coming around that bend and shooting us both on sight?" she angrily replied.

"Because the men with the carriage are taking it back to London. I only hired them and the carriage for the week. Any longer and I shall lose my deposit on the carriage. The horse I rented for a few weeks longer." Freddie held her gaze. "Oh, and as for Osmont Firebrace, he was arrested long before anyone else, held along with several other men at a secret location outside of London. The rest of the members of the Bachelor Board assumed they fled the country and tried to follow. The men in the Tower of London were caught trying to seek passage onboard ships bound for Ireland."

A slow burning anger began to grow in Eve's brain as her mind processed what he had said.

"Now, would you like to come down from the cart so we can talk this out?" he said.

Eve clenched her fists, silently wishing she had a knife or a gun hidden somewhere in her skirts. She batted away his offered hand and jumped down from the cart.

As soon as her feet hit the ground, she spun round and landed a well-thrown punch in the middle of Freddie's chest. "You bastard! You bloody bastard! You had me kidnapped!" she roared. He had set the whole thing up.

She walked away, the roar of anger in her ears making her deaf to his words. For two days she had feared for her life, all the while desperate with worry as to what had happened to Freddie. Two days during which he had followed the carriage, until deciding on the opportune time to *rescue* her.

Freddie followed her. Once she reached a field of flat, green grass, she gathered pace.

"Stop. Stop."

She whirled round as he took a firm hold of her cloak. "How could you? How could you do that to me? Do you have any idea how frightened I was?" she bellowed.

The laughter was gone from his face. In its place was a hard seriousness she had never seen before.

"Yes, I know you were frightened. I told you not to come to the house, knowing full well you would ignore my words of caution. Why did I do it? I did it to make you understand."

"What? What do I need to understand?"

He sucked in a deep breath. "The whole time I have known you, you have been furiously pushing boundaries. You constantly chase the thrill of scandal and danger. You lust after it. I gave you exactly what you wanted. I took your virginity while you were bent over a kitchen table, which is as about as scandalous as it gets with an unwed woman of your social standing. Then I showed you real danger by having you kidnapped. I gave you exactly what you wanted, Eve," he replied. He let go of her cloak and did not follow her as she walked farther into the field.

Once far enough away from him, she sat down on the grass. The view back toward the cart was very much like the one on the road from Rosemount Abbey, where she had sat and raged over his cruel heartbreak. This time it was Freddie, not her mother, who was standing in the middle of the field wondering what an angry Eve would do next.

She pulled at a blade of grass and sat rolling it between her fingers. When Freddie moved closer and sat beside her, she ignored him.

It hurt to know he had caused her pain once more. That he had seen through her game of continually upping the ante with more and more scandalous behavior.

What hurt most of all was that he was right.

She had a taste for danger. Even now she was forced to accept the passion that had heated her blood the previous night with him, had been a result of having been abducted. In his arms she had exalted in the knowledge she had cheated certain death. Sex with him in their bed at the inn had been soul-changing.

"I hate you," she said.

"I hate you, too. I also hated lying to you, but I did it to make you see sense and stop blindly chasing danger. I don't regret it. You have to ask yourself, what if this hadn't been a fake kidnapping? You have to learn to trust that I am here to keep you safe, but in that you have a role to play."

She reached out and took a hold of his hand. It was a gentle hold, offering unspoken forgiveness. He had beaten her at her own game. It was time she conceded.

"Now what is to happen?" she asked.

If he had planned her kidnapping so well, then he would have other plans no doubt. She was still mad as hell at him, but true to nature, she was keen to know what else he had in mind.

He got to his feet and stood in front of her. Her heart began to thump in her chest as he went down on bended knee. "Evelyn Saunders, I love you. I want to spend the rest of my life with you. I want us to forge a life together being respectable members of society, while at the same time allowing us to privately indulge in all that sets our blood on fire. Will you do me the greatest honor, and agree to be my wife?"

She had to hand it to him. He had a gift for the unexpected. A marriage proposal in a field in the middle of nowhere was not something she had considered. It, of course, was scandalous. He had not asked her father's permission. They were not on any formal footing when it came to courting. They were well and truly outside the boundaries of acceptable behavior in the eyes of the *ton*.

It was perfect.

"Yes."

He reached inside his coat pocket and took out a small box. Sitting beside her, he took a hold of her hand and slipped a ring on her finger.

Eve clasped her hands together and stared at the ring. She had seen her mother wear it many times. It had once belonged to Marie Alexandre, Eve's French grandmother. Freddie could only have got it from one place. Her parents knew where she was and with whom. They had given their blessing.

"Oh, Freddie."

He put his arms around her and held her against him.

"You didn't think I would put your family through hell just to perform an elaborate proposal and elopement, did you?" he said.

Through the sheen of her tears she looked at the ring shining on her finger. Her grandmother had lost her husband during the French Revolution and she had braved a dangerous escape to safety in England.

"Your father thought this should come to you. His mother was a brave woman and while she faced dangers far greater than I hope you ever will, he thinks your heart is as bold as hers was," he said.

"I am humble and proud to be its new owner. If I could have ever chosen a ring for myself, it is this one. Thank you," she said.

Their lips met, sealing their agreement. The encounter soon became more heated and she felt Freddie's fingers begin to work on the lace of her gown.

"Here?" she murmured.

"Yes, here. I am going to make love to you in the middle of a field, and you are going to take me deep and beg for me to ride you hard. We know who we are, Eve, and nothing will change that," he replied.

His words had her biting down on her bottom lip with anticipation. When he kissed her neck, she knew she was powerless against his need to worship her body once more.

She looked up at the placement of the sun. He followed her gaze, then chuckled softly.

"I turned the horse to the north as we left the inn. Two days from now, we will cross the border into Scotland. What better way to seal a scandalous relationship than by getting married over the anvil at Gretna Green? You and I will be the cautionary tale of the season for all the good mothers to tell their daughters."

Eve slipped the knot on her cloak loose and let it fall behind her onto the grass. She lay down and greeted Freddie with a sultry smile as he rose over her. "Come to me, my lord. Show me how much mischief you can make."

The End

Epilogue

LONDON 1818

"Welcome to all our friends and family today. It's with great pleasure that we open the second of the Rosemount Bakery shops this morning."

Freddie smiled as a ripple of applause went through the gathered crowd.

"A year ago, who would have thought that an experiment in trying to provide gainful employment for the young members of the parish of St. John's would be such a resounding success. I am truly humbled by the support the people of London have given us."

"Could we please get on with the ribbon cutting ceremony, my back is killing me," chimed in Eve.

He chuckled.

"It would appear that my good lady wife would like to get the formalities over and done with."

He looked to where a heavily pregnant Eve was standing, holding a pair of scissors in her hand, and gave her a friendly wave. She beckoned him to join her.

Reaching her side, he gave her a bow.

"Let's get the ribbon cut, then you can put your feet up," he said.

Eve huffed.

"I haven't seen my feet for weeks, what I need is for this baby to hurry up and be born. Three weeks overdue is scandalous."

He took hold of her hand and their gazes met. Eve's eyes shone with love and happiness. "Well considering the scandalous behavior of its parents is that any surprise?" he said, and leant in to kiss her.

Sasha Cottman

Thank you for reading this book! I hope you enjoyed it as much as I did in writing it.

Sasha xxx

Join Sasha's mailing list to receive news of new releases, special give-aways and other exciting news at www.sashacottman.com.

For a full list of books by Sasha Cottman
  https://www.sashacottman.com/books/
  The Duke of Strathmore Series
  London Lords Series

J